THE WOMAN IN THE WATER

Bath, 1761: When the body of a woman is found in the River Avon, the authorities quickly declare it is merely a nameless pauper who committed suicide. However, maidservant Lizzie Yeo is worried; she hasn't seen her friend, Nancy, for a while. Intent on bettering herself and escaping her past, Lizzie accepts a job as housekeeper for the Reverend Jonathan Harding, a widower with a young son. Harding, too, is concerned about the identity of the dead woman, particularly when news reaches Bath that a local squire's daughter has vanished and the leading lady in a visiting production of *Macbeth* is missing. While Harding attempts to solve the case with logic, streetwise Lizzie's sharp wits lead her to the truth about the woman in the water, but someone is clearly out to stop her . . .

WILL AND SHEILA BARTON

◆

THE WOMAN IN THE WATER

Complete and Unabridged

CHARNWOOD
Leicester

First published in Great Britain in 2016

First Charnwood Edition
published 2018

A catalogue record for this book is available
from the British Library.

ISBN 978–1–4448–3567–0

Published by
F. A. Thorpe (Publishing)
Anstey, Leicestershire

Set by Words & Graphics Ltd.
Anstey, Leicestershire
Printed and bound in Great Britain by
T. J. International Ltd., Padstow, Cornwall

This book is printed on acid-free paper

Table of Contents

Prologue

Even though it was already well past nine o'clock, there was still a rim of red at the edge of the sky. Sunrise had been spectacular — clear and fiery above the frost-encrusted ground. Now the early February sky above him was a bright, cold blue, with only the rose-tinged horizon a reminder that he'd already been labouring for three hours. At least the lifting, the pushing, the pulling, the shouting to his mates to hold steady kept him warm. It was absolutely freezing.

The stone was pretty much loaded onto the waiting boat now. The last of the railway trucks had been emptied and was ready to be pulled back up the hill to Ralph Allen's mines and be filled up again. The railway was one of Bath's wonders — though a simple enough idea — and people came to watch the open carriages steadied by brakes, running on iron wheels and wooden rails from the top of the hill to the bottom to deliver their contents to the wharf. There the soft, yellow blocks of stone, already hardening in the air, were transferred by a wooden crane on a boat, which was waiting to carry them away. Building, building, building — they had never known a time like it. Just as well for him — it meant plenty of employment for men strong enough to dig and cut and load and unload. Week on week, the stone that didn't go to Bristol or London was transformed into the terraces of houses that hung like golden necklaces on the slopes of Bath, a city apparently held by nature in the cup of its green and prosperous hand. Fine streets, squares and walkways, as well as stylish rooms for gambling and dancing rose month on month in a seemingly never ending parade of elegance and prosperity.

He and his mates stood back from the trucks and he pushed his hat to the back of his head before signalling to the crane operators to swing in the last load and guide it expertly onto the deck of the boat. Then he sat with the other railway men, unwrapped the cloth that held his bit of bread and cheese and started to eat. They passed a flagon of ale from hand to hand and he hooked in a finger, tipped it back over his shoulder and took a swig. Soon the cold began to gnaw at him again so he rose and went onto the boat. He liked to check that the blocks of stone were steady and well balanced on the deck. Finding it all well stacked and secured by firmly knotted rope, he stood back to admire his city, the city that he, in his way, was helping to bring into being. His eyes went first to the hills above and then to the buildings below, glowing in the winter sun. From there his eyes came down to the water winding between the gold and green, dark and shining, almost still, on this windless day.

Then something caught his eye. Lining the banks, trees hung over the river, spare at this time of the year, but still gracefully dipping the ends of their branches into the water. Under one,

2

not easy to make out, there appeared to be something wedged. It bobbed occasionally but remained stuck between branches and bank. He shielded his eyes and squinted into the light. All sorts floated down in the winter storms, but there was something strange about this bundle. It was long — a good four and a half feet — and appeared to be swathed in some kind of once white wrapping.

'What d'you think that is then?' he asked, touching the boatman's shoulder.

'What?'

'There.' He pointed. 'Stuck against the bank there. It's big.'

'Aye. It'll be some rubbish.'

'It's big, though.'

'Aye.'

He was drawn from his curious thoughts by a shout from one of the other men.

'Thomas, you done, me lad? We're ready for the uphill now.'

'Aye, I'm with you.'

He jumped from the deck onto the wharf and turned to wave the boatman on. Then he re-joined his mates, harnessed the horses to the wooden trucks and eased off the brake as they began the journey back up the hill.

1

The black plumes on the coffin quivered in the fading afternoon light as six pallbearers lifted it — one, two three, now — onto their shoulders and settled it in readiness. A light drizzle was turning to steady rain as the cortège assembled outside a house in Saw Close. City council men, hospital beadles, Abbey churchwardens and minor clergy busied themselves in arranging and ordering the mourners. The city, normally quieter at this time, while the people of quality dined and their servants waited upon them, was today packed with people of all classes, intent on watching the great civic display. Crowds thronged around the Guildhall market, blocking the roads where stagecoaches were trying to set down their passengers. Horses snorted fretfully, their breath hanging in the cold air like the smoke that poured from the chimneys of every house. Their hooves slipped and scraped on the damp cobblestones as coachmen and ostlers struggled to restrain them. Sedan chairmen, doing better business than on any day they could remember, jostled through the crowds to set down their fares at the side of the route. Their passengers were dressed in their best finery, vying to be, not mere observers of the pageant, but a part of it.

At five o'clock a single funeral bell rang from the Abbey, then its half-muffled companions began to peal. Under the direction of the churchwardens, the procession began the final journey of the late 'King of Bath', the gambler, libertine, scoundrel, gentleman, philanthropist and benefactor Richard 'Beau' Nash, from the house of the last of his numerous mistresses, via a funeral service of sedate municipal ceremony, to an unmarked pauper's grave.

As the bells were ringing out, Jonathan Harding left his house on Duke Street to attend the funeral. In his mid-thirties, with clear, brown eyes under a short, powdered wig and above a plain white collar, he was easily recognizable as a clergyman. Turning into the elevated walkway known as the North Parade, he continued past the Assembly Rooms and gaming houses and through the disciplined lines of trees that formed the Orange Grove beside the Abbey church. Harding's eyes were drawn by the funeral bunting decorating the buildings around the Abbey. The town was strangely bright in mourning, about to witness not just a funeral but a triumphant procession. It seemed to him quite appropriate that such extravagance should end the story of the man who had, perhaps more than any other, shaped and steered the city to its present fame and prosperity. The man who had invested in roads and gambling, this latter to be his downfall.

Beau Nash had not put up the elegant golden terraces, although he had filled them with musicians, dancers and card tables. Neither had he developed the curing waters, the baths and their attendant hospital, although he had worked hard alongside the men who did. The man who was to be laid to rest today was an altogether more extraordinary person — a master of ceremonies, a king of revels, who had come to Bath in the 1730s when its social life was rough and unrefined and had transformed it into the elegant place it now was. Now, in this second year of the reign of King George III, men no longer carried swords in the streets, or wore their spurs in drawing rooms. The slightest disagreement over status, etiquette, cards or dice was no longer inevitably followed by a squalid duel the following dawn, which had constituted the precise downfall of Captain Webster, his predecessor. Beau Nash, an irascible Welshman of no social standing, had, by sheer force of character, succeeded in what many would have thought impossible — he had civilised fashionable English society.

Harding turned and looked about him towards the ring of hills surrounding the city. *I will lift up mine eyes onto the hills, whence cometh my strength* the psalmist had written. The strength that came from these hills, he reflected, was the soft, golden stone that clad all the great new buildings of Bath, making it a unique and impressive sight — a wholly new city designed and built for a new kind of life in a new kind of world. No longer a centre of monastic life or the shabby market town that had remained for two hundred years after the monks had gone, it was now at the centre of fashionable life in England. All classes of society came: from the barely respectable to the most high-ranking; from country landowners to royalty; from soldiers of fortune to dukes. For Beau Nash had eased the rigidity of class in this place. If you had money you were welcome to pursue what this city could now offer: healing allied to hedonistic diversion, fashionable company, new styles in clothing, music, dancing, and gaming — and Europe's premier marriage market.

Harding wore a black coat — the best of his three — not the old one he wore at work in his garden or when walking or riding about the countryside, or the plain but respectable one he wore on most other occasions. This one was of fine wool with shiny buttons which he wore in the presence of better society. His wife had once almost persuaded him to obtain a blue coat to wear to fashionable engagements but in the end he felt it would not be proper for a clergyman and now she was gone he had no taste for such engagements. Today, as he stepped briskly across Orange Grove and entered the Abbey he was grateful for the warmth of his best.

★ ★ ★

Lizzie Yeo was considerably less well protected from the weather as she stepped out of an apothecary's shop on Cheap Street with the last of her deliveries. Shivering, she pulled up the hood of her old, brown woollen cloak to cover her cotton cap, walked briskly up the street and turned the corner. She knocked sharply on the door of a house giving out onto the pavement

8

and stepped in quickly when it opened. Within two minutes she was out again but without the bottle she had been carrying. She judged that she would be just in time to catch a glimpse of the funeral procession if she moved fast.

The funeral cortège wound its way out of Saw Close as the muffled bells wove in and out of the children's dirge. First came the charity girls, two by two, then the boys in their uniform coats and badges. At their beadles' direction they began to sing:

Most unhappy are we here,
Full of sin and full of fear,
Ever weary, ne'er at rest,
When, O Lord, shall we be blest?

Their wavering trebles were taken up by the marching musicians who came after them, made up both of the City Music and the remnant of Nash's own band. The procession moved off towards Westgate Buildings then turned left down Westgate Street, crowded with onlookers, some of whom had come to honour the memory of a prominent citizen, some to mourn the passing of a benefactor and philanthropist, many to see the spectacle and to be a part of the occasion, and not a few to take advantage of the crowds to proposition, solicit or pick pockets. Among them, Lizzie, having pushed her way to the front, stood for a few minutes to watch. Her clear, young face was still hidden by the hood of her cloak, from which brown, wet curls escaped.

Earth's a clog, a pageant life,
Fill'd with folly, guilt, and strife;
'Till we all unite in thee,
With ourselves we disagree,

sang the charity girls and boys. Three clergymen followed the musicians, robed in heavy cloaks, and behind them followed the black coffin, borne on the shoulders of Bath's six most senior aldermen. Its sable plumes, increasingly weighed down by rainwater, bobbed to the rhythm of the pallbearers' footsteps.

The masters of each of Bath's two assembly rooms, in their roles as chief mourners, followed the coffin. Behind them marched the beadles of the hospital, each in a heavy coat and tricorne hat and brandishing his ceremonial staff of office. And last, behind the beadles, came the poor patients of the hospital, the beneficiaries of Nash's largesse. Limping and shuffling, they wept openly for their loss.

Lizzie, absorbed for a few moments in the splendour of the procession, turned her head suddenly. She thought she had felt a tap on her shoulder, and there was someone likely to be about who she was most anxious to evade. The throng was dense and the light almost gone. It was hard to see clearly through the veil of rain, but it seemed to her that a few feet back in the crowd was a dirty face, pitted with smallpox, that she particularly wanted to avoid. She turned her head calmly back and continued to watch the cortège. It would take him a minute or two to push his way through to her, and besides she was sharp-witted and quick on her feet. If she timed it right she'd be fine.

What's our comfort here below?
Empty bubble, transient show,
Wrapt in the body's vile disguise,
None truly is until he dies.

As the last of the processing mourners passed her, Lizzie took her chance. Quickly and silently she lost herself in the crowd, slipping behind the last of the hospital patients into an alleyway and disappeared into the darkness. As she turned into Avon Street, it became clear to her that its inhabitants were marking the funeral of Beau Nash in their own style. All eleven of its taverns were heaving with customers, with crowds of people outside each one. As Lizzie passed the first on her way to the rooming house where she lodged, she was forced to step round a number of men in various stages of inebriation, one of whom was relieving himself into the stinking gutter. Another lunged towards her, without losing a drop from his tankard. Sighing, she dodged the unsteady hands and walked on, holding her skirts up a little. The steady drizzle had at least settled the dust that usually rose from the street, but it had turned it to mud mixed with droppings from horses and pigs and churned up with slops thrown from the houses and urine from the drinkers. When Lizzie reached her front door, she turned her head, checked that all was clear, and knocked to be let in.

11

★　★　★

As the funeral procession approached the great west door of the Abbey, it seemed as if even the carved stone angels climbing up and down Jacob's Ladder above it were animated by the occasion. Some appeared to be scurrying headfirst down the ladder to stare at the spectacle, while others were fleeing back to heaven in distress at the pomp and piety being shown to so flagrant a sinner. At the head of the cortège, the charity children were directed to their places in the abbey by Mr Harding and his colleagues. Cold and damp, they struggled to maintain appropriately solemn faces. The musicians wheeled off to the side of the great west door as the Rector of Bath greeted his fellow clergymen, and then preceded the coffin into the Abbey church, intoning the opening words of the liturgy for the Burial of the Dead:

I am the resurrection and the life, saith the Lord: he that believeth in me, though he were dead, yet shall he live.

The coffin was set down before the pulpit as the Rector's sonorous voice continued:

I know that my Redeemer liveth, and that he shall stand at the latter day upon the earth.

Harding stepped to one side of the pallbearers who now formed a guard of honour around the coffin:

12

We brought nothing into this world, and it is certain we can carry nothing out. The Lord gave, and the Lord hath taken away.

Harding had officiated at many funerals and the words of the service were completely familiar to him. On many such occasions he realised that he had recited long passages completely correctly and clearly, yet without any conscious memory of what he had done. But each time he heard them now, he was shocked back into the world by the memory of the funeral he had conducted only a year after arriving in Bath. Then he had laid to rest his young wife, taken from him in childbirth, with one of the twin children she had delivered. They had been married for a mere eighteen months. Death was a common enough thing and especially in childbirth. A clergyman saw much of it and while he had never become completely hardened, he had learned a sort of reserve. But Jonathan Harding's marriage had been a love match, long-awaited and made possible by the bishop's gift of this position in Bath, and then so short-lived as to twist a knife in his heart whenever he thought of it.

He had been strongly urged to remarry. He was a young man with good prospects, favoured by Septimus Wellbeloved, the bishop, and popular with the congregations of the Abbey. He had a young son who had no mother and a household with no mistress. A clergyman, it was often said, ought to be married, not least as a guard against temptations of the flesh, with which Bath was well provided. But Harding did not want another wife. He remained faithful to the one whose memorial plaque hung above him on the Abbey's north wall and whose body lay in the Abbey graveyard.

In Memoriam
Jane Harding
1732–1753
Beloved wife of Revd. Jonathan Harding
and mother of George

He lived modestly in a small town house with only a housekeeper as a live-in servant. He preached two or three sermons a week at the Abbey, and assisted with other matters when requested by the rector. He read and prayed, took his exercise by walking each day around the city and occasionally rode about the countryside on a horse kept in the livery stables in Widcombe Village across the river. He maintained a keen amateur study of mathematics and logic that had stayed with him since his days as a student at Cambridge. Sometimes he was called upon to deal with business arising in one of his three parishes — Ponting Magna in Wiltshire, a large and prosperous village from which he had £400 a year, Lower Pother, a little to the west, near the Welsh border, a more modest settlement but still worth £220 a year and Rayleigh-in-Marsh in Somerset, which was to all intents and purposes deserted. But mostly he lived a quiet and reasonably contented life in Bath.

The Abbey organ played as the Rector led the choir and congregation in singing a psalm. Harding's thoughts drifted away. His house was modest and required little management but such as it needed was left in the capable control of his housekeeper, Mary Yeo. Now she was determined to leave the city and to return to her family in Bradford on Avon to care for her ailing brother. Of course, Harding recognised that she felt a duty to do this but he could not help wishing she had not. He knew he should be busying himself to find a replacement for her, but the management of a household was a complete mystery to him. He had asked Mary if she could suggest a replacement but she seemed unwilling to nominate one. He himself had no idea how to go about the task of appointing a stranger to a position so important to his and George's wellbeing, and so he remained paralysed as the days went by and Mary's departure grew ever nearer.

The psalm came to an end, the notes of the organ seeming to cling like mist to the pillars upholding the great roof, and to linger in the magnificent fan-vaulting. The Rector strode to the lectern and began to read from St Paul's epistle to the Corinthians:

Now is Christ risen from the dead, and become the first-fruits of them that slept. For since by man came death, by man came also the resurrection of the dead. For as in Adam all die, even so in Christ shall all be made alive.

To complicate things further, Harding's son, George, would soon be home from his Latin school to prepare for his entry to Rugby. Mary Yeo had so exactly suited him and his son and so expertly managed his household, that it was hard for him to see how anyone else would replace her. Certainly the few people who had been recommended to him had been entirely impossible. How had he come to have so suitable a servant in the first place? Had an angel found her for him? Yes, an angel called Jane Harding. Each night Harding said his prayers and went to bed, determined that in the morning he would find the solution to his dilemma. Each day he found himself unable to see a path forward and each evening he found himself no further on. He continued to ask Mary if she could not reconsider — she could not — and if she could not delay at least until George was sent up to Rugby School — this was not possible. At each turn he felt himself blocked.

The coffin was taken up again by the pallbearers and the Rector led them from the church towards the graveyard, intoning:

O death where is thy sting?
O grave where is thy victory?

Behind the coffin came the mourners, the charity children, the beadles, the hospital patients, the aldermen, the congregation, the onlookers, the rich and powerful, the poor and humble, the great and the good, the halt and the lame, the respectable and the common. They wound along to the side of the open pit into which the bodies of paupers were placed and the remains of Beau Nash were committed to it. Harding was glad now that it was wintertime. In summer these communal graves stank abominably, as they were not covered over until they were filled. The king of Bath, having been seen off with due civic ceremony was, at the end, despatched into a communal burial pit alongside common paupers, the criminal, the insane and the destitute. The Rector, sensible of the dismal surroundings and the bitter weather, cut short the ritual, moving swiftly through the committal:

In the midst of life we are in death . . . ashes to ashes, dust to dust; in sure and certain hope of the Resurrection to eternal life . . . in thy eternal and everlasting glory . . . through Jesus Christ, our Mediator and Redeemer. Amen.

Then all of Bath turned away to resume its pleasures, its business and its recreations.

2

The next day dawned just as cold, but dry and bright. Lizzie's cloak, though, was still damp and clung to her skirts as she left her lodgings. She looked cautiously to right and left before venturing into the street, but she saw no-one she need fear. Ragged children were playing in muddy puddles. As she turned into Westgate Street, she passed a pie vendor, carefully balancing the tray that hung round his neck as he began his walk into the more salubrious parts of the city. In the dark, pokey rooms lining the street, seamstresses sewed, working to provide the ladies and gentlemen visiting Bath with the never-ending parade of fashion they required. A couple of people called out a 'good day' to her and she waved back.

Crossing the street, she saw no evidence of the great procession of the evening before. All was back to normal — the rich and middling taking breakfast and preparing for a day of visiting, attending church and taking the water cure; the poor working to provide what was necessary for all of this to run smoothly. Lizzie delivered water for Mr. Leslie, an apothecary who prescribed for each patient a specific amount of the water that sprung miraculously from the earth beneath Bath every day, and which had to be delivered and drunk at particular times. He might also recommend some time spent in the mineral-rich waters of the baths. Lizzie was very glad of this job. Her life since she had left her family in Bradford on Avon eight years ago at the age of sixteen had not been easy, and her existence since she had fetched up in Bath had been a precarious one. Now at last she had a regular source of income — a respectable one at that — and she hoped to extricate herself from her current trouble in the near future. Until then she must keep her not inconsiderable wits about her.

Arriving at the apothecary's shop on Cheap Street, she knocked and pushed open the door. Mr Leslie, the apothecary, looked up from his books and smiled above the eyeglasses perched on his nose — not ones with plain glass worn by the most fashionable ladies and gentlemen — but essential to him for the reading of his ledgers.

'Good morning, Lizzie. So, did you see the funeral procession?'

'I did, a very grand affair, though they say it was a pauper's grave for him.'

'Ah, 'twas mostly show, with him, I fear, but a grand one — and one which still keeps us busy! There's water for the Reverend Jones first, my dear, and then Mrs Castlemaine. You may as well take both together.'

He indicated two bottles on the dark wooden counter and Lizzie took them. As she turned to go, he added, 'I heard from Mrs Dawes that Mrs Castlemaine is showing some improvement. Would you tell her that I recommend an hour in the King's Bath as soon as Mrs Castlemaine is

19

well enough to leave the house? Tell Mrs Dawes to be sure to pass this on to Mr Castlemaine.'

'I will, sir.'

'A very impatient gentleman, Mr Castlemaine. Perhaps he carries too much concern about his wife. Perhaps an improvement in her will also help him.'

'Perhaps, sir.' As far as Lizzie was concerned, many gentlemen were impatient and she had never felt it was caused by concern for their wives. She turned and left the shop.

★　★　★

Jonathan Harding rose at half past six on that same morning and breakfasted on some cold mutton washed down with a glass of beer. It was served by the girl Eliza, who crossed the river by ferry each day from her father's cottage in Widcombe village to perform the services of maid of all work under the supervision of Mary Yeo. Eliza's father and mother worked in the stone quarries of Squire Allen and hoped that domestic service in the employ of a clergyman would give their daughter the chance of a life of less back-breaking toil than their own. From time to time Harding pondered the possibility that when Mary left his service, he might manage by simply hiring one or two more such servants and overseeing their work himself. He always realized ruefully that there was a fatal drawback to this plan, namely that he had very little idea of what those duties were, or how they were to be carried out.

Lizzie set out from the apothecary shop to deliver water to the Reverend Jones. She gave the bottle to the housekeeper at the door.

'He must drink it immediately,' she said and the woman nodded, handing over yesterday's empty bottle. 'Aye, 'tis doing him good, I believe. He got up and sat in his chair for a while yesterday.'

Lizzie nodded. 'I'll return at four this afternoon with the next bottle. Be sure and have the empty one ready for me.'

The woman nodded and closed the door.

Next Lizzie set off towards the house which the Castlemaines had taken — a substantial one in the High Street, fronted with mellow stone like all the new buildings in Bath. On each side of the solid oak front door with its well-polished brass knocker was a pillar, and above it was a triangle of the same golden stone. For most of the two weeks that the Castlemaines had been in Bath, Lizzie had delivered water from Mr Leslie to their house. For Mrs Castlemaine, he had told her, suffered badly with various ailments of the joints and was quite unable to leave the house. Lizzie, on her last visit, speaking to the housekeeper, Mrs Dawes, on the doorstep, had caught a fleeting glimpse of the poor woman sitting in the parlour. Small and frail, her hands were bent completely back on themselves and she was painstakingly lifting a cup to her lips using the backs of her knuckles. Mr Castlemaine — the impatient gentleman himself — had closed the door on his wife and sharply instructed the housekeeper to stop dallying at the front door. Today, Lizzie mounted the two narrow steps to the door, knocked, and then waited for longer than she was expecting to. She had never found the housekeeper particularly friendly, but she usually opened the door promptly and had the empty bottle ready for Lizzie when she arrived with the next dose.

When the door finally opened, Lizzie was surprised to see Mr Castlemaine himself in the doorway. A large gentleman, he was bewigged but without his frockcoat, and for a moment Lizzie was quite taken aback. Gentlemen did not answer their own front doors.

'What?' he said.

Lizzie bobbed. 'Please sir, the water for Mrs Castlemaine.'

He scowled, and repeated, 'What?'

'The water from Mr Leslie the apothecary, for Mrs Castlemaine, sir. I bring it twice a day.'

'Oh, yes.' He grabbed the bottle from her and started to close the door.

'If you please, sir.'

'What?'

'The empty bottle, sir.'

'What?'

'The bottle from yesterday afternoon.'

'Oh, yes. Wait a minute.'

She waited again. Surely the housekeeper had left the bottle to be given to her? It was strange for her to be out at this time. Mr Leslie was quite inflexible about the times the water must be taken, and she delivered it regularly day on day.

Mr Castlemaine reappeared with yesterday's empty bottle.

'Is this it?'

'Yes sir, thank you.' She bobbed again and just as he was closing the door said, 'If you please, sir.'

'Now what?' Two red spots appeared on his plump, sleek cheeks.

'Mr Leslie said to tell you that he recommends an hour in the King's Bath as soon as Mrs Castlemaine feels able.'

'What nonsense — he knows she is not able to leave the house!'

'Yes, sir, begging your pardon, sir, but Mrs Dawes said there had been some improvement.'

'Well, Mrs Dawes has gone. I await her replacement.'

The red spots darkened. 'And I thank you to mind your business. I will know when my wife is improved. She is not. She is in very poor health. Tell Mr Leslie I will consult him when I please and not to send serving maids to ask after me.'

'Yes, sir. Sorry, sir,' then a moment later, 'Mrs Dawes didn't say she was going, sir.'

Mr Castlemaine's eyes widened at such impudence and Lizzie turned quickly to leave but, just as the door closed, turned her head to say, 'I will collect the bottle tomorrow, sir.'

The door was closed sharply. Lizzie didn't see the man's purple cheeks but she guessed they were there and smiled. Then she hurried back towards the Cheap Street shop.

Distracted by her encounter with Mr Castlemaine, she let her attention wander. Her thoughts were suddenly pulled back to her present situation, when she became aware of a shadow behind her. She stopped to look into the window of a mercer's shop and the shadow stopped. She started off again, and so did the shadow. Then she slipped down an alleyway, doubled back on herself, and arrived a little out of breath at the safety of the apothecary's shop.

★ ★ ★

After breakfast and feeling rather out of sorts, Jonathan Harding put on his second-best coat and walked through the bright, cold morning air to the Abbey to hear the eight o'clock service of Morning Prayer. The service was uneventful with an indifferent sermon, all of which, Harding was slightly shocked to realise, he had forgotten before he left the building. All in all, it seemed that the day was beginning badly, but he brightened at the prospect of his next appointment, or at least of its location. Slipping out of the Abbey, he walked briskly towards Milsom Street and Mr Stephens' coffee house.

Coffee houses had proliferated in Bath during the eight years Harding had lived there. Like the toyshops, milliners, and apothecaries, some enjoyed brief lives, coming and going within a few seasons, but some put down sturdy roots and became established features of the city. Some were little more than a room with a table or two. Others were much grander — public meeting places where business matters and politics were debated daily — with private rooms available for smaller gatherings. Some were aggressively masculine, others more refined — and into these women occasionally ventured. Bath even boasted something quite unique in England — the Ladies' Coffee House beside the Pump Rooms in the shadow of the Abbey's great west front. Such a thing was unheard of even in London.

The Parade Coffee House of Mr Richard Stephens offered a comforting blast of warm air to those who entered. Towards the back of the room against the side wall a huge cauldron of water hung on a stout metal rod over a blazing fire, its contents simmering. On the warm bricks in front of the fire stood a row of large black coffee and chocolate pots. A man sat in one of the seats by the fire, smoking a pipe. Two trestle tables were taken by a crowd of men engaged in lively conversation. Waving their pipes and sipping at their coffee, their animated talk caused their long curled wigs to quiver as a serving man refilled their cups. Around the table nearer to the door sat an animated group discussing the political, commercial and theological consequences of the recent accession to the throne of King George III. There was widespread agreement that the new regime promised some much desired stability. The union of England and Scotland was final and indissoluble and the future could only now be seen as that of an entirely united Great Britain, unified under a single crown and ruling over an American Empire which would bring wealth and power in the world.

At the smaller table, nearer to the counter where Mr Stephens dispensed tea, coffee and chocolate to his customers, sat a smaller group, concerned with matters perhaps less weighty as the world goes, but of great importance in Bath — namely the arrivals and departures in the city. The countess of Marlborough, it seemed, had been heard to say that she would not come to Bath again but would instead grace the rival attraction of Tunbridge Wells. Some of the men were visitors to Bath and wondered if this presaged a change in fashion that they should follow. Those whose livelihood was built on Bath's prosperity were adamant that Tunbridge Wells had little or nothing to offer by comparison. After all, the waters at Tunbridge were cold. The curative properties of Bath's water were undoubtedly connected to the constant temperature of the hot spring, and such a thing was to be found nowhere else in England.

Harding passed between these two tables and went through to a private room to one side of Mr Stephens' counter. Here he met the men he had come to see; Mr Strang, the attorney representing Squire Allen, Mr Arbuthnot, a beadle from the Girls' Charity School and Dr Sloane from the mineral water hospital. With them was someone Harding had not met before — a large, florid man in a red and gold brocade coat who was introduced as Mr Henry Castlemaine, an Irish gentleman recently arrived in the city for the sake of his wife's health.

* ★ ★

As Lizzie hurried into the shop, Mr Leslie looked up and noted her flushed cheeks and agitation. She was not a young woman given to explanations or complaints but Mr Leslie was an observant man, despite his failing eyesight, and a kind one too. As he looked at her above his spectacles, he thought he saw something else. He couldn't be sure, just as he hadn't been absolutely positive on the previous occasions, but it seemed to him that a shadow lurked outside the shop — a man, it seemed to him, waiting. The light in the shop with its old wooden shelves and counter, its scales and jars of medicaments, was dim and Lizzie always took a moment or two to adjust. She forced her breathing to slow, wiped her hands down her skirt, then stepped towards Mr Leslie.

'Here are the bottles, sir.'

'Thank you, Lizzie. Did you speak to Mrs Dawes?'

'No, sir, she's gone.'

'Gone?'

'Yes, and I think the manservant, too. Mr Castlemaine himself opened the door to me.'

Mr Leslie raised his eyebrows. 'How very strange. Did she say she was going?'

'No, sir, she never said much, but she gave no indication that she planned to leave.'

'And how fares Mrs Castlemaine?'

'Bad, sir, Mr Castlemaine says, and he'll speak to you when he thinks there's an improvement.'

'Ah, I see.'

There was a pause as Mr Leslie went back to

his ledger and Lizzie hesitated. 'Can I help you with anything?' she asked.

He looked at her for a moment. 'Yes, you can, my dear. Just get me down the senna please. Remember the letter?' He drew an S with his finger in the air.

'I do, sir.' A rare smile as she turned to the shelves of brown glass jars and lifted one down onto the counter. The old man passed her a pestle and mortar as she opened the jar.

'Five seeds,' he said, as Lizzie counted them out and began to crush them before carefully wrapping the powder in paper, ready for Mr Leslie's next constipated customer.

Half an hour later, the door at the back of the shop opened and Mr Leslie's wife stepped in and smiled at them. She had a round shiny face and a brilliant white mob cap and was, like her husband, in her fifties.

'Hallo, my dear.' She nodded at Lizzie. 'Will you take a bite?' she asked her husband.

'I will, I will.' He rubbed his eyes. 'I fear my sight gets worse. Lizzie is helping me with the powders.'

'Would you like a bite to eat, Lizzie?' Mrs Leslie's grey hair, escaping from the cap, framed her smile.

'Oh no, Ma'am, thank you. I must go now.' Lizzie stood up and reached for her cloak.

Husband and wife exchanged a meaningful glance.

'Well, it would please me if you were to eat a little breakfast with us. I have something of a favour to ask of you,' Mr Leslie said.

Lizzie looked surprised, but put down her cloak. 'Well then, of course I will,' she answered and followed the couple through to their living quarters at the back of the shop.

At the end of the meal, Mr Leslie put down his small mug of ale and pushed his plate away. 'Lizzie, Mrs Leslie and I have had some conversation. We wondered if you might come and live here with us.'

Lizzie started in surprise and for the briefest second looked up at them both. Then, just as quickly, she lowered her eyes, remaining silent, her face closed and blank. Mr Leslie looked at his wife. This was what they had expected.

'We have a bed that could be put in the passageway behind the shop. It's quite warm there and you could eat with us.'

The averted face remained blank and Lizzie said nothing.

'It would help me to have you here sometimes in the evenings,' Mr Leslie continued. 'My eyes are not good, as you know, and you could help me with the ledgers and the measuring.'

Lizzie looked up sharply, defiantly.

'You are coming on well with the letters and if we carry on while I can see, you will be able to assist me when I cannot. You can think about it perhaps and tell us in a day or two. We would take your board out of your wages, of course, but I think you will find yourself better placed if you would agree to help me in this way.'

Lizzie nodded. 'May I think on it, sir?'

'Yes, of course you may. Now shall we prepare the next deliveries?'

She nodded again and went back into the shop. Mr Leslie smiled at his wife.

★　★　★

The meeting in Mr Stephens' coffee shop was convened for the purpose of discussing the use of some bequests recently made to the charity school. The committee hoped that these would finance a number of extra places for girls, as there was a clear need for them. Mr Arbuthnot told them that this would require some building work to provide more accommodation, for which the bequests were not sufficient. It was for this reason that Mr Castlemaine had been invited to attend the meeting, having expressed to Dr Sloane at a chance meeting over cards at the Old Assembly Rooms, a desire to make a small contribution to the city in which he now lived. He was not — he said — a wealthy man, but if two or three others could be persuaded to match his donation, they should be able to raise sufficient funds. This struck Jonathan Harding as a generous gesture from someone who had only recently arrived in Bath. Castlemaine was an expansive and lively man with a ready smile and the hint of an Irish brogue. His fine coat and carefully powdered wig, buckled shoes and silver-topped cane showed him to be a man of fashion, yet he was clearly also one with a sense of duty.

'We are most fortunate, Mr Castlemaine,' he said. 'Or rather I should say the orphan girls of Bath are so, that you should make so kind an intervention on their part. Many of those who visit Bath see only its pleasures and not its needs. This is most generous of you.'

'I have not been here long, sir,' the Irishman replied. 'But I see a city much to my liking and I am minded to think of settling here for some time if my wife's health continues to respond to the treatments of the waters. I should like to think that I may make my contribution to the city.'

Mr Harding and Dr Sloane nodded happily, while Mr Arbuthnot kept to himself the rather more cynical thought that it was not so great a sum to spend in expectation of being introduced to the better parts of Bath society, not least since it was said that Castlemaine's money derived entirely from his marriage. He had remarked something to the effect to the doctor before the others arrived. But Sloane had only said that the money of fortune hunters did as much for orphans as any other man's, and that the charities of Bath would be much the poorer if they chose to make fine distinctions in what they would accept.

'Then to business, gentlemen,' announced Mr Strang, opening a large, card-bound volume of accounts. He laid before them the figures and the possibilities, as the conversation progressed, about how much was needed and who might be approached to match the sum now offered. A list was drawn up of likely donors and Dr Sloane and Mr Harding took three names each to approach.

Lizzie set out on her next two deliveries, but scarcely had time to consider the Leslies' offer to move in with them before she needed to use her wits for quite another purpose. This time she was quite sure — sure she was being followed and sure by whom. The bottles of water were in her hands and she couldn't afford to drop them, but she hurried as fast as she could, dodging in and out of doorways and down alleys. The streets of Bath were mostly newly paved with fine, large, flat stones, making them considerably easier to walk on. But the alleys weren't. Bath, the 'valley of pleasure', was a confection of appearances — the alleys, like the backs of the buildings and even the fronts under their façades of gold, were rough and in marked contrast to the elegant streets. Narrow, stinking and full of foul puddles, the alleys required some negotiating, especially by a young woman in a hurry, carrying two precious bottles and with her only cloak catching at her feet. She felt some relief after the deliveries. She had only to return the empty bottles and get back to Avon Street where she could lock her door and think properly.

'Lizzie.' She felt a hand on her arm, started, then relaxed.

'Oh, Jenny,' she smiled at her friend. 'Are you going along this way? Walk with me to Mr Leslie's and then we can go on together.'

'I cannot Lizzie. More errands. She has me at it day and night. No sooner has she decided, then I must go back and change the silk for another, or have another feather put in the hat. You'd not believe the fuss every day before she leaves the house! Still it's clean and regular and — as well you know — better than before.'

Lizzie did indeed know. She and Jenny had fetched up in Avon Street at the same time, both with no source of income. They, and a third young woman called Nancy, had lodged together, sharing a bed as well as food and company. The girls had encouraged and supported each other and somehow managed to laugh a great deal through this time. Nancy was a little older and had the measure of Avon Street. Without her, Lizzie sometimes thought, things would have been even worse for her. Hungry and short of rent money, they had all reluctantly taken up the offer of what a local man had described as 'an arrangement of mutual benefit'. Thus they had entered into a form of employment that may have been regular but was most certainly not clean.

'Here I am, Lizzie.'

The seamstresses in the High Street worked in much better conditions — light and clean ones, even if the hours were still long. Jenny knocked and entered one such workshop for her latest sortie in her mistress' campaign of fashion. And just as Jenny disappeared into the shop, Lizzie finally felt the hand of fate and Dirty Jack on her shoulder. He was well named. Dirty hands, dirty face, dirty clothes, dirty business. He held tight as she wriggled and brought his pockmarked face close to hers. She recoiled at the stink from his breath.

'Now, dear Lizzie Yeo, I think you know we have business together. Four shillings' worth of business, as I recall.'

'Three!' she spat back, wriggling but unable to release his grip.

'Four with interest, my dear. That room is good and clean. You know you'd have struggled to get it without me. It was kind of me to help you, you know. You and that Jenny — you were very down on your luck when I came along and helped you out.'

'Helped? You ruined us for your own advantage. We got away from you, though, and I for one, am happy without your vile company.'

'Well there's gratitude. You'd've starved if it wasn't for old Jack. There's still the matter of the room, though, m'dear. I'm not so flush I can afford to forget about four shillings.'

'That room stinks!'

'Oh come, dear Lizzie, don't you be getting airs and graces now you deliver to the gentry. I got you that room for a price we agreed and you haven't paid it. You know I'm a reasonable man. You can pay me,' he paused, 'in kind, if it suits better. Like the old days. Four good nights should do it.'

Despite Jack's menacing air and tight grip, despite the fact that she was shaking uncontrollably, Lizzie spat at him and, as he wiped the saliva from his face, stamped hard on his foot and wriggled out of his grip. She ran — the bottles must take their chance — across the Orange Grove, past the back of the Abbey, into

North Parade and along the backs of the houses in Duke Street, till she got to the one where her aunt Mary worked. She pounded hard on the door.

'All right, all right, I'm coming.'

Never had the calm, down to earth tones of Aunt Mary sounded sweeter. The door opened and Lizzie pushed her way in.

'Why, whatever's the matter, my dear? Come in, come in.'

Lizzie followed her into the warm kitchen and sat breathlessly on an old wooden chair. Every wall was covered in shelves, groaning with cooking pots and crockery, all spotlessly clean. Kitchen utensils, gleaming in the firelight, hung from hooks. Over the fire, meat turned on a spit and on the wooden table, scrubbed to within an inch of its life, were several earthenware bowls covered with worn but neatly darned, snowy white cloths. Mary Yeo went to the corner of the big room and turned the tap on a keg there, holding a small pewter tankard to catch the ale. She handed it to Lizzie without a word and sat opposite her on the other side of the fire. She looked at her niece inquiringly but asked no more questions while Lizzie took the drink and then looked up and smiled at her aunt.

'Sorry, Aunt. Just in a bit of a hurry. Got late with the water.' She indicated the two empty bottles she had put on the table.

Her aunt looked and nodded. 'Drink it down then. Are you hungry?' She went over to another counter and removed the earthenware cover from a plate. She cut Lizzie a piece from the bread and then went out into a small cold store off the kitchen and cut a piece of cheese. She put both on a plate, handed it to Lizzie, then sat down again. Lizzie nodded and ate.

'I had breakfast with Mr and Mrs Leslie.'

'Aye, they're good folk. You're in luck there.'

Lizzie nodded again. 'Yes, I'm in luck for a change.'

'Well, don't you be doing anything to spoil that good luck.'

'No, I won't.' Lizzie avoided her aunt's eyes. 'I won't.'

They sat in silence for a while, Lizzie looking to the high windows from time to time. It was impossible to see out of them. 'How's Uncle Silas?'

'Not good, not good. I've told Mr Harding, I must go soon to him.' She sighed. 'I never knew a man to struggle so long over the plain facts. He must find someone else. And Master George comes home soon.' Lizzie looked up with a flicker of a smile at this. 'He'll be needing all sorts for this school. The lad and the father need a woman here to take care of it all — and there're plenty of good women looking for work in Bath. But he won't shift. I shall just have to get up and go. Then he'll have to sort it out.'

Lizzie looked down again, distracted from her present troubles by a flood of memories. Her aunt sighed. As usual, there was nothing forthcoming from her niece. Life's hardships had closed her up like an old, cobwebbed book and Mary knew from bitter experience that it would open when Lizzie decided it would and not before.

'Why don't you come with me to Bradford?'

'What?'

'Well, when I go to Silas. Mr Leslie could get someone for a few days.'

'Mr Leslie needs me.'

'He does, he does, but just for a few days. I know your father would be pleased.'

Lizzie looked scornful but didn't speak. Mary ploughed on. She, like her niece, wasn't a woman who was easily pushed off course. 'A few days away from Bath would do you good. The winter fogs are a trial to us all. Your mother hasn't seen you in two years and Becky's that grown. She won't know her sister if you leave it much longer.'

Lizzie shook her head as if a fly buzzed round her. She felt so very weary. Mary spoke more quietly. 'Bad blood, Lizzie, bad blood in a family — that's not good for all concerned. We've nothing else we can be sure of this side of the grave.'

'Wasn't my choice.'

'No, but it could be yours to end it.'

'Well, what if I go? What if I ask Mr Leslie and lose my sixpence a week. What if I walk there and back for nothing? What good'll that do me?'

Mary shrugged. 'Think on it, Lizzie. Kin are all we've got for certain in the end.'

'I'll think on it, Aunt. I'd better go. Mr Leslie will wonder what ails me.'

Her aunt rose. 'Come out the front. The house is empty.'

'Yes, I will.' She followed her aunt up the stairs and to the front door, looked about her as the afternoon light faded, and stepped out into Duke Street.

★ ★ ★

Once the business of the bequest was concluded, it only remained for the men gathered in Mr Stephens' coffee house to review the monthly accounts and sign the necessary papers for the income and expenditure of the school. While the committee busied themselves in doing this, Mr Castlemaine bought coffee and chocolate for all of them. Harding thought this a generous action and he warmed still more to his new acquaintance. So he was pleased, when the time came to leave, that Castlemaine turned in the same direction as he.

'Where do you live, Mr Harding?' Castlemaine enquired.

'Just along here, past the Abbey, and around that corner in Duke Street.'

'Then let us walk that far together — I have business in that part of town. I much admired the sermon you preached last week. You have a great facility as a speaker of reason and balance. Your words were well chosen.'

'You are very kind, Mr Castlemaine. I hope my preaching is satisfactory. It is, you know, the reason for my being here. It is my lord bishop's desire that the Abbey should be a place of

38

rational and protestant instruction.'

'It is most important that it should be so. In my own land, you know, we are much beset by papistry.'

'It is the persuasion of most of the common people of Ireland, is it not?'

'It is — although you may depend upon it that Rome's star is declining. As all the islands of Britain are now united under a protestant king, and as we all prosper under that wise rule, there can be only one future assured. Reason and industry will lift the peasantry of Ireland from their ignorance. In two or three generations they will find their true home in the Church of England and Ireland. But I see that we have reached your house. I have much enjoyed making your acquaintance, Mr Harding. I should like to continue our conversation. May I presume so much as to invite you to breakfast with me tomorrow?'

'I would be very pleased to do so but tomorrow I am engaged. I plan, though, to attend divine service at half past four this afternoon and then take a glass or two in the New Assembly Room, if you would care to join me.'

'I would be delighted, sir. I've been too much around sickness since we arrived in Bath.'

Before Harding had a chance to reply, his front door opened and Lizzie Yeo stepped out.

'Why, Lizzie!' Harding smiled but Lizzie looked quickly down.

'Yes, sir, beg pardon sir, my aunt thought it'd be quicker through the front.'

'Oh, don't mind that. Are you well?'

'Yes sir, thank you.'

'Does the apothecary business suit you?'

'Yes, sir. Please, I must be going.' Only then did she look up and see Mr Castlemaine standing with Harding. She hid her surprise, nodded to Mr Harding, bobbed to them both and hurried on her way.

3

Henry Castlemaine arrived at the Assembly Room ahead of Jonathan Harding and was already deep in conversation with a group of men when the clergyman entered. The talk was lively and concerned racehorses, a subject on which Castlemaine was deemed to be an authority. On seeing his new friend, however, he broke away from the group to greet him.

'It's a pleasure to see you again,' he beamed. 'Will you take a glass of wine with me?'

Harding was happy to do so and they found seats near the end of the elegant, high-ceilinged room. A number of small tables around them were occupied by ladies and gentlemen playing cards, some of the ladies appearing to perch precariously, so large were their skirts. On a dais at the end of the room, two violinists, two viola players, and one flautist provided a background of pleasant music to set the mood for the evening's dancing, which would soon start. Harding sipped his wine appreciatively. Although he did not consider himself a connoisseur, he had drunk often enough with the Bishop of Bath and Wells to recognise a superior vintage, and he settled into his chair with a smile.

'This music is pleasant,' the Irishman said. 'But I think that the ladies are impatient for the dancing to begin.'

'I am sure of it,' Harding replied. 'And you, sir? Do you like to dance?'

'I'm a little heavy of step to dance well, Mr Harding. You perhaps have the bearing for it?'

'I was never much for moving lightly, and besides I am out of practice. I have not danced since my wife was taken from me and I think I shall not do so again.'

The Irishman nodded sympathetically. 'Perhaps you should marry again. It isn't good for one to be alone. A man such as yourself — admired, respected and comfortably settled, would find a wife without difficulty I am sure.'

The story of Jane Harding's death and the long, slow widowerhood into which the clergyman had sunk was the stuff of common gossip about the town.

'But not, I fear, one who would make me forget my Jane, and so not one I could do honour to. I am somewhat melancholy and would be poor company for any young woman. But how is your wife, Mr Castlemaine? Are the waters of Bath working to her benefit? It seems to me you must find much advantage to being here if you contemplate settling on a long-term basis. Most of our visitors, you know, take the cure then return from whence they came.'

'She is still weak but I have hopes that there may be signs of improvement. It is my dearest wish that she will one day be well enough to enjoy not only the health-giving waters, but also the lively pleasures of Bath . . . ' Castlemaine broke off suddenly. From the other end of the room voices could be heard raised in anger. 'It is

42

my friend Pocklington of Road. What can be the matter with him?' So saying he moved swiftly towards the commotion and Harding followed him.

They eased their way through a small crowd gathered a few discreet yards from the source of a noisy exchange. Illuminated by a sumptuous chandelier, burning candles of the finest beeswax, they came across a curious tableau. There was a man dressed not in the affected manner of much Bath society, but in the more robust style of a prosperous landowner, a younger man in a red frock coat and a very fashionable wig, and a young woman of no more than twenty, blushing and on the edge of tears. The older man, to whom Castlemaine immediately attached himself, was scowling angrily at the younger. 'How dare you presume to make advances to my daughter? We are not your silly water-takers and dancers of quadrilles. We are people of substance and native to these parts. I do not come to town for my daughter to be importuned by a scoundrel. I will not bear it!'

It was plain that he had discovered his daughter in close conversation with the younger man and had immediately assumed the worst — that here was an attempt to approach her and gain her affections without reference to her family. Soldiers of fortune of every kind were, Harding knew, to be found in Bath, and the city's reputation as a marriage market was common knowledge. He gathered quickly that Pocklington's rage — for it was obvious that he was the acquaintance Castlemaine had spoken of

43

— was as much to do with territory as general outrage. Not only did he object to a man speaking to his daughter who had not first been introduced to him, he was furious that an outsider had presumed to speak to a lady of local standing. The younger man stood his ground and looked angrily at his aggressor. He was a tall man with a military bearing, although his dress showed him to be conscious of the latest fashions. His coat was decorated with fine brocade and his wig was powdered to perfection. His stockings were white, yet almost unspotted with mud, despite the season, and his shoes were fastened with highly polished gold buckles.

'Sir, you embarrass yourself,' he snapped. 'Here a gentleman may surely address a lady without asking the permission of her father. This is not the court of France, stuffed and puffed with popish artificiality. We are at Bath, where modern manners prevail and one true subject of the king may speak to another.'

The young lady who was the occasion of this unpleasantness seemed to shrink in fear of the tempest breaking about her head. She wore a cream silk dress, tight at the waist and with a wide skirt, decorated with gold embroidery. Her stiff bodice was similarly decorated and her hair was high with a few ringlets falling onto her pale shoulders, complementing her unexceptional but pleasant features. On her nose a delicate pair of gold spectacles was perched. There were tears in the corners of her eyes and she was deathly pale. Silent and anxious, she did not move either towards her father or her admirer, maintaining an exact distance between them. It was clear that a point in the exchange was fast approaching which could only lead to some irrevocable action. Squire Pocklington's face was crimson with rage. He was a powerfully built man of middle age, with the air and bearing of a country squire used to robust manners, roast beef dinners, and riding to hounds. Between him and his enemy it was hard to judge who might triumph were they to come to blows.

'I would know, sir, the name of the man who so presumes to speak to his betters!'

'I am William Cosgrove, sir, lately Captain Cosgrove of the Fusiliers, and not afraid of any man in this room.'

While this violent confusion built towards a crescendo and the ladies and gentlemen around them watched with a mixture of alarm and amused anticipation, Harding saw some way behind them the figure of Mr Collet, the new Master of Ceremonies, trying to push his way through the crowd towards them.

Disagreements leading to confrontation were by no means unknown in Bath society. In a town whose principal distractions were dancing, gaming and the pursuit of rich spouses, and where wine flowed as freely as the famous waters, Mr Harding had seen many such incidents. Often he had witnessed their prevention or diffusion at the hands of Beau Nash, whose reputation, and that of the city, had been built on the civilising and the gentling of behaviour. Mr Collet, Harding feared, was struggling to achieve the same easy control. He

45

seemed to be unable to make his way through the press of onlookers. Harding caught the eye of Castlemaine, who nodded almost imperceptibly.

As Squire Pocklington reached for his glove, exclaiming, 'Why, then sir, I'll ask you to . . . ' the big Irishman caught his arm, restraining him with a powerful grip, while Harding stepped briskly between the belligerents, blocking the path for the gauntlet to be thrown down.

'I hope you will excuse my intrusion, Captain Cosgrove,' he said, calmly. 'I have heard many stories of the recent wars in the low countries and wonder if you might one day dine with me and explain some points of those engagements upon which I have pondered?'

Castlemaine had by now pulled Pocklington a good six feet away and Mr Collet had at last made his way to the scene to ask, 'What's here? Who raises voices in this place?'

'Why, Master Collet,' said the clergyman quickly, 'only a discussion of military victories. Our pardon if it shocked anyone.'

He turned to Cosgrove. 'I think, sir, you must be leaving now. I understand you have delayed your departure on my behalf too long. I must no longer detain you from your business.' So saying, he began to manoeuvre his somewhat confused charge towards the door. 'I beg you to leave now in peace,' he said in a lower tone. 'There's no shame in walking away from a man the world can see you'd best in a fight. Everyone will think better of you for sparing his daughter than they would of your fighting a man the age of your father.'

The logic of this seemed to impress itself upon the captain, along with the knowledge that there is no certainty in a duel. He had seen enough of wounds, slight at first, turned gangrenous and ending fatally, to know that no one drew a sword without placing his health and his very life at risk. He allowed Harding to accompany him to the door and push him gently into the street.

Castlemaine was meanwhile giving urgent advice to the enraged Pocklington. 'This is barbarism, Tom. We'll have no duelling here. The man's a scoundrel, no doubt, but there's no harm done and God be thanked for that. And what good to Emily is a father with a rapier in his gut? You'd have given him choice and he'd have chosen swords. He's half your age, man, he'd run you ragged then run you through. And for what? A few stolen words. Did you never do so much?'

By the time Harding returned to them, the squire was pacified at least to the extent that he would not seek to follow Captain Cosgrove with his glove. Emily was sulking, bitter to be so shown up, although this demeanour was beginning to be replaced by the awareness that she had almost been the occasion of an affair of honour. At the thought that men might fight over her, even to risk their lives, the colour was returning to her cheeks.

Already planning the way she would recount the incident to her younger sisters, she made a show of obedience to her father and to his orders that she would now immediately pack her things and prepare to return home to Road. Squire

Pocklington intended to rise at dawn, ride back to the manor and then send his man John back with the carriage to fetch her. That was to be the end of her playtime in Bath for this year. With that, the enraged squire and his outwardly chastened daughter withdrew from the scene and Bath society, cheated of one set of diversions, returned to their more usual vices.

'Well done, Mr Harding. You handled him consummately.'

'I fear I have seen such things more than once; often with sorrier outcomes. It was good you knew the man and we were at hand.'

They returned to their seats and to their wine, which they despatched promptly, Castlemaine immediately calling for another bottle. They talked of duels, of young ladies and of soldiers of fortune, of Bath and its society. They talked of their lives before coming to the city, Mr Harding of his student days at Cambridge, Castlemaine of the rolling hills of County Down and the horses they bred there. At the end of the evening they decided to meet again and go riding. Mr Harding was sure that the stables in Widcombe village would find a mount for Castlemaine. They arranged to meet at the South Parade ferry in three days' time and went their separate ways to sleep deeply in their beds.

4

Lizzie had not lit the candle in her room. She was standing by the grimy window looking out at the street. It was noisy and crowded with men and women picking their way through the mud and rubbish, carrying bundles and stopping to chat to each other, the women lifting their skirts a little above the dirt. Children and dogs played at their feet, either indulged or shouted at. Women called to each other from high windows across the narrow space of the street. There was a strong smell of cooking and ordure. She sighed. She had friends here — people like Nancy who had helped her when she had arrived in Avon Street, naïve and unused to the trickery of some of her neighbours, although not as entirely innocent as she appeared. She also had, amongst those neighbours, enemies and people she wished she would never have to see again. How good it would be to sleep in a clean bed, her few possessions safe, not looking behind her for Jack every time she left the house. How good it would be to get on with her letters. Imagine being able to read! Lizzie was quite determined to make herself a better life, and even more determined never to lie on her back for money again. She rubbed her face absently in memory of the extras that went with that particular profession. The bruises had faded, but she would never lose the faint scar on her temple she had acquired in the course of her employment in Jack's business. Also, she thought, she could save the money she owed him quite quickly if she took up the Leslies' offer. She would be free of him at last. But what would she give up? Most people would say nothing. Most people would grasp at the offer. Lizzie, though, did not like to be on the receiving end of charity. She might not have much to be proud of but, all the same, it mattered.

She sighed as she took up her candle, locked the door behind her and went down to the kitchen to light it. A large woman had her back to the door, but turned as Lizzie entered. Her face was red and her sleeves pushed up beyond her plump elbows. Her mob cap was dirty, and greasy wisps of hair escaped from it. She had discarded the neckerchief of muslin, the 'modesty piece' worn by most women, and her cleavage glowed pink and moist with warmth and the effort she expended in working some pastry on the table in front of her. She had flour on her face.

'Good day to you, Lizzie. How goes it with you?'

'Oh, well, Mrs Pardoe, well. I came to light the candle — and to get a little small beer, if I may.'

The older woman inclined her head towards the fire burning at the end of the kitchen. 'There's a tankard by the keg.' She regarded the younger woman for a moment. 'We hardly see you from day to day, my dear. I think you must creep in and out of the house. And you do not grace us with your presence in the tavern any more. Are you still delivering the water for the apothecary?'

'Yes, for Mr Leslie. It is a good business.'

'Well, you fell on your feet there. Not the way Jack liked to see you!' She laughed coarsely and went back to her pastry, chuckling.

Lizzie pulled herself some beer and hastened to the fire, where she pushed in a taper and lit her candle from it.

'I'll be back up to my room, then,' she said.

'Aye,' replied Mrs Pardoe, rolling her pastry on the wooden table. 'I never see young Jenny, either. Does she deliver the water as well?'

'No,' replied Lizzie, backing towards the door, trying to shield the candle and not spill the beer. 'She serves a lady in the High Street, here for the season.'

'Well maybe she will be back when the season's over. Haven't seen much of Nancy lately either, now I come to think of it, although she hasn't got herself a new station. She's got no airs and graces, that one. She's still one of us.'

'Yes, she is.'

Lizzie saw fleetingly in her mind's eye the sallow face of her friend, a faint purple fading round one of her eyes, watching Lizzie as she explained her new found fortune. Nancy had not been friendly, had merely shrugged and turned to fill a pewter mug from the barrel behind her, which she had handed to a man standing beside Lizzie in the tavern. Lizzie shook her head slightly, pushing away the memory and a flicker of guilt at the way Nancy had been left behind when she and Jenny escaped. Nancy always

51

waved when she saw her, but now she rarely stopped to talk. Lizzie hadn't seen her, she realized, for a few weeks now. She hunched herself over the flame as she went up the stairs to her room and carefully lowered herself to put the tankard on the floor. She unlocked the room and took both candle and beer in with her. The smell of the tallow — like burning offal — soon filled the room, but she was able to light her fire and get out the frying pan as well as the two sausages Mrs Leslie had wrapped in paper for her.

★ ★ ★

Mr Leslie did not refer to their conversation the next day, and it passed peacefully enough. But after the last delivery, Lizzie felt restless and decided to visit her aunt again.

'Well, I do not understand why you hesitate, my dear.' They were both settled in front of the fire discussing the Leslies' offer. 'Avon Street's not a place a young woman should choose to live.'

'Well, I have friends there.'

'And enemies?'

Lizzie hesitated, then replied, 'I don't like . . . '

'You, Lizzie Yeo, don't like to see what's staring you in the face!'

A rare smile. 'No, perhaps not.'

'Well now, I've been thinking. If you do not wish to take up the offer of Mr Leslie, then why not let me suggest to Mr Harding that you replace me here? I really must go to Silas soon and Mr Harding is sometimes as poor at facing the obvious as you are.'

'Oh no, really Aunt, please do not suggest a thing like that to Mr Harding.'

'And why not, may I enquire? Young Master George still dotes on you and you know the household.'

'No, I could not, Aunt, really. Mr Harding would not agree, I am sure.'

'He might. Really Lizzie, you are too proud!'

'No. It is not pride.'

'Well then, what is it, may I ask?'

'You know he will not have me.'

'I know no such thing. He often asks how things go with you. You know, Lizzie, you may have been mistaken. He may not bear you any ill will.'

'It's done, Aunt, finished long ago. I must think over Mr Leslie's offer now.'

Her aunt sighed. How a bright young thing like Lizzie could not see what was staring her in the face quite defied reason.

Lizzie left, as she had arrived, by the back door of Duke Street, climbing up from the kitchen to the outer door and into the small garden. She opened the gate and looked around wearily. Why must everything be so difficult? Why must she always escape from one predicament by entering into another? And why did her aunt have to hark on the past? Poor motherless George had doted on her it was true, but he must be a strapping lad by now. It was years since she had seen him. And she was quite certain that Mr Harding would not entertain the idea of her as a housekeeper. As she made her way along Pierrepont Street, lost in her thoughts, she did not see Mr Castlemaine watching her from across the street. She would not, even had she noticed him, had time to ponder his scrutiny, for as she turned the corner into Westgate Buildings, she was forcefully pulled from behind into a doorway, her neck yanked back by a strong and very dirty arm. This time, there would be no spitting or stamping. He had her by the throat. She could hardly breathe.

'Now, young Lizzie, let us try again. As you see, my patience is all used up. I promise you that you will regret any fighting or scratching of old Jack. Bitterly regret. Old Jack has been kind to you — yes you. He gave you employment in your hour of need. He helped you find a room, even though he lost money on you. He gave you time to pay. And what gratitude has he had? You took advantage of an old friend. That is what.'

He loosened his arm a little and Lizzie could breathe again, although her heart raced.

'Now, about my money. You pay me — one way or the other. That's fair, I'd say.'

'I'll pay you,' she gasped.

'When?'

'Fourpence a week from tomorrow and then more as soon as I can.'

Jack dropped his arm, but held tightly onto her wrist. His filthy nails dug into her skin. 'You about to come into money, my dear? You'd not be trying a little trickery on old Jack, would you?'

'No, I have an improvement in my circumstances.'

54

'How's that, then? You working for someone else?' With his free hand, he had grabbed the back of her cap and wrenched her head back. 'I gave you good rates, young lady. It's a well-known fact that I treat my girls well. I wouldn't think well of you joining any other.'

Lizzie tried not to show her fear as the grip on her wrist tightened painfully, but she knew she should push him no further. 'No, no, not that, there is no other. I am still with the apothecary but I can pay you from tomorrow. It is the best I can offer. Fourpence a week.'

'Tomorrow, then. You will regret it, my dear, if you try any more of your trickery.'

'I will not.'

He let go of her then and started off down the street. Turning his head for a moment, he grinned at her, looking uglier than ever. She looked down at her bruised wrist and then made her way to the apothecary shop.

★   ★   ★

Jonathan Harding was seated in his study, deep in thought, when he heard a knock at the door and Mary Yeo brought in a letter, which had come from London by Mail Coach. He broke the seal and began to read:

My Dear Harding
  It is now some five years since last our paths crossed at old Wellbeloved's Castle. Forgive me, Dear Fellow, for being so remiss as to leave so long the renewing of

our acquaintance. Your reputation as a preacher has grown so that by now you are Quite Famous, whilst I, a simple theatrical player, languish in obscurity, awaiting still the moment when the world shall recognise my art. Ah me, but — On with the Motley!

I am to come to Bath in four days' time to take the lead in the Scottish Play at the Theatre Royal, with Mr Josephs' Company. Will you come to see our poor efforts, or does your Calling proscribe such Frivolity? Here in London, Gentlemen of the Church think it no shame to be seen at the Theatre — at least, I believe, some do — others put on plain dress and disguise their vocation whilst sampling our entertainments. Perhaps we shall disguise you — but, no. I pray you take no Offence at the chirruping of one of Nature's empty-headed songbirds. Whether or not you will come to see me strut my hour upon the stage, I mean surely to come to hear you preach again and Hope for Wisdom of it.

As soon as I am arrived, I shall call upon you and desire greatly to renew the friendship we enjoyed in our Salad Days in that great seat of learning!

Forgive the brevity of this letter — I am called again to Recite my Lines in rehearsal.

Until my arrival, I remain

Your Good Friend

Richard Radleigh

PS — I'm to lodge at the Bladud Inn — but that I am sure is not a Respectable Place *to receive a man of the church — I will call on you! RR.*

Harding had mixed feelings about this letter. On the one hand, he had pleasant memories of student days idled away in the public houses of Cambridge with his college friend, whose carefree way of life had livened up his own university career. Until, that is, Radleigh was sent down, after which, Harding's studies advanced rather more successfully. On the other, he was concerned that too close a public acquaintance with Radleigh might have a negative effect on his own reputation as a moral and spiritual pastor to the already hedonistic citizens of, and visitors to, Bath. As much as Radleigh's letter might claim obscurity, he was well known to society, if not as a rake, then at least as a dilettante. It would be necessary to be clear from the start that the respect in which Harding was held was in no way to be compromised. He folded the letter and placed it in the drawer of his desk and, giving it no more thought, applied himself to the writing of his next sermon.

5

The morning was dry but very cold. Harding arrived first at the ferry, a little ahead of the agreed time. A bright February sun was shining, bringing the honey yellow of the stone-faced buildings into glowing life. Over the river, the leafless skeletons of winter trees splayed spectral fingers against the blue sky. The bustling sounds of the city behind him — horses, carriages, the cries of street peddlers and sedan chair men — were answered from the far bank by birdsong. The ferryboat was moored to a wooden jetty built out over the mud of the river bank. It was a simple vessel, big enough to take about twenty passengers, covered by an awning but open at the sides. It bobbed at the end of its painter and was crewed solely by a small boy of nine or ten. This lad, in answer to Harding's enquiry as to the whereabouts of the ferryman, had pointed to the tavern nearby.

''E's having 'is breakfast, your reverence,' he said.

Harding walked over to the inn and peered inside. It was a small taproom with some bench seats and three tables, one of which accommodated the only customer of the morning, the riverman, seated in front of a bowl of oysters and a tankard of ale. He looked up briefly from his meal and nodded to Harding, gesturing that he would be at his service once he had eaten. It was at this point that Castlemaine arrived, wearing a brown riding coat. He wore high boots with polished spurs and carried a crop. Harding's only concession to their outing was to wear boots instead of his usual buckled shoes. He wore no spurs and had on his older coat.

Seeing that the ferryman's breakfast was not to be hurried, Castlemaine and Harding took seats on a bench and called for tankards of porter. Harding asked after the health of Castlemaine's wife.

'She does better,' he replied, 'I have hopes she may soon recover enough to venture out of the house.'

'That will be a great joy for you both, I am sure.'

'It will, my dear sir, and you can be sure that if her first visit is to the waters, her second will be to the Abbey to hear you preach. I have told her of the great depth and reach of your sermons.'

'You are too kind, Mr Castlemaine,' Harding said, but he was pleased. He took some pride in his reputation as a speaker. He knew that people sometimes included his sermons alongside Bath's more secular activities — music, dancing, gaming and theatre — as examples of the civilized and stylish life of the spa town. Flattered, but embarrassed, he turned the conversation back to the subject of Mrs Castlemaine's health.

'She has been ailing for some two years now,' the Irishman told him. 'The doctors each have their names for her condition, yet none that means much or that they could cure until we tried these waters. Slowly but certainly, her strength is returning and the bloom is coming back to her cheeks. I bless the day we thought of coming here.'

'It is a great sorrow to a man when his wife falls ill. And a great solace when she recovers,' Harding replied. 'Not a day passes that I do not think of my Jane.'

Castlemaine nodded his head and remained silent for a moment or two before speaking again. 'It is hard to live alone. A wife brings many comforts. I find it hard to run a house with my own so ill, the more so since both my housekeeper and manservant have deserted me — run off together without notice and I am hard put to find new servants. You are fortunate in having the services of Mary Yeo. She seems an eminently capable servant.'

'She has been invaluable to me, but now she wishes to leave. In truth, I cannot stand in her way — she has a sick relative who needs her care — and yet I find myself at a loss to know what I shall do when she goes. There is a possibility, perhaps, that her niece might take her place — the young woman at my house the other day, just leaving as we arrived.' Harding looked enquiringly at his friend. 'But I am not convinced she would do.'

He took a deep draught of his porter. His friend became solicitous. 'That girl lives in the town, I think. And not in a good part of it.'

'I suppose she lives where she can. She is poor.'

'A girl like that may be poor and virtuous . . . or not.'

'I have no reason to believe ill of her. I think she is honest. She seems to be wary of me, though we were on easy terms once . . . ' Harding suddenly decided not to continue with this story. Only he and Mr Leslie knew of his part in finding Lizzie the situation with the apothecary some time after she had left his service and found herself in deep waters.

'She is, anyway,' he continued, 'too young to manage a household and I cannot think it would be right to have her under my roof.'

'Why indeed, it would not. A man of the cloth can so easily be subject to the cruelty of loose tongues.'

Harding reflected that this perhaps overstated the case, knowing, as he did, of a number of clergymen whose domestic and, indeed social arrangements were rather more unconventional than the hypothetical one he had described. But he decided not to share that thought with his friend and was happy to let the matter rest there.

Castlemaine was easily diverted into conversation about the goings-on of Bath. 'Squire Pocklington,' he remarked, 'was off at dawn the day after our discussion in the Assembly. Went back to his estate in Road, I believe, and sent the carriage back to collect his daughter. She was despatched home the next day, post haste, much to the delight of the gossips. Her suitor's gone, too. Back to London, I shouldn't wonder, or else to Tonbridge to try his gallantries there.'

'That is, perhaps, the best for all of them,' Harding said.

'So many comings and goings in this city, eh Mr Harding? Have you heard about the great actress, Mrs Maltravers? Coming to play for us in Shakespeare this season, along with her swain, Mr Radleigh, I understand. She is a great beauty and he a rising star in thespian circles. But perhaps you do not concern yourself with such vulgar entertainments?'

Harding was about to tell his new friend about his acquaintance with the actor, when the ferryman, having finished his breakfast, stood and, draining his tankard, led them to his boat, beside which three lady passengers were waiting. Each carried a small basket containing ribbons and buttons, indicating that they had made a successful visit to one of the new high street shops that were becoming as much a feature of Bath as they already were of London. Harding and Castlemaine took care to ensure the ladies were safely boarded and seated and then took their own seats as the boy cast off. The ferryman took hold of the great oar at the stern of the vessel and paddled out into the stream. The crossing only took a few minutes, but as they came to the other side, the boatman seemed momentarily lost in thought as he stared upriver. Then he whispered something to the boy and brought the ferry into the bank, throwing a rope around a pole at the end of the jetty. He, with his gentlemen passengers, helped the ladies ashore and as soon as they were safely on solid ground, the boy set off towards the village. As Harding and Castlemaine were about to do likewise, the ferryman put a hand on Harding's sleeve.

'Beggin' your leave, sir,' the ferryman said.

'What is it?' asked Harding.

'I thought perhaps, as a parson, you would wish to be told. Just up there against the bank is the body of a woman. Been in the water some days, I'd say. I've sent the boy for the constable.'

Harding paused, quite shocked. 'You seem very sure about this. Did you see clearly?'

'Oh yes, sir. I've seen bodies a plenty in this river in my time. Most times the current just carries them along and they end up on the way to Bristol but sometimes they get trapped, see?' He lowered his voice to indicate that he was imparting the arcane lore of the river. 'The water in their clothes weighs them down and they sink. Then after a day or two they starts to change.'

'Change?' Harding was horribly fascinated.

'There's like a gas builds up inside them, you see, and they floats again. This one done that but it's got tangled in the branches of the willow. She weren't there yesterday so I reckons she'd have gone in some way upstream, got stuck, got unstuck when she floated up, then come down here today and got stuck again.'

'Dear God, man. And do you mean you see this sort of thing regularly?'

'Oh yes, sir. I reckon I've pulled more than a dozen bodies out of the water.'

'A dozen! Great Heavens. And were they all women?'

'Oh no sir, two of them was. Both young 'uns and in the family way if you see my meaning.

63

Last 'un was ten year ago. I expect this un'll be the same sort of thing.'

'How awful. But what of the others?'

'Well sir, they was mostly sheep.' Harding's involuntary smile left his lips at the sight of his friend's face, suddenly jolted into a realisation of the seriousness of the situation. In no hurry to approach the object of their attention, the three men stood silently contemplating it for some minutes. Their reveries were interrupted by the return of the ferryman's lad, accompanied by a tall, heavily-built man in working clothes and a leather apron. Harding knew him for David Rees, the village blacksmith and constable and he greeted him with a nod. Rees looked for a while at the bundle in the river and then turned to the ferryman. 'You and me can get 'er out then.' The ferryman nodded and they made their way along the riverbank, whose mud came up to their knees and overtopped their boots. The constable took a firm grip on the corpse, holding it by the shoulders, and tugged it free of the hanging vegetation. Then the ferryman took it by the ankles and together they swung the body up onto the path and laid it as gently as they could on the ground. Harding and Castlemaine approached and looked down at what only a few days before had been a young woman.

'She's been dead two days or more in the water,' the constable remarked. Seeing Harding's questioning look, he elaborated: 'It takes that time for them to go stiff and then go back.' He demonstrated the limpness of the corpse's forearm. Harding looked away. Castlemaine's face was drawn and grim.

The ferryman went to his vessel and came back carrying a sheet of the same material that covered the ferryboat, the great oar that propelled it, and some lengths of rope. He and the constable lifted the body onto the cloth and then passed the ropes under it, tying them above so that the oar, passed between the ropes, could be used to carry it with as much dignity as possible.

The woman's body was smothered in mud and waterweed. Her hair and clothes were tangled with twigs, leaves and rubbish from the river. With a surprisingly gentle gesture, the constable scooped up a handful of water and brushed it over her face, washing away the mud. Harding felt a sudden shock. Until now this had been an anonymous corpse, a thing, floating in the river. Now with a start he saw it as a woman, about the same age as his Jane had been when she left this world and him. A great sadness swept over him, he felt faint and clutched the mooring post for balance.

'Are you all right, yer reverence?'

'Yes, I . . . ' Harding recovered his composure. 'I wonder if I should say a prayer. I don't know what would be prescribed for such . . . ' He tailed off.

'The shepherd one, Parson?' suggested the ferryman, so Harding produced his prayer book from the pocket of his coat and read aloud the twenty-third psalm.

The Lord is my shepherd: therefore can I
  lack nothing . . .
Yea, though I walk through the valley of

65

the shadow of death, I will fear no evil;
for thou art with me . . .
thy loving-kindness and mercy shall surely
follow me all the days of my life; and I
will dwell in the house of the Lord for
ever.

Then the two workingmen hoisted the grim bundle on their shoulders and all four men made a melancholy procession to the Blue Boar Inn, where the body was laid in a back room.

'What will happen now?' Harding asked the constable.

'Coroner's Inquest tomorrow, your reverence, then we'll bury her.' Harding nodded, and the other added, 'It were good as you said that prayer.'

Harding nodded again, but something in the tone of voice made him aware that there was something unsaid. He raised an eyebrow.

'Vicar here won't bury such a girl,' the constable explained. 'She'll be buried outside the churchyard with no prayers.'

'But she must have family — people she knows. Will no attempt be made to discover who she is?'

'If she were missed, someone would have been looking for her by now.' The constable's tone was level but resigned and world-weary. His was the voice of one who had had this conversation before. 'We've had three or four like this in my time. None of 'em were ever claimed. If anyone did know 'em, they didn't want to own it.'

The realization of his meaning dawned on Harding. A suicide could not have Christian burial. 'But how can anyone be sure?' he asked. 'Surely it were better to err on the side of generosity?'

'Not as how Mr Andrews will see it.' The constable's tone was flat.

Harding knew that it was hardly for him to question the judgement or ruling of the vicar of Widcombe in matters relating to that parish, but he felt troubled as he and Castlemaine left the inn. They walked up Widcombe Hill to the livery stable where Harding's mare was kept and from where they had arranged that Castlemaine should hire a mount.

They collected their horses, saddled and mounted them, and rode further uphill, intending to make a circuit of Bath and enjoy the views from the hills over the city. But both men were subdued by their experience. Castlemaine, normally as loquacious as his countrymen were famed to be, was quiet and contemplative. Harding became more and more troubled as he rode. The similarity in age, if perhaps not of station, between the unfortunate woman over whom he had read the psalm and his own dear wife, whose loss seemed the more hard to bear with this fresh reminder of mortality, had shaken him. Alongside this was the constable's assessment of the likely fate of the corpse — to be buried without ceremony in unconsecrated ground. It seemed harsh and even cruel that a woman who for all anyone knew might be blameless and a true Christian soul, should find her path to eternity hindered for want of a charitable interpretation of circumstances and events. The determination began to grow in him that he would attend the coroner's hearing the next day. More, he began to feel he must make enquiries and find out who the unfortunate woman might be. He wasn't sure how he would go about this, but it must not be left a silent mystery for no better reason than that no one cared. The Lord had said that he marked the fall of every sparrow. It seemed to Harding that he should be the person through whom the Lord marked the fall of this young woman.

The two men rode on, around the rim of the hills surrounding Bath, but their hearts were not in the ride and their minds were not on the view. Harding's conviction that he must do something to dignify the humanity of the poor soul they had dragged from the Avon became stronger, seeming to him to become linked somehow to his memory of his wife and the pain that still burned fiercely inside him when he thought of her. As the morning turned to afternoon, they turned their horses back towards Widcombe, buried in a silence that neither seemed able to break more than to exchange remarks about the route, the weather or the state of the path. Eventually they returned their mounts to the stable and made their way back to the ferry. As they reached the jetty, the boatman, perhaps chastened by their sombreness, immediately abandoned the account he had been giving to his lad of the history of gruesome finds in the river and rowed them silently back to the city. They parted at the jetty and Harding made his way home to boiled beef and port wine, filled with a new and sober determination.

* * *

Later that day, Lizzie found herself once again knocking on the door at the back of Mr Harding's Duke Street House.

'Lizzie, my dear, come in. Well, I don't know. I do not see you for weeks on end and now here you are again.'

'Are you busy, Aunt Mary?'

'No, no.' Lizzie's aunt kissed her on the cheek. 'It's all the better to see you. I shall not be here much longer and I will want to give current news of you to your father and mother.' Lizzie ignored the reference to her family as she followed her aunt down the dark passageway to the welcoming kitchen. 'We're all agog here, anyway, my dear. Sit down, sit down. I'll get you a drink and then tell you.'

'Well, I came to tell you something. I'm moving in with Mr and Mrs Leslie.'

Mary spun round. 'Why Lizzie, I am so pleased. Even more pleased this day. You will know why in a moment.'

Once the two women were settled, Mary continued, 'Well, my dear, you will find it hard to believe what has happened here today. There was a body, Lizzie, a poor young woman, washed up in the river.'

Lizzie paled. 'Who is it?'

'We don't know that. Why my dear, are you cold? Move nearer to the fire.'

'No, no. I'm not cold. Just . . . it's a shock. How do you know about it?'

'Well, Mr Harding went riding this morning with that new friend of his — that Irish gentleman, big, hearty fellow.'

'Mr Castlemaine? He isn't always so hearty.' Her aunt looked at her quizzically and Lizzie added, 'I deliver water for his wife.'

'Oh yes, Mrs Castlemaine is an invalid, come to take the water. I expect he is worried about her.'

'Mm, what about the body? What has the riding got to do with it?'

'They went down to the ferry to cross to the stables in Widcombe but when they had crossed the ferryman held them back and asked them to look at a body floating in the river. The ferryman's boy ran to fetch the constable and Mr Harding went with him to lay out the body. Very wan, he was, when he returned, very shocked. He's a kindly man, Mr Harding is — quite worried that there was no way of telling who she was and what terrible despair had driven her to do such a thing. Young women — there is too much freedom for them these days. It always leads to the bad.'

Lizzie looked down.

'Well,' her aunt continued, a little disappointed in her niece's reaction. 'I'm very glad you're to live with Mr and Mrs Leslie. I shall sleep more easily knowing you are not alone in Avon Street. It will be good news to give your father.'

Again, Lizzie didn't answer and Mary looked perplexed. Lizzie's reaction to this exciting news was disappointingly subdued. And yet at the same time she seemed very anxious about what was, when all was said and done, the death of a stranger in circumstances that were certainly not unknown in Bath and, she was sure, in many other towns and villages with a river flowing through them. It was sad to think of young women reduced to such acts of despair, but that was life.

'Thank you, Aunt. I will be going now. I am glad my news pleases you.'

Mary looked suspiciously at her niece, but all signs of her discomfiture appeared to be gone. 'Well, goodbye then, Lizzie. Come soon and tell me how it goes in Westgate Street. Now with all this trouble, I suppose there will be another delay in Mr Harding's search for a housekeeper.' She sighed.

Lizzie hardly noticed the walk back towards her lodgings. Her mind was racing. As her aunt had appeared to guess, she did indeed have experience of deaths such as that of the woman in the water — rather more than she had ever felt the need to inform her aunt of. Added to this, her encounter with Jack had shaken her up more than she liked to admit. Memories of violence needed to be suppressed if a young woman like her was to keep her nerve and determination to survive, but they left memories below the skin as well as scars upon it. Like most people in her situation, Lizzie had seen women reduced to wrecks by poverty, by beating, by endless pregnancies, by the diseases of the poor. She also had a working knowledge of the levels of violence that they could be subject to.

She turned into Westgate Buildings, deep in thought, and then changed direction abruptly and went back the other way. Her pace quickened and her face took on a look of more focused anxiety. She took shortcuts through a couple of alleys and was virtually running by the time she reached the back entrances of the houses on the High Street. She counted the backs of the houses and then slipped into the small garden of the one she was looking for. Slipping past the brick-built privy, she went down the steps and through the back yard. Quietly she opened a door and came face to face with Jenny carrying a chamber pot. The girl stopped abruptly and eyed the pot nervously. It slopped but didn't spill.

'Why Lizzie, you gave me a fright — and almost a tumble. You should take care, coming up on a body like that! This is one spill I would not relish the clearing of!'

'Sorry Jenny. But I am glad to see you.'

Jenny looked puzzled. 'Wait,' she said, and carrying the pot carefully, went up the steps to the privy. 'That's better,' she said on her return. 'Madam is too grand to come down the steps herself, so I must empty the pot three times a day. What it is to have folk at your beck and call day and night! I am run off my feet, Lizzie, as usual. What can be the matter? I have never seen you here before.'

A bell rang imperiously.

'There — you see, I have taken too long. What is it Lizzie? Be quick.'

72

'Nothing . . . well. I just wanted to see you.'

Jenny raised her eyebrows. 'And now you have seen me?'

'Have you seen Nancy?'

The bell rang again.

'I must go. No, I have not. I have not seen her in weeks. But how should I? I am here now and have precious little time to run around Avon Street and no inclination to do so. I do not wish to lose this position, Lizzie. I really must go.'

And with this, she turned and hurried off.

Lizzie walked slowly back to her lodgings, but she was only in her room for a few minutes before she left again and went into the adjoining tavern. Mrs Pardoe looked up as Lizzie entered and folded her red arms across her ample bosom. 'Why, Lizzie Yeo, twice in two days. I am honoured. I thought you were no longer a frequenter of taverns now you have gone up in the world.'

'I have a message for Nancy — have you seen her?'

'No.' The woman turned back to the kegs at her back and turned the tap, holding a cracked mug underneath it. Then she carried it over to a table and put it in front of a man who took it without a word and downed it in one. Mrs Pardoe returned to the kegs.

'Are you here to drink?' she asked aggressively.

'No. I am very sorry to bother you.' Lizzie hesitated. 'Have you seen Jack today?'

'No.'

'Yesterday?'

'Yes, I saw him walk by in the morning.'

'And in the evening?'

'What is this about? Why do you wish to know?'

'Did you see him yesterday eve? He comes here every evening, does he not?'

'Depends on whether he has business.'

Lizzie turned to go. Mrs Pardoe called after her as she reached the door.

'He did not come here yesterday.'

Up in her room, a grim-faced Lizzie lifted the floorboard and took out two small cotton bags. She pulled out her box from under the bed and put one bag into it. The other, she opened and from it took a few coins. Then she tied it inside her skirts, closed the box, opened the door and dragged the box onto the landing. She locked the door, lifted the box, went down the stairs and into the tavern next door. Mrs Pardoe looked up at her and stared. Lizzie put down her box, walked across to the landlady, reached into the cotton pocket and drew out three pennies.

'Here is what I owe you, Mrs Pardoe, and here is the key to my room. I will be leaving now.'

'Well! Don't you think you can come running back, Miss Lizzie Yeo.'

'You can be sure I will not.'

Lizzie carried her box to Westgate Street, opened the door of the apothecary shop and went in.

'Ah,' said Mr Leslie, rubbing his eyes. 'And I am mightily glad to see you here, Lizzie. Come and measure this out for me, will you my dear?'

Lizzie put down her box and walked over to the counter.

6

On Monday, Jonathan Harding got up early, dressed and breakfasted. He then put on his wig and coat and left the house on Duke Street to walk briskly in the direction of the ferry. During Sunday, he had had plenty of time to think about his experiences, especially during morning worship. The story of the woman taken in adultery was read from the New Testament and Christ's teaching still resonated in his memory: *He that is without sin among you, let him first cast a stone at her.* He was the ferryman's only passenger at this early hour and as they crossed the Avon, he engaged him in earnest conversation. Before he disembarked on the Widcombe side, Harding gave the man clear instructions and a sum of money to carry them out. Then he strode along the riverbank — not towards Widcombe, but in the other direction to the parish of Bathwick, where he called on the vicar, Mr Snape.

Bathwick was a tiny parish of a hundred and twenty people, who scraped a living as smallholders. Its vicar was paid only seventy pounds a year, with the use of a rather rundown vicarage and a small area of land, which supported the cultivation of a few vegetables and the keeping of a dozen hens. Despite this frugal endowment, Mr Snape was satisfied with his lot, supplemented as it was by frequent burial fees.

Indeed it was said that his ministry was concerned more with the dead of the city of Bath than the living of Bathwick. There was little space within the city for graveyards. Burial at or near the Abbey was prohibitively expensive — a privilege of the rich and the well connected. Those of the departed who escaped the anonymity of the paupers' mass grave but could not aspire to the Abbey's stone-walled vaults were generally laid to rest in one of the adjoining parishes such as Widcombe or Bathwick. Hence the principal support of Mr Snape's family was the steady stream of funeral fees from the city's deceased inhabitants. It was in this capacity that Harding and he were acquainted, the latter having often been involved in the arrangement of such funerals and having often officiated at them. Their conversation was brief and business-like. Harding purchased a grave plot, paid the funeral fees and the cost of the sexton, exchanged polite greetings with the vicar, and took his leave. As he walked back towards Widcombe, alongside the river, his expression was set and determined.

The coroner's court was convened at eleven o'clock in the Blue Boar. The presiding coroner was none other than the attorney, Mr Strang, known to Harding through their joint interest in the administration of the Girls' Charity School. Also present were the two constables, the innkeeper, the ferryman, a Dr Gumble, whom the coroner had requested to examine the corpse, and a few idle residents of the village with nothing better to do. Mr Strang opened the proceedings and took evidence from the boatman as to the discovery of the corpse and from the doctor, who gave it as his opinion that the unfortunate woman was of the lower classes and had drowned. There were no marks of assault or injury to suggest this was anything other than either an unfortunate accident or a suicide, the latter, in his opinion, being much the more likely. Mr Strang was aware that this evidence articulated the assumptions of most people in the room, but he pressed the doctor a little further.

'What was the basis of your opinion, concerning the manner of her drowning, Doctor?'

'Enquiries have been made in the village and the city, sir, and no one knows of a missing woman. Why should a stranger, known to no one, be walking alone by the river and be so careless as to fall in and be unable to save herself?'

'Quite so, Doctor. Thank you,' said Mr Strang drily. 'Has anyone else made enquiries for a missing woman?'

The elder constable confirmed that he had questioned people locally and had conferred with two of the city beadles. He agreed with the doctor's assessment that she was a stranger.

'Then it seems,' declared Mr Strang, 'that we may safely assume that this poor creature's death was not the result of foul play, nor the work of any third party. In the absence of any good reason to assume or attribute any intent on her part, I feel safest in recording her death as due to misadventure and to release her body for burial. I have received a request for the body to be given into the care of the Reverend Mr Harding for removal to a site of Christian burial in another parish rather than in the ground reserved for strangers beyond the churchyard. Unless anyone has cause for dissent, I shall so direct.'

This was the cause of considerable surprise to the people in the room. There was much speculation as to why — and on whose behalf — the clergyman had taken this interest. Josiah Walters, Churchwarden of Widcombe exclaimed:

'But our sexton be ready to put 'er in the ground 'ere!'

'That is precipitate on his part, sir,' chided the coroner. 'It is no part of my duty to decide whether Christian burial is appropriate here. I represent the county of Somerset and leave matters of religion to the men of the church. Mr Harding, are you prepared to take charge of the body?'

'I am, sir,' replied Harding. 'A coffin has been prepared by Mr Sykes and I have engaged the services of Mrs Tolley of this parish to lay out the body. As soon as she is done, we can take it to Bathwick for burial.'

'Then,' declared the coroner, 'I order that this shall be done and I declare this coroner's inquest closed.'

He gathered up his documents, put on his hat and indicated to the ferryman that he now wished to return to Bath. As he left the inn, the impromptu courtroom was filled with excited debate. Mr Harding, however, stepped quietly away to instruct Mrs Tolley to begin her task. By mid-afternoon the old woman's melancholy work was completed. The nameless corpse was laid in her plain wooden box by Mrs Tolley and by Mr Sykes's apprentice, Tom, who nailed down the lid and then, with the aid of two other men engaged by the ferryman, on Mr Harding's instructions, placed the coffin on a handcart brought for the purpose to the inn yard. Mrs Tolley then informed Mr Harding, who was waiting in an upstairs room, that all was prepared, and he gave her two shillings for her trouble.

Mrs Tolley was a farmhand's widow who was known to have skills in midwifery and in the care of women's troubles. In the course of her life she had seen much to make her cynical about men and women. She took the coins and studied Harding's face. He was not so unworldly as to fail to read her thoughts.

'I know no more than you, who she was,' he said. 'Our Saviour said, "in as much as ye have done it unto the least of these my brethren, ye have done it unto me.' Whoever she was, He saw her fall, be she no more than a drudge of Avon Street.'

'Perhaps, sir, she were more a gentlewoman than that . . . '

Harding was angered by the implication. 'You know the doctor's evidence!' he exclaimed. 'One of the common type,' he said.

'I dunno about that, sir,' the old woman muttered. But, reflecting on her two shillings, decided to leave the matter there.

The men took the body on the handcart to the riverside and, led by Harding and accompanied by the ferryman, along the path to the little riverside church of Old St Mary's, where they were met at the gate by Mr Snape's sexton. Harding took out his prayer book and began: 'I am the resurrection and the life . . . ' The same words that, just a week before, had been read in pomp and ceremony in the great Abbey Church, in the presence of gentlefolk and dignitaries, were now recited in the presence of five working men, standing in the gathering gloom of a February afternoon as a light drizzle began to fall. The wind was getting up, shaking the branches of the yew trees, and Harding moved as quickly as was decent through the service as they progressed from the gate to the church door, and from there to the newly-dug plot, where the nameless coffin was lowered into the ground. By the time he had reached 'earth to earth, ashes to ashes, dust to dust . . . ' the spadeful of earth cast onto the coffin by the sexton was turning to mud, the drizzle was becoming rain, and the evening was growing cold.

Harding felt sorrowful that this should be anyone's end — a hurried succession of prayers, a perfunctory burial, everyone wanting it over quickly so they could return to their lives, to light and warmth. Yet he, too, was grateful to lead them in the final words of Grace, to see the sexton shovelling earth hastily into the grave, to dismiss the workers, each with an extra sixpence, and to walk back along the river in silence to cross by the ferry, along with a group of passengers complaining at having to wait so long for the ferryman in such bad weather. When he stepped onto the jetty on the city side, he was, at last, alone with his thoughts. It was dark and cold and the rain was lashing down. His coat was soaked through and he was shivering. But he felt a grim satisfaction that, in some way he could not put into words, he had performed an act of charity out of love for the memory of his wife. At the same time, something still troubled him. There was something about the events that left him uneasy. A nameless body in an umarked grave was not an unusual thing and yet, having taken it upon himself to see the woman decently buried, he now saw that anonymity as an injustice. There was, he supposed, little he could do about that but it continued to trouble him as he arrived at Duke Street, to a fire, dry clothes, and to a hot punch prepared by Mary Yeo.

★　★　★

Later, after Mary had served him his dinner, there was a loud knocking at the door. Mary went to open it and was confronted by a man dressed in a bright blue coat with velvet collar and cuffs and a canary-yellow waistcoat. Both his black breeches and his shoes were adorned with silver buckles, although the white stockings between the two were well spattered with mud. He swept off his black, felt hat, releasing from his curled wig a shower of white powder.

'Radleigh — I am come to visit my dear old friend Harding. Would you be so good as to apprise him of my arrival?'

'Sir,' Mary said, averting her face and hiding her raised eyebrows. 'Please wait a moment and I will tell him you are here.'

But Harding had come into the hall at the sound of is old friend's voice.

'My dear Harding! Here I am at last. How are you, my fine fellow?' Radleigh thrust out a large hand which emerged from a sea of lace, and grasped Harding's, who was rather surprised that his old college friend had not timed his arrival to coincide with the evening meal. Unless, he reflected, better fare had been on offer elsewhere.

'I have come hot foot from dining with a gentleman name of Anderson. You are acquainted, I'm sure?'

He assumed a look of puzzlement at Harding's obvious ignorance of Anderson's existence. 'Big name in the theatre, don't you know. Says he knows Garrick well. He was going on to play cards at the Assembly Room and would insist on my going with him, but I said, no — I must call on my good friend Harding, before I attend on any others in this city.'

Harding considered ruefully that it might not have been quite so hard for Anderson to part from Radleigh as the latter implied, but was, anyway, grateful for the visit of someone who would lift his spirits and distract him from the melancholy memories of his day. He called for a bottle of port and the two men settled in the library to renew their acquaintance in front of a roaring log fire. Radleigh sat opposite him, spreading the tail of his coat as he did so. His brass buttons glinted in the firelight. Some years had passed since their last meeting and they had both changed. Harding, whether as the result of bereavement, of riding, of his frequent walks around Bath or of a combination of all three, had retained the trim figure of his youth. Radleigh, despite the physicality of his profession and his tendency to rely on the goodwill of others to provide him with regular sustenance, had noticeably spread. Harding raised his glass.

'To old friends.'

'Indeed. To friendship!'

They had plenty to talk about — news of shared acquaintances and the events that had passed in their lives. When Harding spoke of the loss of his wife, Radleigh was solicitous.

'Will you not marry again?' he asked. 'A clergyman should have a wife and George a mother.'

'It is not my wish,' replied Harding quietly and firmly. The actor sensed that this was not a subject he should press his old friend on. But he decided privately that he would try to see to it that Harding was introduced to a woman who would make him reconsider his position. He already had one in mind. In the meantime, he turned the conversation to his own situation, which he portrayed as a tragi-comedy of high drama.

Harding listened to the much embroidered account of his friend's many romantic attachments, remarking only that it was much to be regretted that Radleigh had not found it possible — no doubt as a result of his somewhat nomadic existence — to entertain the possibility of marriage, with the comforts and consolations it can bring.

'Why, on the contrary, Harding, I assure you that the matter has been of a constant concern to me. Nothing could be more earnestly desired, and I have often had cause to hope, but it was not to be. In the thespian world, one meets, of course, many beautiful ladies, but the fact is, my dear fellow, that those who'd have married me were not quite respectable, or were without any property, or indeed often both at once — and those I'd have wed never seemed to find me — how shall I put it — a serious proposition — as a husband?

'Really, Richard?' Harding tried to make his voice solicitous as well as amused.

'In truth, perhaps they find me to be less respectable or less well provided for than they hope for.'

'Or, indeed, perhaps both at once?' suggested Harding lightly, much to his friend's amusement. He had noticed, as they had talked, that Radleigh's waistcoat was worn in places and his cuffs a little ragged — that, in fact, all of his clothes were not as pristine as their grandiosity might have led one to expect. As the port went down and the evening drew on, Radleigh turned the conversation to safer topics, regaling Harding with endless stories of theatrical triumphs (largely his own) and disasters (usually of his rivals), interspersed and enlivened by verbal cameos of theatre managers, actresses and their admirers, cronies, colleagues and creditors, by wry reflections on the way of the world and by a sprinkling of scandal and gossip.

Harding was, as always, disarmed by his friend's frivolity. There was in it, he believed a kind of innocence, a freshness — an almost child-like quality. On the other hand, he could not be quite at ease with Radleigh. What might be an attractive frivolity in an undergraduate could look close to irresponsibility in a grown man. The lightness of touch with which the actor contrived to get himself into and out of entanglements, financial and romantic, could so easily slip into something more serious, with grave consequences for both his immortal soul and his earthly liberty. At the same time, he was bound to consider the implications for his own reputation of an association with such a man.

This made it all the more problematic when Radleigh broached the question of whether Harding would attend his performance at the theatre. On the one hand, Harding agreed with his friend that it was by no means unheard of for a man of the church to enjoy a night at the theatre — although, of course, not all productions would be suitable. Shakespeare, he conceded mentally, was quite acceptable. There were also, though, those in the clergy who condemned all theatre as sinful, along with such vices as dancing, hunting, music and gambling, although they were in a minority in Bath. Then again, it would not do to be too closely associated with theatrical types. That such people led lives of licence and intemperance was commonly understood. For the Reverend Mr Harding to sit in a box at a performance of *King Lear* was perfectly respectable. For him to mix afterwards with the cast as they caroused in the Cock Inn would be unthinkable.

This train of thought led Harding to remember what Castlemaine had told him about the famous actress who was supposed to come to Bath with Radleigh. 'Did Mrs Maltravers accompany you from London?' he asked. 'People here are quite excited at the prospect of seeing her perform, I have heard.'

His friend's smile died and he looked down. 'I came alone,' he said. 'Truth to tell, I have not seen Mrs Maltravers for four days and I do not know where she is. Ask me no more, I pray you. I am quite out of sorts with her.'

His tone and demeanour so contrasted with his behaviour up until this point, that Harding decided not to pursue the matter further. Instead he produced another bottle of port and they passed more time in reminiscence of their student days and of gossip in Bath. Harding told his friend about the averted duel in the Assembly Room and about the body found in the river. This last he passed over quickly, not wanting to introduce too solemn a note into an evening that had quite improved his mood, nor to discuss his unusual involvement in the burial of the body. Radleigh informed his friend of his intention to take the waters whilst he was in the city — since he was experiencing a regular aching in his bones. Finally and late at night, Radleigh made his unsteady way from Duke Street to the Bladud Inn and Harding made his equally unsteady way to bed.

7

At the same time as the unfortunate woman's body was being buried in Bathwick, Squire Pocklington's carriage rattled to a halt outside The Bear Inn at the top of Stall Street. John, his groom, reined in the two horses, nodded to the boy beside him and jumped down, calling, as he did, for him to run round the back of the building and find the stable lad. A cloud of yellow dust filled the air and settled on his topcoat and hat, already spattered with the mud they had gathered on their way in from the large village of Road. The golden limestone that was transformed into the beautiful new buildings of Bath was soft, and, when being worked, polluted the air as thoroughly as it pleased the eye. The pounding of horses' hooves on the newly improved roads added to the fine mist that hung in the air — a compound of stone dust, sawdust, powdered lime and sand. The lungs of the citizens of Bath, as well as those of its visitors, paid the price for the improvements they saw all around them.

Robin reappeared with a stable lad, as thin and shabbily dressed as himself. They took the reins and led the horses round into the yard behind the inn. As a fine drizzle started, the horses were unharnessed and led, each by a small underfed boy, from the cobbled yard into the comparative warmth of the outbuildings, to be watered, fed and settled for the night, sharing the hay with their diminutive guardians. A woman carrying a basket descended from the coach, followed by a man carrying a bundle under his arm. Then all three, carrying their paltry luggage, ducked their heads beneath the lintel of the door and entered the inn.

'Well, then.' A middle-aged man, red-faced and fat, appeared from a back room just as their eyes were becoming accustomed to the gloom. He wiped his hands on a dirty apron and ran them through the strands of greasy hair covering his wigless head. 'You'll be wanting to put up for the night, then? Where's the master? I've one good room free and can make shift for the rest of you.'

Sam, Squire Pocklington's Estate Manager and, to all intents and purposes, the head of this little band, removed his hat and answered gruffly, 'There's no master, although we're on his business.'

'Mistress, then?' The innkeeper turned his puzzled eyes to what appeared to be a lady's maid without a lady, accompanying two manservants in a gentleman's coach without a gentleman. Molly, pretty and wearing what was once a very good dress, now much darned and very dusty, raised her brown eyes and answered clearly, 'There's no mistress, either. We seek news of her here.'

The fat innkeeper rubbed his already flushed face and shook his head doubtfully. 'Well now, I know not what this nonsense means. State your business or be on your way.'

Sam drew from inside his coat a leather bag and loosened the drawstrings. 'This is all you need to know, landlord.' He withdrew two coins and placed them in the flat of his hand for all to see. 'We are Squire Pocklington's men and this is Miss Pocklington's maid. We are here on the good squire's business. We require two rooms and watering for the horses. Our lad will watch them with your boy. We shall be here two nights. Here is money. Now show us where we may rest.' The landlord reached for the money as Sam closed his hand, drew it back and replaced the coins in the bag. 'Rooms where we may bed for two nights and food for our empty bellies. Then you will see the good squire's money. We are here on his business. He will want to know that it was well spent.'

The landlord shook his head and indicated with a nod that they should follow him up a narrow staircase to a dingy corridor. He opened a door and nodded to Sam, who entered the room with John. The bed would sleep two. Molly followed the landlord up another vertiginous flight of stairs to an attic room where she put down her basket and closed the door on the doubtful face of her host. She then lay on the straw mattress on the floor of the tiny room and sighed. She couldn't imagine how they were to begin this task, yet all three had reason to be very anxious about the idea of returning to Road empty-handed.

The good squire's habitually florid face had flushed to a deep purple on the fateful afternoon of Miss Emily's expected return with her chaperone Miss Jane, Pocklington's spinster sister, when John had opened the door of the coach to reveal — nothing and no-one. Miss Emily's two large boxes and Miss Jane's small one were still strapped to the roof of the coach, but of the two women and Miss Emily's jewel box, which she always kept with her inside the coach, there was no sign.

'Where is my daughter? And where is my sister? And where in God's name are the jewels? What have you done, you asses? How have you lost your passengers and their wealth? How have they been magicked away? Answer me!'

His bellows could be heard all over the house and through a good part of the grounds, and were accompanied by blows about the head of the unfortunate John, who had not the slightest idea how he had achieved this piece of sorcery. The line of servants, headed by Bertha the housekeeper and Molly, Emily's maid (left in Road because Emily had insisted that Jane could do as both chaperone and maid), averted their heads and flinched as the blows rained down. But later, gossiping in the kitchen and stable, they were inclined to the squire's opinion, if not his manner of delivery, that it was a rum thing and no mistake and that it took a particularly negligent type of servant to lose a mistress, her aunt and all her jewels on a day's journey.

Later, in the privacy of his rooms, but still audible throughout the household — for he was a man of the countryside, more used to, and much more comfortable with, calling to hounds than making polite conversation in elegant

91

rooms — the squire had also railed against Jane. 'My own sister — taken in, saved from penury, given a home and the warmth of family — she is deep in all this. I am betrayed twice over, twice over, I say!'

And so he ranted, walking from room to room, shouting at the walls and the servants. For Emily's mother had died in producing one of her younger siblings and left all the responsibility of a young girl's upbringing, and eventual marrying off, to a man who preferred the company of dogs and horses to that of women and children. He had prevailed on his sister, plain, unmarried and entirely dependent, after the death of their parents, on the goodwill of the squire, to take charge of Emily's upbringing, to see that she acquired the refinements necessary to a young woman who might make a good match and then, once the product was finished, to accompany the young woman as her chaperone until such a match was achieved.

John, his ears ringing with the squire's words and throbbing from his blows, had been certain he had lost his livelihood — and probably the chance of ever finding another. Sitting in his cottage that evening, head in hands, with his wife and children standing solemnly around, he went over and over again his journey from Bath to Road. His wife feared that spells and witches had been involved as the woodland between Bath and Bradford was known to be home to both, and she personally had always feared for her husband on this journey. But John knew that this was human trickery and he suspected that blackguard William Cosgrove was involved — as indeed did everyone else. And he knew that they had passed without incident through the so say haunted woods, because the lady had alighted at Bradford with her chaperone and taken some refreshment while he saw to the horses. They had halted there barely an hour and then continued on their journey. And yet, somewhere between here and there, the two women had disappeared. But how?

★ ★ ★

This was precisely what the three servants and the boy had been sent back to Bath to find out — how, where, when and how to reverse the trickery and magic back the disobedient young woman? She could not have stayed in Bradford or any other village on the way. For a young lady to be lost, she needed to be in a city and so, all concurred, she had gone, or been taken, back to Bath and perhaps from there on to Bristol and from thence, who knew where? But, it was decided, the search would begin in Bath, where she was known. John's, and indeed Molly's, livelihood depended on finding the young woman and returning her to the bosom of her family. But how were they to do it? They would not be able to question gentry and it was amongst gentry that Emily had spent her time. They must, Sam had opined, start by question-ing the servants at the Squire and Miss Emily's lodging place and, at the haunts they frequented, find out anything they could about Captain

William Cosgrove and concentrate on Miss Jane, who must have been complicit in this deception and who, one might assume, still accompanied the missing lady.

Very early the next morning, the three servants and Robin, running along to keep up with them, began their investigations, beginning at the fine set of rooms Squire Pocklington had rented in order to parade his daughter at genteel events in the city. There they were able to establish the names of the servants who had waited on and kept house for the Pocklingtons, and to find them in their new employments. The initial wave of hope that rose in them at so easy a beginning to their investigations soon crashed onto the shore.

'Well now, you want to know what they did here and who they met with?' asked a puzzled Mrs Fox, found keeping house only a few doors along the street.

'Why are you asking such a thing?'

The three servants looked at each other and Molly said, 'Squire Pocklington returned to Road early . . .'

'Yes, I know that.' Mrs Fox laid aside the linen she was folding, but tapped her foot impatiently. 'Thought I was set for the season, and then they hie off back home. What a commotion! Lucky my sister knew of this situation — and mark you, I don't want to lose it through wasting my time with folk telling me things I already know!'

'Well,' Molly looked at her companions again and John shrugged. 'The squire sent for Miss Emily.'

'Oh, be off with you.' The woman turned back to her linen.

'No, please listen,' Molly continued. 'Miss Emily's coach arrived in Road without her.'

At this, the woman finally gave them her full attention. 'What do you mean, without her?'

'When the squire opened the door . . . '

'Yes?'

'She wasn't in the coach. Nor was Miss Jane. The squire is . . . well he sent us to ask if anyone knows of her whereabouts.'

The little brown eyes in Mrs Fox's rough, red face had widened as she spoke. 'Well, I certainly don't! Don't you accuse me of knowing things!'

'No, no, we just . . . want to know where she went and what she did while she was here.'

'But everyone knows that. She rose late and breakfasted then attended service at the Abbey.'

'With the squire and Miss Jane?'

'Why, yes. Then, let me see, they walked on the North Parade or the squire took coffee at one of the new houses, and the ladies went to the shops or the dressmakers. And Miss Jane went to the dressmakers a lot on her own, on errands for the young lady. Then, in the evening, they went out in all their finery to the Assembly Room or to some play at the theatre. Miss Emily usually had a rest in the afternoon — and that's when Miss Jane went on the errands. Ain't nothing unusual in their doings. It's how all the fine folk go on here. What will the squire do?'

They had her complete attention now. This bit of gossip would keep her going for a good few days.

'The squire will find Miss Emily and bring her home,' said Sam decisively. 'Is there anything more you can remember — about Miss Emily, about anywhere she went?'

'No, I don't know nothing more. The gentry don't tell the likes of me what they be up to!'

With this they left and made their way to Stall Street where they separated, the men and boy making their way to the Assembly Room where a duel had recently been averted, and Molly continuing along Westgate Street to begin enquiries in the shops and the market where servants and gossip gathered.

At the back of the Assembly Rooms, Sam, John and Robin came across a number of men, sleeves rolled up and hatless. For even in the damp chill that pervaded Bath for much of this dismal month, they were warm. They were unloading from carts and barrows the crates of fine wine required to accompany the evenings of cards, dancing and concerts that took place in the building. One man stood for a moment, wiped his brow and looked enquiringly at the two men.

'Good day to you,' Sam began.

The draymen hadn't heard about the trouble between Pocklington and Cosgrove, but were soon able to find someone who did. The women and men who went in to clean, to refresh the flowers, to wash the glasses and replace the packs of cards, worked strictly behind the scenes, but although the footmen who stood with trays of drinks, announced guests and carried messages may have seemed to be invisible to the society

96

that gathered there, they heard and saw everything.

'Can I be of assistance to you?' There was no doubt that, once adorned in his footman's uniform — his velvet jacket and white stockings, his buckled shoes and powdered wig — this man would have looked quite something. But in his every day, he seemed what he was — little higher in the ubiquitous hierarchies of class than Sam himself. But Sam, who prided himself on his ability to assess the character and worth of other people and on his plain speaking, needed to get information and, for this reason, he suppressed his smirk and spoke with respect to the jumped up flunkey who stood at the door.

'Be quick. I have tasks to attend to.'

'Why, to be sure, and thank you for giving me your time. I have come here on behalf of Squire Pocklington of Road.'

The flunkey gave a slight nod of his head as though he were well acquainted with the gentleman. 'I remember the squire well. I was privileged to serve him during his visits here. A most generous man.'

Again, Sam suppressed his immediate reaction. He had worked for Pocklington for more than ten years and knew for certain that any hopes of generosity this glorified waiter at tables entertained would most certainly be dashed.

'My business concerns an incident that took place here some few days ago — an unpleasant incident, which might well have led to bloodshed had it not been halted. My master was here with his daughter, Miss Emily. There was another gentleman,' his voice betrayed his doubt that this was the correct definition of the man in question, 'who engaged Miss Emily in conversation and who behaved in a most ungentlemanly way towards her. I seek news of this gentleman — a certain Captain William Cosgrove.'

The footman smiled a small smile. 'I do indeed remember this incident and I know a little of this gentleman.'

He spoke for a few minutes, leaning close to Sam and tapping his nose on two occasions. 'You will remember my help when you return to the squire?'

'You can be assured of that.'

'But you have not asked my name!' the man called to Sam's retreating back. 'I am called Robert Norton. Be sure to remember.'

'Robert Norton, I will remember.'

Leaving the Assembly Room, John, Sam and Robin crossed the High Street, dodging between horses, hawkers and dirty puddles, and stopped in an ale house for a jug of small beer and some refreshment before making their way towards the address they had been given. Robin, who was enjoying himself immensely and intended to detail every part of this adventure to his new companion that evening, looked and listened. They came quite suddenly onto a square, bounded by houses and fine pavements. And such a grand square! The houses on each side were very large — one long façade was the size of six or seven dwellings, and stretched along the whole side of the square. A generous road, offering plenty of passing room for the carriages on it, ran in front of the houses. In the middle of it all, surrounded by a stone balustrade with four iron gates was an area of gravel walks and lawns with an imposing obelisk at the very centre. Seeing a man sweeping the gravel, Sam sent Robin to run to the balustrade and call to catch his attention. Having never been in Bath before, Sam looked around in wonder. The Assembly Room had been a revelation and here was another wonder not more than few yards from it! For once he was lost for words and John, who had lost his customary jauntiness in the face of the calamity that had befallen him, now pulled himself together to speak to the sweeper who had come to the railings at Robin's request.

'Good day to you.'

'And to you.'

'What is this place?'

'This is Queen Square.'

'And it is fit for a queen!'

The man smiled as he leant on his broom. 'It is that.'

'We seek a certain lodging house.'

After listening carefully to the directions given by the sweeper, they set off up a steep street that was even dustier than the one they had come from. On every side could be heard sawing, hammering and the raised voices of masons, carpenters, glaziers, plumbers and painters. From a wooden crane on a plot to their right swung large blocks of smooth yellow stone, caught by men positioned high on a wooden platform, supported by wooden poles. Smaller blocks of the same stone were being carried in wicker panniers on the backs of men straining to climb ladders with their heavy loads. These smaller stones were being used to face the building's already completed shell with small amounts of lime mortar. Already, the stone surrounding the doorway on the lower floor of the building was being worked into fine patterns by masons. Adjacent to this building was the shell of another house, hardly begun. The crane swung round again, its load narrowly missing a man reaching the top of the ladder. Sam, John and Robin flinched as they watched, but disaster was averted and the masons carried on as though nothing untoward had happened. They looked around this scene of dangerous industry for a few moments more, and then continued on their way up the steep street of finished, half-finished and barely begun housing. Eventually they came to a quieter street and approached the door of a respectable looking lodging house.

Over the door a neatly-painted sign informed them that this was Daunts Lodging House, with six fine rooms to rent, £1.5s.6d for the week. Sam and John raised their eyebrows at such prices. The profligacy of the place! Perhaps Captain Cosgrove was a gentleman after all? If he had such wealth at his disposal, then perhaps all was not lost even if he was with Miss Emily? Perhaps they would find Miss Emily here and all would be reconciled with the squire? Robin rather hoped not, but Sam and John felt their hearts beat faster. They knocked at the door and were let in by a maid.

Back in the city centre, Molly began her

search. She had been to Bath before, in the company of Miss Emily, and could remember a little of the shops and parades. She walked along Westgate Street till it turned into Cheap Street, where her progress was suddenly halted. The air was full of shouts and smells, some good, some considerably less so. There were makeshift stalls of fish or saucepans, barrows with spinach and carrots and men and women with trays round their necks selling pies, gingerbread and flowers. A man and woman stood in well-worn shoes and ragged hats, holding brooms and brushes over their shoulders. Another man, his tricorne hat pushed back on his head, sat on a box holding a tall basket of leeks between his knees. Each one shouted out the quality and availability of their wares. The ground was covered in squashed vegetables, bits of pastry and large clods of mud. In between the legs of townsfolk and servants haggling over tonight's supper of ox tongue, mackerel or pigeon, children and dogs darted or scrapped over a piece of fat or the rind from a cheese. And beyond, past the Orange Grove, in front of the elegant Guildhall, coaches, carts, horses and pedestrians all struggled to turn or cross in the congested space. For a country girl it was almost overwhelming, but Molly, pushing and shoving between the vendors, was in many ways as headstrong as her mistress and she knew she had to make some progress in this investigation. So, bearing in mind her mistress's fondness for the sweetmeat, she decided to start with gingerbread.

The man wore a dull green coat, cut away to

reveal what was once a yellow waistcoat. His barrow was two-tiered — the bottom layer enclosed to keep his wares warm for as long as possible. A young girl stood by him and smiled at passing manservants when prodded by the older man.

'Spiced gingerbread, good an' 'ot! Buy my spiced gingerbread!' he shouted. 'Gingerbread, my lovely?' He leered at Molly.

'No sir, I seek news of . . . '

The man shrugged and turned decisively away from her. 'Move on, then. I don't sell news.'

'But you might have sold some of your fine gingerbread to the person I seek. Have you seen Miss Jane Pocklington, chaperone to Miss Emily Pocklington? Please sir, it is an urgent matter.'

'No, now be away with you. I've wares to sell,' and he began to shout again, precluding any possibility of further conversation.

Molly turned away and was wondering where to try next when she felt a tug at her sleeve and was surprised to see the girl who had been with the gingerbread seller. Molly looked towards him and saw him scowl, but asked the girl to repeat what she had said.

'There were a lady with Miss Pocklington, mum. She came two or three mornings to buy. She talked a little to me.'

The girl's face was reddening as she tried to ignore the threatening gestures of the seller.

'Yes,' said Molly. 'Please tell me anything you know.'

'She said it were for 'er niece, couldn't get

enough of our gingerbread.' Her face shone with pride.

'Have you seen her in the last few days?'

'No, Miss, ain't seen her in a week.'

Molly sighed but she said, 'Thank you for your help.'

The girl turned back towards the barrow and the angry face of the vendor. But as Molly was about to step off into the scrum of people, the girl looked back and called, 'She did like to buy fine ribbons, that Miss Jane. Always 'ad some new with 'er. S'pose they were for Miss Pocklington, but she did love 'em.'

Molly waved to her and pushed her way back through the market to emerge on the High Street and the shops of silks and ribbons.

★   ★   ★

Sam and John conferred together outside Daunts Lodging House while Robin looked from man to man as they spoke.

'That's a rum thing.'

'Aye, well that fellow at the Assembly Room was well above himself. He was mistook, no doubt about it. Where now?'

John shrugged. He had no idea where else to try. But Robin was tugging at his sleeve. 'John, John.'

'Be quiet, lad, cannot you see we are conferring?'

'But John . . . '

'I said quiet!' The exasperated John, despairing of his future, raised his arm, but lowered it when he saw a young woman approaching them.

'She wants to speak to you,' said Robin. 'She's been waving at you.'

The girl looked anxious, turning to look back at the lodging house. She was about fourteen and very nicely turned out in a clean petticoat and white mob cap.

'What is it, Miss?' Sam asked.

'Well, sir, I heard as you were asking after that gentleman, that Captain Cosbooth.'

'Cosgrove.'

'Yes, well him. Dressed like a soldier, very fine and like.'

Sam looked puzzled. 'But your master said he had not seen him, that he did not lodge here.'

'No, he didn't in that way, sir.'

'What do you mean?'

'Well, it was like this . . . '

'Sarah!'

'Oh, 'tis my uncle. I mun go.'

'No, tell us first.'

'Well, I saw him every morning, sir, when I swept outside. He came from the corner and stood on our doorstep. I thought it queer but that's what he did. Every morning, he stood there and looked about him. Then he walked off, towards the square, all stiff and proper like. Never spoke to me.'

'Sarah! Come here and be about your work or I shall have words with your father. Now, I say! This is a respectable house.'

'I must go, sir, but I heard say he was staying at Lock's, further up, you see, staying there but walking out from here. T'was strange.'

One more shout from her uncle and she was gone, leaving the three men staring after her.

'Then, on to Lock's, I think,' said Sam and they prepared to walk further up what was by now a very steep hill.

Lock's was a quite different proposition from the first boarding house. Where at Daunt's there had been a spruce front door, here was peeling paint; where there had been a brass bell, here was a tin plate hanging from a rusty nail; where there had been trimmed lamps, here was a single candle holder, and where there had been a brightly painted sign, here was a rotted piece of wood on which could just be made out 'Lock's Boarding House, rooms 5s 6d a week'. Sam rapped on the tin plate with the spoon attached to it by an old piece of string, but they waited a long time for an answer. He banged again and they were almost ready to give up, when the door creaked open and an old woman appeared.

'Yes? You want rooms? Well I'm full,' and she began to close the door.

Sam grabbed it and it shuddered under his grasp. 'No, Mistress, we are not looking for rooms but for news of a gentleman who lodged here a week or so ago.'

The old woman's face, grey and almost covered by a mob cap of a similar colour, broke into a crooked grin. 'Gennerman?' Then her face closed down again and she started to close the door. 'No, no gennerman here.'

'His name is Cosgrove — Captain William Cosgrove.'

'Don't know no Cosgrove.' The door was now barely ajar.

Sam reached into his bag again and at the sight of a penny the door inched open slightly. 'What did he look like then, this so called gennerman?'

'Well, he had a red coat and a wig like — well like the gentry — and, well like a soldier. Quite a fine-looking gentleman.'

The cackle startled Sam, who stepped back. 'That ruffian ain't no gennerman, and if you're friends of 'is, you can pay me what money he owes!'

'Owes?'

'Yes, owes. He owes me and a deal of other people. Gennerman indeed! Yes, got up like one in clothes not paid for either. They'll be a lot of people pleased to see friends of his. Cosgrove, you say? I'll remember that.'

'No, no, Mistress, you mistake me. We are not friends. We are servants of Squire Pocklington. We'll bid you good day now.'

And with this, they hurried off down the hill.

★　★　★

That evening, while Robin lay in the hay with a piece of bread and told his new friend all about the adventures of the day, the three other servants ate an indifferent mutton stew in the inn and discussed their findings. They had no news at all of Miss Emily, but they had quite a bit of information about the subsidiary characters in their little drama. Molly had started a systematic trawl of the seamstresses in the centre of the city as soon as she left the market. In each, she described Miss Jane Pocklington and asked if anyone had seen her. The first two shops had yielded her nothing and the seamstresses, busy with dresses that were needed for balls, and the mantua makers busy constructing the strange apparatus that went beneath them, were impatient of someone who did not even come to buy ribbons. But in the third shop, she waited patiently while a young, pretty, fair-haired woman explained that her mistress had changed her mind again and now wanted cream lace on the sleeves of her petticoat instead of the pink that she had first wanted. She nodded to Molly as she opened the door to leave the shop, but turned back when she heard Molly's question.

'I know that woman.'

Molly looked up just as the seamstress looked down and began the change to the lace sleeves.

'Have you news of her?'

'I don't know about news. Is this lady older than her niece by some years, with a . . . ?' The young woman hesitated and then patted her chin with her hand. Both women giggled and Molly nodded. Miss Jane did indeed have a large, hairy wart on her chin.

'Have you news of her?'

'What has happened? Why do you seek her?'

There was something she liked about the young woman, some kind of sympathy for another caught in the web of the whims of masters and mistresses with money to spend on them, and servants to run around fulfilling them.

107

'Will you walk with me? My mistress is very impatient and will be unhappy if I am delayed. My name is Jenny.'

'And mine is Molly.'

The two young women smiled at each other in sympathy at the trials of servitude to fashionable ladies, and walked together towards Jenny's place of employment.

'The woman you seek bought a great many ribbons. Also thread, lace, feathers, buttons an' all — a great many. I thought maybe she served more than one mistress — I saw her many times,' Jenny smiled ruefully, 'for my mistress is very . . . ' She paused for a moment. 'She has a great need for change. I am every day at one seamstress or another for the altering of things. So, I was surprised to see her — this — Miss Jane did you say?'

Molly nodded.

'This Miss Jane, then. I saw her often and so I asked her if her niece liked to be in fashion — just by way of talking, you see?'

Molly nodded again.

'And she said the ribbons were for herself! Very haughty she was. But I never saw her wear any. She was plainly dressed — not as plain as . . . ' She indicated her own hand-me-down garment. 'But not as a real lady.'

Molly was puzzled. 'Why do you think she told you this?'

'I do not know. But she could have set up shop with all she bought! We are arrived at my mistress's. I must go in.' She smiled and entered the house.

Sam and John continued to look at Molly in a puzzled way as she recounted her day. They had failed to grasp what she had quickly surmised.

'So then I went to all the other seamstresses I could find.'

'Why, and what could this have to do with Captain Cosgrove?'

'It has nothing to do with that gentleman.'

'No gentleman,' John muttered. 'Why, you have wasted your day then.'

'My day was not wasted. Miss Jane was buying stuffs to set up. Do you not see? She plans to be a seamstress. I'll wager she's no longer with Miss Emily. I do not think she's here, though.' She thought for a moment. 'I do believe she is gone to Bristol!'

* * *

The next day, the horses were harnessed. Robin said a tearful goodbye to his never to be seen again friend and then jumped up to sit beside John on the road to Bradford, where they would break their journey and make more enquiries. None of the party felt happy about returning to Road and to Squire Pocklington, but return they must, and hope that their findings would obviate his terrible rage.

There was one more enquiry to be made. They must try to find out what happened at Bradford. For, wherever Misses Emily and Jane were now, it was certain that they started out from Bradford. And to have done that, they must have had at least one accomplice, if they were willing partners in their flight or at least two abductors, if this most awful of possible occurrences took place. But the hour they spent at Bradford, while the horses were fed and watered, was a frustrating one. Yes, the landlord at the inn had seen the two ladies and indeed served them refreshments but, no, he had no idea what could have happened to them after that. However, his wide-eyed look of shock when informed that the two ladies had not been in the coach when it arrived at Road, appeared overdone and, they suspected, an act put on for their benefit. But they could get no more from him, nor from the serving maids or stable boy.

Sam thumped his fist on the seat of the coach as it turned out from the inn yard. 'Money has changed hands here, I'll wager,' he fumed.

Molly merely sighed as she nodded her agreement. And thus they reluctantly returned to face the wrath of the choleric squire.

8

Harding slept badly and woke feeling out of sorts with the world. His rest had been fitful and his dreams grotesque and disconcerting. It was not his habit to drink so much port or to drink so late into the night. His head throbbed and his stomach lurched queasily. As he dressed and made his way downstairs to breakfast, he went over in his mind the events of the last few days. The city of Bath was a busy, bustling place where — more than anywhere else in England — a man could never be sure what novelty, surprise or innovation he might encounter on any day. In the time he had lived there — only eight years — it had grown prodigiously in size and grandeur. Every day, it seemed, new and ever more imposing buildings appeared. Fashions in clothes, in music and in gaming came and went with bewildering speed. Even religion was in flux, as the new evangelical enthusiasts extended their influence, particularly under the patronage of the Countess Huntingdon, who was now, it seemed, proposing to build a chapel for them in the city.

In the midst of so much change and innovation, many people felt disoriented and adrift. Never before in history, it seemed to him, had human life been so volatile, so unpredictable. Harding, however, found it bracing. He was happy to be in a city at the forefront of the new ways. All around the nation, it was true, great changes were afoot. Common land was being enclosed to create more efficient agriculture; engines and machines were being employed in manufacture, enabling craftsmen to produce much greater quantities of goods. Communication was faster, with improved roads including the new turnpikes, stagecoaches and the new system of mails. And all of these advances fed into the fashionable centre of English society in Bath. Even in his subdued moods such as the present one, Harding thought it a great and exciting place to be.

In spite, however, of his pride in being a man who could deal with the unexpected, he found himself disconcerted by the events of the last few days. This world in which people were thrown out of their traditional habits and habitats, where they travelled speedily from one place to another, settling and resettling at will, was also one in which people could become lost, anonymous and ignored. How could it be that a young woman could be so alone as to die unknown and unrecognised? What sort of new world was this, where no one would claim or acknowledge her, even in death?

If he had hopes that this day would improve with his breakfast, they were dashed by his housekeeper. Mary Yeo had been patient and had tried for some weeks now to ensure that her departure would not cause too great a difficulty for her employer. She had made great endeavours to suggest ways he might find a suitable replacement for herself, and was exasperated by his almost wilful inability to act upon her advice.

Her patience was now at an end. She was determined to return to her family in Bradford and would postpone her departure no longer. In vain did Harding plead that he could not be left alone with no one to run his house. In vain did he plead with her to give him longer to make arrangements. Mary cared a great deal for her master but she knew he would never resolve his domestic arrangements unless and until he was compelled to do so. She now presented her final offer of a solution to the situation:

'Sir, my niece Lizzie is a strong and capable young woman. She were in your household when Master George were a babe and you know her to be honest and reliable. I know there was that business before, but that's over and done now and I think you know she's more than paid for that. She could do this work as well as I and fill my place here finely. I know she's spoke of well by Mr Leslie as she works for and that he'd commend her to your service.'

Harding, remembering his new friend's reaction to this suggestion said, 'I do not think she would wish it.'

He did not know why it was so, but he was sure that there was some dislike or resentment that Lizzie felt towards him and he still sensed a discomfort between them when they had met on the previous day. He pushed from his mind the idea that it was his own fears for his reputation that lay behind the unease.

'It would be a way, though, wouldn't it, Sir?' Mary continued obstinately. 'And you'd be . . . forgive me . . . '

The housekeeper looked down, avoiding his eyes. She knew she had overstepped a limit. Harding, however raised a smile from somewhere beyond his dyspepsia and ennui.

'I know, Mary, that you speak from goodwill and that you have a care for my wellbeing. You need not fear to speak honestly to me. We have known each other some years now.'

There the matter rested for the moment. Mary's determination to go was unwavering. Harding remained resolute in irresolution, unshakeable in his uncertainty.

★　★　★

It was the custom of people taking the waters in Bath to go to morning service first. Radleigh, telling himself that his evening with Harding had been a kindness to that poor, lonely gentleman, that the lateness of the hour when he finally got to bed and the amount of port they had drunk had been matters of gentlemanly civility, failed to attend the service at the Abbey before he made his way to the King's Bath. And, although it was certainly true that he suffered increasingly from aches and pains in his limbs late at night and that he fully intended, as recommended by his physician, to drink of Bath's miraculous waters as well as bathe in them, the concomitant recommendation of abstinence from alcohol was not one he intended to act upon. Despite his headache, he felt cheerful as he entered the building in which the bath and the pump were situated. He wondered what it was in particular about Bath that so lifted his spirits, in spite of his lovelorn heart and less than full pocket. Was it the buildings? No, he had seen grander in London and Dublin. Was it the way the golden stone caught even the slightest glimmer of sunlight and made the coldest day seem warmer? Perhaps a little. Mostly, he thought, it was that any place so devoted to the finer things in life, to music, fashion and theatre, would cheer any man of culture, such as himself. Meanwhile, he was looking forward to a good soak in the warm water, and to the gossip that would inevitably attend on that recreation.

After donning a jacket and breeches of coarse linen, Radleigh, still wearing his hat, was guided to and helped into the King's Bath. It was a strange sight. Men and women stood unsteadily, some clutching at protuberances of stone, some attempting to sit, or at least perch, on the submerged shelf around the edge of this pool of steaming water. A warm cloud rose eerily in the cold air making the roofs and walls of the surrounding houses move in and out of view. It was like being in another world. People, up to their chests in the water, conversed beneath their hats as though they had just encountered each other in a recreation in a park. The water, though, was comfortingly warm and felt pleasant to Radleigh. It was renewed every morning and so, at this hour, was relatively clean. He found a space against the wall and managed to prop himself against the shelf. The stone behind him was stained a reddish brown from the minerals in the water and the linen clothing that most people wore would soon bear similar stains. Radleigh closed his eyes for a while and let his mind bathe in the babble of conversation around him as his body bathed in the health giving waters. A little mild flirting was taking place on the other side of the bath, but on Radleigh's side the men chatted to the men and the women to the women. Several of the women wore little trays round their necks on which were kept, relatively dry, nosegays, diaries and handker-chiefs. Radleigh, startled by a cry, opened his eyes to see that one woman had, instead of a tray across her chest, a tiny babe clutched to her bosom. He hid his amazement quickly — for he was, when all was said and done, a gentleman — closed his eyes again and allowed himself to eavesdrop gently on the conversations around him.

'I tell you, she has disappeared. There has been no sight of her since the coach stopped at Bradford.'

'A lady cannot disappear — except by her own arranging!'

'Or that of another . . . '

'She took no luggage — nothing but her jewels.'

'I believe, sir, that she will be discovered in Bristol — or London, with that blackguard Cosgrove. He's to be found somewhere in this.'

'Perhaps. But will she be found married or abandoned — or even dead? A young lady may believe that a gentleman desires her heart when all along it is her jewels which are a greater prize to him. It may be that once the jewels are obtained, the heart, and indeed the lady herself, become a burdensome thing.'

'She would not be the first young lady to have her head turned and her reputation ruined by an adventurer such as Cosgrove.'

'Well I, sir, believe not a word of the fusiliers. That man was an imposter if ever I saw one.'

Radleigh let his thoughts drift for a while and he was almost asleep when two young women entered the bath and waded slowly across to a space beside him. He raised his hat and the ladies nodded and hid their blushes behind their hands. They put their heads close together and began to whisper loudly.

'But what if it is her? What if it is Emily found in the river and no one to recognize her? What if that gentleman stole her jewels and then . . . '

The voice became indistinct.

'Oh, how very dreadful. It is to be hoped it is not.' The other young woman's voice was high with excitement.

'But my father says he was a fortune hunter to be sure and that Emily Pocklington had not the sense of a . . . '

Again, the speaker placed her mouth close to the ear of her friend.

A clock struck and Radleigh saw that it was time to leave. It had been a diverting hour but the bath was becoming crowded. Besides, he was now tiring of the clammy linen and was hungry. The attendant pulled hard on the rope around his waist and eventually Radleigh was able to exit the bath, dress in his own clothes and join the crowd in the Pump Room.

Minstrels played in the gallery and Radleigh looked around him at the elegant room and the similarly elegant crowd and smiled in contentment. He drank two glasses of the hot, sulphurous water to the pleasant accompaniment of viols and flutes. Then he became suddenly focused on another conversation going on behind his back — for it concerned the very friend with whom he had spent such a convivial evening.

'Harding you say? Surely that cannot be right? Did he know the woman?'

'No. She was known to no-one. It is believed that . . . '

The voice became too quiet to hear as its owner leant towards his companion and a crescendo rose from the musicians. Radleigh concentrated hard. Harding had told him a woman's body had been found and that he had been present, on the way to Widcombe to ride, when it was pulled from the river. He had said that, as a consequence, he had inevitably been involved in the inquest and the burial. After that, he had made it clear that he wished to discuss the matter no further. And, as with the remarrying theme, Radleigh had suppressed his natural inclinations and let the matter rest. But this was a different slant on the tale.

'He would have her buried in hallowed ground and so he paid for it himself. I call it damned odd!'

'But who was she?'

'Some poor unfortunate. Dr Gumble thought her a suicide — driven to it by disgrace but Harding would have her buried properly.'

Radleigh glanced behind him and nodded to the two men. There was no doubt at all that they were gentlemen of the highest class. Their frock coats, sober for this medicinal activity, were nonetheless of the most superior quality. The men moved away and Radleigh pondered his friend's involvement in this strange affair. Soon, though, moving aside to allow a gentleman of military dress and bearing to obtain a glass of the water for his wife, he was distracted and then engaged in polite conversation with the colonel and his lady. The clock struck again and, sweeping low, hat in hand, he took leave of his new acquaintances and returned in a sedan chair to his lodging.

★　★　★

Lizzie had to admit it to herself — life with the Leslies was a good deal more agreeable than living on Avon Street. For the first few days, she woke and wondered where she was but she soon became accustomed to the quiet regularity of the Leslie household. Mrs Leslie told her husband that she could see the difference in Lizzie almost immediately and her husband nodded in happy agreement. They would have been less happy had they seen her meet with Jack and hand over the first of her instalments, but Lizzie made sure that they did not. She herself was not aware that the tight set of her face had relaxed and that she looked behind her a good deal less. She was warm, well fed and secure. Lessons in her letters could take place much more frequently and she even occasionally joined in conversation with the Leslies at mealtimes.

'It is sad about the woman found in the river, is it not?' Mrs Leslie checked that everyone had enough food and then sat down as she said this.

'Yes, my dear. Shall I say grace first?'

All three bowed their heads while Mr Leslie said a few words. They repeated his 'amen' then began to eat.

'I believe it was Mr Harding who conducted the burial,' Mrs Leslie continued. 'Is he not the gentleman your aunt works for, my dear?'

'Yes, he is.'

Mr Leslie said nothing. Keeping his word to Harding, he had not even told his wife of the way Lizzie had come into his employ.

'And no-one to claim her. Such a great sadness. It is hard to think that a young woman may pass to the next life with no single person to mourn her.'

They ate in silence for a while.

'And there has been no news of Miss Emily Pocklington. What a worry that must be to her poor father.'

'Lizzie, I have a little mixing I'd like help with this evening.' Mr Leslie tried hard to divert his wife. It was unusual for her to be so obtuse.

'Yes, sir.'

'I do hope . . . .'

'What do you hope, my dear?' Mr Leslie's voice betrayed an uncharacteristic irritation.

'Well just that . . . . No, it could not be, could it?'

'Could not be what, my dear?'

'Well, the body — the woman in the water. I do hope it is not poor Miss Emily.'

Both faces shot up in amazement.

'Really my dear, I think this most unseemly talk.' Normally so mild, Mr Leslie flushed.

'Yes, yes, you are right, of course. It is, nevertheless, what is being said.'

★ ★ ★

Harding, Castlemaine and Radleigh were taking a glass of wine in the Lower Assembly Rooms. Radleigh was beguiled, just as his friend had been before him, by Castlemaine's geniality, witty conversation and, even more than these two, by his generosity. The three men sat at the side of the room, half watching the dancing that was taking place, a much pleasanter activity to watch or take part in these days. For not only had Beau Nash forbidden spurs and swords to the men on the dance floor, but large hats and hoops to the ladies, all of which had greatly improved the experience for all concerned. The dancing and the card playing took place in candlelight, which added to the general sense of civilised comfort. There would be no trouble this evening leading to violence at dawn. Radleigh wondered how he could move the conversation round to the body found in the river and to the disappearance of Miss Emily Pocklington. He found he could not get the stories out of his head. He loved gossip and the possible involvement of his oh-so-respectable friend in

121

this piece of it was a lure he could not withstand.

'You are deep in thought, Richard.' Harding smiled. He was not used to this quietness.

'I am, my friend, musing upon a story I heard whilst taking the waters.'

'Ah,' said Castlemaine. 'Do you find them to be beneficial?'

'I am quite sure they will be, sir, quite sure. But this tale — 'twas of a young lady quite disappeared on her way home from Bath.'

'Miss Emily Pocklington — indeed I have heard the same,' Castlemaine replied. 'I am acquainted with her father — the man must be distracted beyond endurance. Mr Harding and I had reason to believe that we had assisted in averting disaster for that gentleman — but now 'tis come upon him even harder.' Castlemaine nodded sadly.

'And are you also acquainted with his family, Harding?'

Harding had not spoken and was surprised to hear this news of Miss Pocklington. He realized with a start that he had been so bound up in the business of the burial that he had thought of little else. He answered his friend.

'No, but there was an incident in this very room between Squire Pocklington and a younger gentleman. It looked to be a duel in the making, but we were able to head it off. The good gentleman decided to take his daughter home — far from the attentions of fortune hunters. But the carriage arrived empty? I had not heard. 'Tis a sad story, indeed.'

'And what of the body found?'

Both of Radleigh's companions looked up in surprise. Then Castlemaine spoke. 'That is another sad story. A poor disgraced woman, dead by her own hand in the river. We were there when the body was found.'

'We do not know that she was disgraced or took her own life,' Harding said quietly.

'My good man, your generosity of spirit commends you — and the charity you have shown this poor unfortunate. But I do not think we are in any doubt as to the story behind this sad occurrence.'

'You do not think it might be Miss Emily then?' Radleigh asked.

His companions looked surprised again.

'Miss Emily? How so?' asked Harding.

'I do not know, I am new to Bath. I only tell you what they are saying in the baths.'

To Radleigh's disappointment, neither Harding nor Castlemaine replied.

'I have not heard of this conjecture,' Castlemaine said shortly. He looked thoughtful for a few moments. 'But enough of gossip. More wine, good sirs?'

He smiled his wide smile and Harding was relieved to leave the subject alone. It was one thing to obey one's conscience but quite another to become the object of gossip because of it. He did not want to think about the way his actions towards the poor dead woman in the river might be construed. As for Emily Pocklington, his immediate thoughts were that she had run away with Cosgrove and that she would probably be found when her money was all spent. The wine

123

arrived, Radleigh made a toast and conversation, and, to Harding's relief, turned to lighter matters.

★ ★ ★

The next morning Harding, wigless and looking much younger with his brown, close-cropped curls, was sitting in his study writing a sermon. That is to say, he was looking out of his window and failing to write much at all. He had been hoping to pen some improving words on the bounty of God's creation and the gratitude that this should inspire in all men. Instead, he thought about the past few days — about the body, about the missing girl, about the need to find a new housekeeper and about his own reputation. He had felt driven to do something for the poor dead girl but perhaps he had not given it enough thought? He had risked causing ill feeling between himself, a well-respected doctor and another man of the cloth. The bishop was sure to hear of it and be utterly perplexed by Harding's actions. And how did he come to be a topic of conversation in the baths? Were tongues wagging about his actions? Was his reputation to be sullied? Was — and this was his worst fear — he to lose respectability amongst the gentlefolk of Bath?

Because he was looking out of the window, Harding saw Castlemaine approach his house. He heard the knock and he heard Mary open the door and bid the gentleman enter. She knocked on his door.

'Sir.'

'Yes Mary, I saw Mr Castlemaine approach. I will come down,' he said, pulling on his wig and hurrying from his study into the drawing room, where his new friend was standing.

'My dear friend — I did not expect to have the pleasure of your company again so soon.'

Castlemaine looked a little sheepish. 'No. But my night's sleep was greatly troubled by the recent events we have been party to. To be truthful, I was disturbed by Radleigh's conversation.'

'Come into the library. Mary will bring us some refreshment.'

They settled down once Mary had gone.

'I share your disquiet, Castlemaine, but I do not think there is anything to be done. Indeed, it is possible I have already done too much . . . '

'Pish sir, don't be troubled by the tittle tattle of idlers. You are a man of honour and acted accordingly. No, I was thinking of my friend Squire Pocklington and of young Miss Emily. It seems to me that precious little is being done to find her. It may be too late — but it may not. I have some time on my hands whilst my wife is recuperating, I thought I might ride out to Bradford and inquire of the missing lady. Whatever is said, it is not possible for a young woman and her chaperone to disappear without trace. There must be a trail to follow. I wondered, might we perhaps ride together out to Bradford and make some enquiries about these events?'

Harding thought this a very strange suggestion. But thinking of the gossip, of the intractable

125

problem of the housekeeper and of the attractions of fresh air when there are sermons to be written, he smiled at Castlemaine. 'Why not? I will join you. We will seek out the answer to this riddle.'

There was an old sermon somewhere that he had not yet delivered in Bath. He believed it concerned the Good Samaritan.

9

At six o'clock Harding rose, ate a simple breakfast, put on a riding cape over his black coat, pulled on his heavy boots and made his way down Duke Street to the ferry. The little frost that had settled on the town was being washed away by a weak drizzle, and as the dawn came up over the city behind him the light was grey and wan. Harding reflected that at least rain was better than snow for travelling in, but he knew that the roads would be muddy and treacherous and that, although his cape and boots were of good quality and his coat warm over the two shirts he had put on for protection from the weather, he would be wet, chilled and miserable by evening. The ferryman, who had by now come to accept that this clergyman was somewhat eccentric, none the less raised his eyebrows to see him embarking on a ride on so foul a morning. No doubt, he considered, this was some new errand of mercy. Neither cleric nor boatman spoke much; somehow the hour, the dim light and the weather conspired to urge silence upon them.

The ostler at the livery stables was taciturn as a rule and under the weight of the prevailing gloom came as close to silent and surly as he reasonably could to his social better. Unconcerned, Harding ordered his horse saddled and hired another to accompany him. Then he set off at a gentle trot along the riverside, leading the second horse. He crossed the river by the old stone bridge into the city. Harding rode on to Castlemaine's house where his friend was waiting with tankards of warm rum punch. Fortified by this, they set off on their mission to retrace the mysterious journey of the Pocklington coach, taking the London Road east towards Bathford and from there following the waggoners' route to Bradford on Avon.

At Bathford, they paused at the tavern and spoke to the innkeeper, but he had no recollection of the Pocklington coach's passing. He was certain it had not stopped there at any rate, nor would he expect it to so soon into its journey. Once out of the city they found the roads slippery and inches-deep in freezing mud, but the drizzle stopped and the sky, though still quite overcast and grey, lightened a little.

'This is an ill time of year for a venture such as this, I fear,' Harding remarked to his companion, more in order to break the silence than for any purpose.

'It is poor weather and hard riding, but it may work for us that so few travellers are out at this time of year — those who are may be more easily remembered,' Castlemaine replied.

'That is true, although in better weather, there would be more people abroad to remember them. Anyway, we must take the circumstances as they are. We must pray that the roads do not become still more impassable or I fear for our return. I am to preach at the Abbey in two days from now.'

They arrived at an isolated cottage next to a stream where travellers often paused to water their horses. Castlemaine knocked loudly on its door with the end of his riding crop, and after some time it was opened by an old woman. She looked at him with a mixture of suspicion and unease.

'We seek to know whether a carriage passed by here four days ago, carrying two young ladies,' he demanded.

The old woman said nothing.

'We mean you no harm,' said Harding. 'We wish only to know if you saw them — if they passed by here or waited here to rest their horses.'

'Well sir,' the old woman began, hesitantly, 'I stays inside this time of year. I can't be sure . . .'

'Oh come, come!' Castlemaine snapped. 'You must know if you saw them or no!'

But the old woman shrank back into the darkness of her cottage. 'I don't know nothing, sir. I didn't see nothing.'

No persuasion by Harding could coax from her anything more. She closed the door and the two men remounted and went along their way.

They continued their journey in the direction of Bradford on Avon, riding through the morning and early afternoon. Leafless trees, skeletal in their winter sleep, screened them and filtered the low light from the sky. The horses' breath rose before them and there was hardly a sound apart from the thud of their hooves and their laboured breathing on the upward climb. Harding was poor company, for he seemed distracted, his mind half on the task in hand and half elsewhere. Castlemaine suspected, correctly, that he was worrying about his domestic arrangements. They stopped for a few minutes when the steep terrain flattened out a little and they came out of the trees.

'It will be easier riding now, I believe,' Castlemaine said cheerfully. Harding nodded. 'You are very distracted, my friend. I fear I have pulled you away from concerns more pressing to you.'

'No,' Harding replied. 'I was glad to be so pulled.' He smiled ruefully. 'I have made no progress at all and for that I must bear the blame. My housekeeper has been forbearance itself. If only I could find a way to move forward.'

'You remain faithful to the memory of your wife. 'Tis an admiral quality in you but, I fear, not a very practical one. Could you not move on it for the sake of your son? A man in your station should have a wife to keep his house and his servants in order. 'Twould be no insult to your dear departed wife. I am certain she would wish it both for your sake and for that of the boy.'

Wearily Harding reminded him that this was not the first time he had ventured this opinion, nor was he the only one to do so. He did not wish to be ungracious but he found it tiresome. Harding disliked having this conversation because he felt it put him in a poor light. That no one could take the place of Jane Harding was not at issue, but that was no reason to live alone. That

130

almost anyone would be better than he at running a household, he readily conceded. That there were in Bath and about many very pleasant ladies who would think him a good match could not be disputed. Yet he resisted the idea implacably and did not want to think about, nor to explain his reasons.

'Well, sir, I do believe you will resolve your dilemma and, I most heartily wish, without the aid of the Avon Street girl.'

Harding's attempt to cover his surprise at the sudden twist of his companion's conversation was poorly done. 'Lizzie — Mary Yeo's niece? Why, what makes you speak of her? 'It's true she was once in service to me . . . '

Now it was the turn of Castlemaine to look surprised. 'I did not know of this, Harding. I must confess to amazement.'

Harding immediately regretted disclosing this piece of information. 'Oh, it was some years ago — she was new to Bath — from Bradford — a country girl. She served me for a while but she would not make a housekeeper — of that I am certain.'

'No indeed not! Then I should truly fear for your reputation.'

Harding fought with the rush of irritation he felt with Castlemaine for refusing to leave this topic alone. He did not reply and they rode on for a few minutes.

'Do not misunderstand me,' Castlemaine said eventually, 'I wish no discourteousness. But a man's household must be above reproach. I myself had cause to replace my housekeeper and

131

my man recently — at great inconvenience to myself. But I felt they wouldn't do.'

Harding nodded and thought to himself, not for the first time, that things may go very differently in a lively and fashionable city to the way they do in rural Ireland. His friend no doubt meant no ill will, and would soon learn that a degree of latitude would work better in his adopted home.

They met few people. No one who could be inside ventured out in this dismal weather. Those they did meet, herdsmen, a tinker and an old woman driving two pigs that had broken out from their sty, they questioned about the Pocklington coach. Their efforts were unrewarded, except that a turnpike keeper was able to confirm that he recalled the coach passing through his gate, though he was unable to comment on any passengers it might have contained.

'My tariff, sir, is on the number of horses, not of persons, you see,' he explained. 'I doesn't need to look inside of the carriages.'

Their task seemed fruitless, their journey dour, and it was with great relief that they arrived eventually at the George and Dragon Inn by the great stone bridge of Bradford, to rest and water their horses and to warm and feed themselves. The innkeeper of the George was as fat as a country publican should be, but spoilt the effect by being far from jolly. He took offence at Castlemaine's questioning and said that his place was to serve food and beer to his customers, not to spy upon them. Harding had more success with the ostler, when he went to check that the horses were getting their feed.

'Why yes, your reverence, I do remember that coach. The ladies went into The George for victuals and the coachman and I smoked a pipe together. They was here about an hour and then the ladies got back in the coach.'

'Both of them?'

'Yes sir.'

'And was there anyone else here at the time?'

'Well sir, ever since I heard from Squire Pocklington's man that the lady were missing, I've been thinking about that and I reckon there might have been a man hanging about here. I saw boot prints in the mud that I didn't recognise. 'Course I didn't think much of it at the time and now they be washed away. Mind you,' he admitted, 'they might have been the coachman's'.

'But nonetheless, the ladies both returned to the coach. You saw them get in?'

'No, sir, but that's what I been told. Anyhow, I thought about it like I said. I reckon that if a lady can enter a coach by one door, she can as easy get back down straight away on the other side and no one would see that from here.'

'You mean she might have simply passed through the coach and met someone behind it?'

'I ain't saying she did, your reverence, but I am saying she could have. And if the coach didn't stop again till it got to the manor, and if she didn't jump out as it were going along, then that's my guess as to how it might have been done.'

Harding conveyed the ostler's theory to Castlemaine as they rode out on the last leg of their journey that day, heading across country to Wormlow Manor where Castlemaine had arranged they would spend the night, having made the acquaintance of the squire at the card tables of Bath and gained his friendship by that most infallible of means — losing money to him. Castlemaine seemed cheered by their progress at Bradford. The idea that Emily might have been stolen away from the carriage there was at least something.

'Captain — as he calls himself — Cosgrove has not been seen since that night at the Assembly Room. He could have followed the carriage, enticed her away and carried her off on his horse.'

'And the squire's sister also?'

'Perhaps not. But then perhaps he had a carriage nearby, just around the corner, out of sight, or a second horse.' He sighed. 'It's a puzzle, I know, but there must have been some such contrivance — or else we are left with magic.' He smiled. 'Not a notion we could entertain! Perhaps he enticed her away here, took her jewels and then smothered her and threw her body in the river. Both riddles would be solved by this solution.'

'But why would he take her back to Bath only to kill her? It makes no sense.' Harding's mathematical, Cambridge mind revolted from the absence of logic in such a course of action.

'Perhaps he killed her and ran off with the Squire's sister? Or maybe the sister is the dead woman?'

Harding felt that his head was swimming. Of course such a thing was possible but it seemed to him more like an Italian romance than a likely explanation for events in an English city, even one so atypical as Bath. Nonetheless, he could see no better way of reconciling the facts as they knew them. Like the ostler's suggestion, it at least didn't require a supernatural explanation. It had been the opinion of the serving maid at The George that Emily had been taken by the fairies.

★　★　★

Lizzie had slipped out of the apothecary's shop and was making her way to Avon Street. Although she knew that the move she had made was for the best and that her life had improved considerably, the day she began living with the Leslies, what she had feared was loss of freedom and it irked her even if she had expected it. The gentle enquiries of the Leslies would be solicitous and merely made in the way of making conversation and showing a basic level of care for their protégée, but it annoyed Lizzie to have to make an account of her comings and goings. Still, it could not be helped. She would think of something harmless to report when the conversation arose. The image of the body in the river haunted her. There were things she needed to make sure of before her mind would rest. It might be the case that her good fortune had created a rift between her and Nancy, but the fact remained that she cared about her and that was all there was to it.

Mrs Pardoe looked up with a face full of scorn when Lizzie entered the tavern. 'So soon back, young Lizzie. Did the company of fine folk not suit you?'

'Thank you for your care, Mrs Pardoe, Mr and Mrs Leslie are kindness itself. They are the only company I keep.'

'Then I wonder how you find yourself here again.'

'I am looking for Nancy, Mrs Pardoe. Have you seen her?'

The older woman looked puzzled and then turned to draw beer for two men who had become impatient. The light in the tavern was very low — the windows were very small and the room went back a long way. Tallow candles gave out almost as much evil smelling smoke as light. Lizzie stood quietly. She knew Mrs Pardoe could not abide a mystery and would soon return to her in the hope of gathering some titbit of gossip she could relay to her customers. She was right.

'So, what is it you require of young Nancy?' Her tone was aggressive. 'Were you not enquiring of her before?'

'I did then and I did not find her. I wished to speak to her then and I do so again.'

'Ooh, you wished to speak to her. You have become quite the lady with your letters and your water. Well, what if Nancy does not wish to speak to Lizzie-come-up-in-the-world?' She spoke the words mincingly and laughed at her own joke.

'You have seen her then?' Lizzie worked hard to keep the interest out of her expression, and anger out of her voice.

'No. Haven't seen her for days — no weeks, now I come to think of it. But when I do I shall be sure to tell her that Lizzie Yeo wishes to speak to her. Now partake of a drink or be gone. You are wasting my time.'

It was the same wherever Lizzie enquired. Most people she asked said first that yes they had seen Nancy . . . now, when was it . . . ? And then realized that in fact they had not seen her recently. In fact, they could not remember the last time they had seen her. Finally, Lizzie found herself at the entrance to a narrow and very dirty alley. She hesitated, for she knew it contained one dwelling and she was not keen to visit it. But she shrugged and told herself not to be a fool. It held no dangers for her now, surely? She was on her way to settling her account with Jack, who would not risk his future payments by hurting her and, although she did not relish the prospect of his company, he would know if Nancy had disappeared. Nevertheless, she shivered when she reached the house. The window to the side of the door and the one above that were both obscured by very dirty cloth. No sound came from within the building. Lizzie almost turned and left. The thought of the apothecary shop and of the Leslies' gentle enquiries suddenly felt comforting and something to which she might return happily. What were these people to her, after all? Was it her place to run around after another's safety? She sighed. She knew that if she left it now, she would return tomorrow. She knocked on the door. Several minutes elapsed and she knocked again before the door opened a crack.

A sleepy-looking Jack rubbed his eyes and peered out. When he saw who it was, a hand shot out and he pulled Lizzie inside the door. It was dark in the house, quiet and noisome.

'Why, my dear young Lizzie. I never thought to see you come a-visiting old Jack. Delighted I'm sure.' He bowed mockingly, but kept hold of her wrist. 'Have you come to pay your second instalment so soon?'

'No.'

'You've come to your senses and think to pay me in kind then?'

'No, not that.' Lizzie felt nauseous and overwhelmed by a desire to get out of that place and run.

'What then?' Jack's voice hardened. 'For what do you rouse Jack from his well-earned rest?'

'I am looking for Nancy.'

He stiffened. 'Why?' he almost spat at her.

Lizzie instinctively pulled back from this unexpectedly fierce response. 'Well, just that I have not seen her for some time and wished to speak with her.'

'Why? What would the likes of you want with Nancy?'

'We are old friends . . . .'

'That was long ago — and so was the last time you sought her. Why have you come?'

'Just to enquire after her. No more.'

'You lie,' he spat again. 'There's some trickery in this. You think to make a fool of Jack again?'

'No, no I do not. Is she here?'

Lizzie found herself shoved towards the door

and was surprised by the force of it. The door was opened again.

'Get away with you, Lizzie Yeo. You are not to be trusted and Nancy will do better without you. Be ready with your next payment and do not come bothering me here again.'

He pushed her hard, almost thumping her back. Lizzie found herself tripping into a foul puddle and before she could turn, the door had slammed behind her.

10

After an hour of slow progress across sodden fields, Castlemaine and Harding finally came to the Manor at Bradford on Avon. It was only when he saw it, that Harding remembered that this was the house in which Lizzie Yeo had been in service before her disgrace. Immediately he felt angry with himself for thinking like this. If she had not had a child and lost it, and if she had not been discharged in shame from Wormlow's service, she would not have been the wet nurse who sustained his poor motherless son. She had done her penance and was no doubt forgiven by the Lord. It was not for him to think of her as a fallen woman any longer.

Squire Wormlow welcomed them and called his groom to see to their horses. Then he took them inside to a room with a log fire and a table laden with cold meat, French wine and brandy. As they ate and drank, he questioned them about their investigations. He was strongly inclined to agree with Castlemaine's construction, having taken a strong dislike to Captain Cosgrove who, it seemed, had once had the temerity to win money from the squire at cards. Whether from politeness, misfortune or want of skill, this was not Castlemaine's fate when, after supper, he and Wormlow decided to play. Harding had excused himself by virtue of his calling, assuring his companions that this did not stem from any

Puritan disapproval on his part, but was simply a matter of decorum.

'I have heard it said that some enthusiasts of religion, such as Mr Wesley, claim to think sport an abomination before the Lord, but I assure you I am not of his company. May you enjoy your games. Still what is proper for a gentleman may not be right for a parson.'

'I am pleased, sir, to hear you say you do not follow the strictures of that renegade Wesley,' the squire snorted. 'One of his men came around these parts last year saying that a servant had as good a hope of heaven as his master and that even the king himself was as much a sinner as the lowest labourer! Of course we kicked his backside and sent him packing. That man would have Cromwell back, I do believe.'

With that he returned to the table and Harding sat deep in thought, turning over and over in his mind the events of the day. Brandy and tiredness combined to send him into a half-waking reverie in which the drowned woman, the Pocklington carriage, the card tables of Bath, Lizzie's disgrace, ranting preachers and roundheads all seemed to swim before his confused vision. He woke up with a start and decided to take himself off to bed. Castlemaine and Wormlow were settling in to play late into the night.

So it came about that he was awake long before his companion or their host. It was a little after dawn when he heard a horseman arrive, loudly and drunkenly call for the groom to stable his mount, and then unsteadily enter the house.

Harding felt sure this must be the squire's son Jeremy, known far and wide as a drinker, a gambler and a womaniser. It was no surprise then to hear him enter the great living room and head straight for the brandy bottle. An hour or so later, Harding ventured downstairs in search of some breakfast. As he was making his way towards the kitchen, he was startled to hear a cry of distress from behind the door to the living room. He tentatively pushed the door open and out rushed a maid in some disarray and apparently in tears. Behind her stood, somewhat unsteadily, a man in his late twenties, still mud-spattered from his homeward journey, adjusting his clothing. Before he could be seen, Harding stepped quickly back from the doorway and continued his search for the cook, the maid having quite vanished.

By the time Harding had eaten a good breakfast in the kitchen, the young squire was nowhere to be seen, having finally gone to bed. It was only after Castlemaine and Wormlow the elder had come down and breakfasted and they were preparing to leave, that Harding caught sight again of the maid, dusting in the parlour. When she saw him, she blushed, turned away her eyes and then left the room. As they rode away, Harding mentioned the incident to his companion, who laughed and told him that the squire had been complaining of the loose morals of his servants, having had, over the last ten years, to dismiss no fewer than three serving girls who had been with child, and had lost another who had concealed her disgrace and then died in childbirth.

'Of course, those girls are giddy and lustful baggages, but I do think that young Jeremy could be a better son to his father by keeping his adventures outside the house,' Castlemaine said.

Harding was silent. They rode back to Bath, breaking the journey at Bradford again, this time at the White Horse, but gained no more information to add to that of the day before.

★ ★ ★

It was a miserable morning when Lizzie left the apothecary shop — nothing extreme, no gales or ice — in truth it was nothing much at all. Damp. Dull. The sort of day Bath could do so well in November or February, swathed in a general dampness, where drizzle merged with mist from the river into a dreary miasma which obscured the hills and weighed on the spirit. As she turned into Avon Street, she smelled its particular stench and thought that she could always turn back and forget all about Nancy. She owed her nothing and her previous attempt to find her had been fruitless and unpleasant. Still, now she was here, she might as well make a few enquiries. Although she had scoffed at Mrs Pardoe's suggestion that she now considered herself above the folk in Avon Street, she was amazed at the assault on her senses as she stepped into the road. It wasn't that life with the Leslies was luxurious in any way whatsoever, or that her walks through the back alleys of Bath to deliver the water were particularly sweet smelling, but

143

there was no doubt that Avon Street had a fragrance that was quite its own. There were piles of horse dung everywhere — the local waggoners used the street, which ended at the river bank, as a place to water their horses — but that smell was sweet in comparison to the underlying stench of ordure. Adding to the foul smells left by the water and sewage that regularly washed up the street and into basement rooms when the river flooded, was the stink caused by the residents' habit of throwing rubbish or emptying chamber pots out of their windows into the street below. You had to keep your wits about you in Avon Street to avoid a shower of urine — or worse.

There were few people about, but that was to be expected in the middle of the day. Most of Avon Street's population would be away at their work in the city. The keepers of the eleven alehouses would be up and about, and in the alehouses she would find the waggoners who, whilst their horses drank water at the river, took refreshment in something a little stronger, and then relieved themselves in the street. The houses were tall and crammed together and she was overwhelmed, as she stepped back into her recent past, by a sense of descending into a dark smelly tunnel from which she immediately longed to escape. Two children of indeterminate gender, both swathed in a collection of ragged shawls, squatted in the street, mixing ash with dirty water to make 'pies'. They didn't look up at her. An old woman sat in front of one of the houses on a small wooden stool. Several layers of

144

clothing — all of them patched and ragged — covered her. She stared down at the ground with rheumy eyes.

In front of the dark houses and beneath the precarious looking overhangs, posts were regularly placed — ineffective attempts to separate people from traffic in a street with no pavement. In fact, it was impossible to stay on the house side of the posts. There simply was not enough room, and so she stepped around the muck in the road, creating a small cloud of ash with each step she took. She held her cloak up a little — the few women around who had not gone into Bath to work had their petticoats pinned up — and stepped around the horse dung and a couple of pigs nosing around the piles of rubbish. She thought it unlikely that she would get any more information out of Mrs Pardoe and so she walked past the first of the taverns, looking around for anyone else who might remember her and with whom she could speak. Anxiety about Nancy had turned into a vague but persistent gnawing at her guts. Jack had sent his 'girls' out every night to look for custom and bring it back to the dingy house Lizzie had already visited. She wouldn't expect to see any of them out and about in daylight. But she would expect people to have seen them in the last few days. She needed to find someone less hostile than Mrs Pardoe to tell her that Nancy had been out and about and no worse off than usual. The grisly image of the woman pulled from the water, white and bloated with weeds tangled in her hair, might then leave her dreams.

She approached the old woman. 'Good day, mum.'

The woman's mouth dropped open a little, revealing two blackened stumps. She sucked and there was a faint whistle as a thin trail of saliva made its way down her chin. Stepping towards her, Lizzie caught sight of the woman's rotting nose and realized that she would probably get little sense out of her. She was also struck by a sense of the complete futility of her search for Nancy. This woman was probably no older than forty but her mind and body were rotten with the pox — a fate almost certainly awaiting Nancy and one from which she and Jenny had so recently escaped.

Lizzie put her arm gently on the woman's shoulder. 'How goes it, mum?'

The woman shook her head as if a fly were bothering her.

'Do you know Nancy, mum? I'm looking for her. Have you seen her?'

The rheumy eyes turned to her for a second or two and then the woman began to rock backwards and forwards, mumbling. Lizzie stooped down to listen.

'An' I told 'im sure. I told 'im good an' proper. I told 'im, I did.'

She began to weep and Lizzie stood up.

'It don't matter, mum. Don't worry yourself.'

But the woman was agitated and Lizzie saw that she was the cause. She sighed and turned away to see the two small children watching her. They were both barefoot and each had a single line of green snot running from nostril to mouth.

Their wide eyes watched her from filthy faces.

'She's cryin',' one volunteered.

'Yes.'

'She cries all the time, Miss, an' 'er nose is gone.'

'Yes.'

'If we be wicked our noses'll go.' The little child scratched its head while delivering this solemn statement. Lizzie lowered herself to their level.

'I'm looking for someone called Nancy.' Now both children looked at her silently. 'She has black hair with a red ribbon in it.' They both scratched and stared. 'Have you seen her?'

They shook their heads. Lizzie nodded, stood up and began to walk down the street.

She decided not to turn into the alley where Jack's establishment was. After all, nothing had come of it before — except threats and violence. She sighed. Why was she doing this? Nancy had made it clear that she no longer considered her a friend. If she and Jenny had managed to get away, why couldn't Nancy? But in her heart, Lizzie knew that she and Jenny had been lucky and Nancy had not. She herself had been very fortunate to go into service at Mr Harding's as a wet nurse to George after fleeing her disgrace in Bradford. She knew she had her aunt to thank for that. And if she had ended up in Jack's employ when Mr Harding no longer needed her, then that was no more than what happened to dozens of serving girls between jobs. It hadn't been that long before the water delivery job turned up and, although she had never asked any questions concerning this piece of good luck, she was certain that her aunt had somehow been instrumental in it. It was also certain, although she would never admit it and was still angry with him, that Mr Harding must have given a good character reference to Mr Leslie before he would have considered employing her. As for Jenny, one of her 'boys', a respectable draper with a kindlier disposition — or possibly a more active conscience — than most of their customers, had taken a shine to her and helped her get her current position in exchange for the occasional 'favour'. If Nancy was not lucky enough to have such benefactors, then her experience was much more commonplace than Lizzie's or Jenny's.

A man and boy — probably his son — walked towards her. From their sore eyes and their brushes and pans, Lizzie knew them to be scavengers. There were areas of the city now where scavengers gathered and disposed of the ashes and other rubbish every single day. Along with safer pavements, lamps above doors, bye-laws attempting to make householders responsible for keeping the street in front of their houses free from filth, and attempts to deal with sewage, daily scavenging kept Bath's visitors happy and very much more likely to return and spend their money there. Needless to say, no such thing occurred in Avon Street. It was scavenged once a week — if that, and was filthy again within minutes. The boy had a dirty hessian bag across his shoulder. Any reusable bits of cinder found amongst the ashes they cleared would be the sole perk of this dirty trade.

'Sir?'

The man turned a weary and cynical smile towards Lizzie. 'What you 'sirring' for, Miss? What d'you want of me?'

'I'm looking for a young woman called Nancy.'

The man stiffened. 'Why do you seek her? Who are you?'

'A friend.'

'Then why don't you know where she is? Come on, Jacob. We've work to do, unlike some.'

He walked on but Jacob hung back. The boy was very thin and his back was bent under his brushes. 'Is she in trouble, Miss?'

'No, I hope not. I haven't seen her for a while, though, and I wonder where she can have got to. I have something to tell her.'

Lizzie realized that she should have thought up a feasible story before she began this expedition. These people were suspicious of anyone asking questions, just as she would have been.

The man turned and saw his son lingering. He walked back.

'She's only looking for a friend, Father, a friend called Nancy.'

'Have you seen her?' Lizzie asked again.

'I may have. I may have seen her in Mrs Pardoe's tavern. Why don't you ask there?'

'I have. She hasn't been seen there for a while.'

'No.' The man looked thoughtful. 'Now I come to think of it, I haven't seen her for a while. But aren't you the girl that left? Weren't you with Nancy once?'

'I was but now I dwell on Cheap Street.'

'Cheap Street? Uppity then! Why d'you seek old friends here?'

Lizzie hesitated. 'I have a message for her.'

'Leave it with Mrs Pardoe, then.' He turned and strode up the street, his son running to keep up with him.

Lizzie sighed and looked down the street. Then, spotting a friendly face, she hurried towards the woman, who was sweeping dust and ash from her house onto the street.

'Abigail?'

The woman looked puzzled before a smile of recognition spread across her face. 'Why, young Lizzie. Now what brings you back here? I can't think it's for the pleasure of our company!' But she continued to smile.

'I thought I would come to see how Nancy fares but I cannot find her.'

'Well, my dear, surely you haven't gone up in the world quite so much as to think Nancy'd be out and about at this hour! You should come back later.'

'No, I know she'd be sleeping now and I can't come back later . . . Is she well?'

Abigail looked puzzled. 'Just the same as usual, Lizzie.'

Another woman, picking her way along the street, eyes down and with a basket over her arm, looked up as Abigail shouted to her.

'Martha — here's young Lizzie come to visit.'

Martha walked across to them. 'Lizzie.' She nodded but didn't smile.

'What brings you back among us? Have you come to tell us tales of the gentry?'

'No, Martha, I spend no time with the gentry. I give the water to their housekeepers and they give me back the empty bottles. I'm looking for Nancy.'

'Why?'

'I have a message for her.'

'Well, she'd be abed now, as no doubt you know. Leave the message with Jack — or Mrs Pardoe.'

'I can't do that.'

'Well then, come back tonight. She'll be in the tavern . . . now and again.' She smirked at Abigail.

'Was she there last night?'

'I don't know. It's not every poor soul living here spends all their time in the tavern! I must take my leave. She'll be there this evening.'

'You know, Martha, now I think, I haven't seen Nancy in a good while,' Abigail said.

'No, well it'll be soon enough for me.' Martha turned and walked off.

Lizzie looked at Abigail anxiously. 'Please think. When do you last remember seeing her?'

'I can't tell, my dear. I'm not saying anything about her — just that I haven't seen her in a while. Don't mean nothing. Is it a serious business, this message?'

'Yes.'

'Then, when I see her, I'll tell her. Can't do no more.' A shout came from inside the house and Abigail raised her eyes. 'He's the one might have seen her. If I can get him reasonable between food and beer, I'll ask. Good luck to you, Lizzie. Don't mind her . . . ' She nodded towards Martha, disappearing round the corner. 'She's jealous, that's all. There's many'd like to put down their head somewhere else.' Another roar came from the house. 'I must go,' and she went.

Further down the street, Lizzie went into a tavern. As she expected, there were a number of waggoners standing around putting away large quantities of ale. One looked up with reddened eyes and called out, 'Ah here's something to brighten the day. Out a bit early aren't ye lass?'

'I'm looking for someone.' Lizzie turned away from him.

'I'm looking for someone,' he mimicked and some of the other men looked towards her. 'Well, now you've found 'im,' he laughed as he lunged towards her.

Lizzie stepped out of his reach and he stumbled before righting himself on a stool. He spat. 'No, I don't want ye — now I come to look at ye close up. Sour and well past it. Now, there's a good bit of woman I could handle.'

He lunged again, this time at a young girl sweeping. The girl stepped back but kept her head down.

'Leave her alone,' Lizzie said.

'Why, you'er mother?'

Lizzie gently pulled the girl to one side as the drunkard mimicked a woman holding a baby. 'She won't want those old dugs any more. Away with ye!'

Lizzie guided the girl over to a dark corner and the men laughed and returned to their drinks.

The girl would not look up, but Lizzie could see that she was about 13 years old. 'What's your name?' The child stood silently, eyes averted. 'I won't hurt you. Are you one of Jack's girls?'

She had noticed the slightly swollen belly. It could be hunger, but she thought not. The girl looked up now, with frightened eyes, ringed with dark shadows. Her cheekbones stood prominent in a face aged beyond its years.

'Why? Who are you?'

She looked ready to run at any minute. Lizzie rested her hand firmly but gently on the girl's shoulder. 'My name is Lizzie. What's yours?'

The girl looked up at Lizzie with suspicious eyes. Lizzie kept her gaze firm but friendly.

'Annie,' the child mumbled.

'Well, Annie, I used to work for Jack, but I got away.'

Again the stiffening at his name. Lizzie knew the girl was waiting for a chance to bolt. She smiled easily at her. 'Come and sit down for a minute.'

'I daren't.'

'I used to live in a house down a few from here. I worked for Jack but now I work for Mr Leslie, the apothecary.' She talked on gently without pausing, hoping Annie would relax a little. 'I deliver water now.'

'Water?' The girl was interested in spite of herself.

'From the great spa. The water can cure people if they're ill.'

Annie's eyes widened even further.

'How? Is it magic?'

'Yes, I suppose it's magic. Folks swear it does 'em good, anyways, and so they keep coming to Bath to drink it. They bathe in it too.' She smiled. 'Isn't that strange? All together they go into the warm bath.'

'Men and women together?' Annie was shocked.

Lizzie laughed. 'Yes, isn't that strange?'

How could this young girl have been long enough in Bath to be with child and not know about the water? But she had relaxed a little and Lizzie loosened her grip. 'Do you know a woman called Nancy?'

The girl smiled and suddenly she was a pretty child who should have been at home in the country, playing with her doll. 'You do, don't you? I expect she is kind to you?' The girl nodded. 'I expect she will help you when the baby comes.'

The girl's face shot up and the fear returned. She started to cry, silently but intently and suddenly Lizzie felt thin arms round her waist, clutching desperately at her. 'There now,' Lizzie said. 'How did you come to Bath?'

The sobs intensified.

'Did you come to work here?'

She felt a nod against her stomach.

'And your master took a liberty with you?'

Another nod.

'And then when he found you with child, he cast you out?'

A fresh bout of sobbing told her this was the case. Lizzie put her arms round the girl.

'And perhaps Jack has told you he'll help

when the babe is born, then give you work after?'

The girl nodded again. Lizzie pushed her away from her side. She held the girl's chin and bent to look her in the eye.

'Listen to me, Annie. You must go home. Where are your mother and father?'

At this a storm of weeping shook the girl. 'I want my mother.'

'Then go to her.'

'I daren't, I daren't. Father'll whip me to kingdom come.'

'Believe me, that will be better than what awaits you here. Your father'll whip you and then he'll forgive you, but you will be safe.'

Lizzie knew that this might well not be true. The child might find herself cast out again — this time in the countryside where shame was harder to hide and work impossible to find for a disgraced girl. She was tiny — she'd probably die having the baby anyway.

'Now, tell me about Nancy. She was your friend, wasn't she?'

'Yes, but I don't know where she's gone. She didn't tell me and I miss her so much.'

Lizzie felt a shiver cross her heart. 'How long ago?'

The girl shrugged.

'After this happened?' Lizzie indicated the child's swollen belly and Annie nodded.

'Who are you, then? What you doing with my girl?' A man wearing a hessian apron strode towards them. He looked Lizzie up and down then scowled at Annie. 'Get on with you. I don't pay you to chat.'

A terrified Annie resumed her sweeping.

'You don't pay her at all!'

The man stepped threateningly towards Lizzie and she saw she would get no more information here. So she turned on her heel, leaving the girl to her sweeping and the men to their ale.

Lizzie decided that she would go the whole way down Avon Street to the river. She would go into one more tavern and ask news of anyone she saw on the way. Then she would return to the Leslies and forget all about Nancy.

Someone was making uneven progress towards her. As he neared, Lizzie saw that the man was using crutches to move along the street. One leg swung and then stepped rhythmically in the ash but the other leg ended at the knee in a dirty bandage and swung above the ground. Over his arm was slung the cap he would use to beg with, probably outside the Abbey until some official shooed him away.

'Good morning to you,' Lizzie said.

The man stopped and wiped his brow. He nodded but did not answer.

'I seek a young woman called Nancy.'

He nodded again, but again said nothing.

'Do you know her?'

He nodded again.

'Have you seen her about lately?'

'Why? Who are you?'

'My name is Lizzie Yeo. I'm an old friend of Nancy and I have a message for her. Something to her advantage . . . . Do ye know of her?'

He nodded again. 'She is a good woman.'

Lizzie smiled hopefully. This man obviously

knew Nancy. He nodded again.

'She is. 'Tis more than can be said for some of those strumpets.'

'Yes. Did you see her yester eve, or lately?'

He shook his head and leant forwards to start again on his journey. 'I ain't seen 'er in a while an' I don't talk to strangers with questions.' He proceeded unevenly down to the end of the street, his crutches making a rhythmic stomping as he went.

Lizzie sighed. She wasn't getting the news she hoped for — she had no desire to meet with Nancy — simply to know that she was alive. But, although the people she spoke to were recalcitrant and unfriendly, they were letting her know in their roundabout way that Nancy hadn't been out and about for a while. She could, of course, just be recovering from an 'argument' with Jack. The respectable gentlemen of Bath who enjoyed her favours didn't mind the odd black eye, but broken ribs or arms made them feel uncomfortable. She sighed and entered the last tavern before the river. Again, once her eyes adjusted to the low light, she saw that the customers were mainly waggoners. They did not live in Avon Street — indeed many came from villages around about — but they were frequent enough visitors to know many of the residents. She approached the table where the landlord was filling tankards with ale, and smiled.

'Good day to you.' All the men looked at her but did not reply. ''Tis a fine day.'

The landlord laughed unpleasantly. 'And what is it a fine day for?'

The other men sniggered

'I have a message for a girl called Nancy. Have you seen her abroad?'

The landlord pulled some more beer, then looked up. 'No, I haven't seen her in a week or two. Leave the message with Jack.'

'Will Jack be in here tonight? Can I leave the message with you?'

'I know not whether he will or no. Changes from day to day.'

'He hasn't been about, then?'

'You're an impudent trollop aren't you? No, he has not, and I doubt he'd be interested in you!' The men laughed again. 'If ye want ale, then buy, if not, then be gone.'

Lizzie nodded and sat with her ale. She closed her eyes for a moment and saw in her mind's eye Annie with her thin arms and swollen belly. Suddenly she felt overwhelmed with sadness. Her own memories, normally kept well locked away, welled up and she longed for a moment to lie quiet in her mother's arms again.

'Young Lizzie?'

Lizzie looked up.

'You're John's girl — John the weaver out at Bradford.'

'I am. Who are you?'

'Matthew. I worked with your father for a while. I don't think it would please him to see you here.'

He nodded towards the ale in front of her. 'Have you no work? Or is this your work now?'

'No, I have respectable work. I'm looking for a friend.'

158

'What friends could you find here?'

'I lived here. It's bad luck brings a girl here and it would not be so if 'twere not for all the fine gentlemen have need of them!'

The man nodded. 'Aye. Still, I'd rather take better news of you to John.'

'Then take me to him! When are you going back to Bradford?'

'In four days' time. Aye, you can sit on the wagon. 'Tis not the carriage of a fine lady — 'twill be rough.'

'Yes. Here?'

'Here — early, mind, before six.'

Well, Lizzie thought ruefully as she made her way back to Westgate Street, she hadn't found Nancy, or any news of her, and now she was off to Bradford. Now she would have to talk to Mr Leslie, who might not be pleased after all his kindness to her, and maybe all for a cold welcome and more sorrow. But at least Aunt Mary would be pleased!

That evening in the taverns in Avon Street, there was some talk of Jack. The women — well, they were here one minute then gone again, abed for a few days then back again. But Jack — he could be relied upon to be drinking somewhere in the street on most nights. And now they came to think on it, he had not been about much at all.

11

The next day, after her water deliveries, Lizzie went to see Aunt Mary to tell her of her plans.

She was sitting in the warm and welcoming kitchen of Mr Harding's house and her aunt was delighted. 'Well, my dear, you could not have brought me better news. When will you go?'

Lizzie told her of the friendly waggoner and that she would be off in three days' time, as long as she could square it with Mr Leslie.

'Hmm.' Her aunt thought for a moment. 'Mr Leslie will give you no trouble, but perhaps we can find a girl to take your place for a few days . . . I'll go and speak with them.'

She looked at Lizzie enquiringly, who nodded assent.

'Come back before you go, my dear. I'll have things for you to take to Silas. You must tell him I'll be there before two weeks have passed. Mr Harding must manage. I cannot wait any longer.'

Lizzie merely nodded again. Mary wondered what was wrong with the girl.

''Twill be for the good,' Mary said. 'Your poor mother grieves so for you.'

Another nod and Lizzie got up to go.

★　★　★

Mary Yeo entered the apothecary shop and stopped for a moment, as everybody did, while her eyes became accustomed to the gloom. When they had, she looked up to see both the Leslies looking at her, and then a smile spread across Mrs Leslie's face. Mr Leslie, she noticed, was still peering myopically towards her and she thought to herself what a sad thing old age could be. Day after day, Mr Leslie dispensed powders and drops to those in bad health. There was nothing he could do, however, to halt his own encroaching blindness.

'Mrs Yeo, how good to see you. How go things with you?' Mrs Leslie walked towards her visitor. 'Come and sit with us for a minute. Lizzie isn't here at the moment . . . Is everything well with you?'

Mary sat down and began to talk to the Leslies. She must, she emphasised, go back to Bradford to look after her brother. She was quite determined to leave in two weeks' time and if Mr Harding could not sort out his affairs whilst she was here, then she must leave him to take his chances. Mrs Leslie nodded. She was sure he would find a replacement — although not one as reliable as Mrs Yeo, she was also sure.

'Lizzie has a chance to go to Bradford for a day or two.' Mary looked enquiringly at the couple. 'Her mother would be so pleased to see her — and she needs to make her peace with her father.'

'That would be a blessing,' Mr Leslie said.

'You know of her . . . Disgrace?'

'She has more than paid for that,' Mr Leslie said quietly. 'She is a fine young woman and she will make her way in the world, of that I am sure.

Does she have company to walk to Bradford? I should not like to think of her alone. It will be quite dark before she arrives.'

'There is a waggoner who will take her.'

'Then she should go.'

'How will you manage with the water?'

'Oh, we will manage.' Mrs Leslie looked enquiringly towards her husband.

'Can we think of anyone who could do for a few days? Perhaps I may deliver?'

'Yes, we will manage,' Mr Leslie said slowly. 'There is a young woman that may do. You would find it tiring, my dear, I think. But there was someone recommended before I found Lizzie. I shall make enquiries and then I shall speak to Lizzie. 'Twould be a mercy if she were to make peace with her father — although I must admit to being hopeful that she will return to us.'

'Oh, have no fear on that score. All manner of things may happen in Bath — many we would rather not dwell on — but I think a young woman of Lizzie's temper would not relish a return to Bradford after living here.'

The Leslies nodded.

'And you have been kindness itself to give her work and take her in. I feared for her living in that midden.'

'She is a great help to us, Mrs Yeo, and a delight to have under our roof.'

There was a short silence. Mary clearly had something else to say. The Leslies waited for her to say it.

'She is very happy here . . . . but I fear there is something on her mind — she won't tell her old

162

aunt. You know that girl can be so stubborn!'

The Leslies smiled at each other and nodded.

'We thought . . . ' Mrs Leslie began. She looked towards her husband who nodded slightly. 'We thought we may have seen someone, outside the shop, a few times. But we weren't sure.'

'Who?' Mary asked sharply, for the body dragged from the river had disturbed her nights as well as Lizzie's.

'We don't know. Perhaps nobody. But Lizzie seemed flustered a little at the time. The journey to Bradford may be a good thing in many ways.'

'Yes,' Mary agreed. 'It pleases my heart greatly to think there will be peace between her and her father, and that whatever troubles her here may be left behind for a while. You know, I did suggest to Mr Harding that he might consider Lizzie as a housekeeper — young George adored her — but he will not hear of it.'

'Yes, it had crossed our minds,' Mr Leslie said. 'Perhaps his new friend thinks it improper?'

'Mr Castlemaine?'

'Aye.'

'Well, it's a fine thing when a gentleman who has only been here five minutes can pass judgement on us. He cannot even keep his servants — good, reliable people.'

'Perhaps the bishop too?' asked Mrs Leslie.

'Fie — Mr Harding has crossed the bishop before now — just think of this burial business!'

'Aye, and I believe Mr Castlemaine was afraid for Mr Harding's reputation then as well.'

Mary tutted. 'Well, he must get to it and make

arrangements. I must go soon and that is that!'

And with that she took her leave of the Leslies.

* * *

It was still dark when Lizzie rose on Wednesday morning. She had spent the last two days attempting to teach Dorcas the ins and outs of delivering water. It had never occurred to her before that anything about the water delivery and bottle collection was complicated, but Dorcas seemed to find it mightily complex and fraught with the possibility of error. Nevertheless, Lizzie was now determined to go to Bradford and knew she must leave Dorcas to do her best. She had slept in her clothes for warmth and had only to drink a cup of water and draw her cloak around her before stepping into the shop. She had a small bundle containing the things Aunt Mary wished her to take to Silas and, just as she was creeping towards the door, Mrs Leslie appeared and thrust a cloth containing bread and cheese into her hands. Then she hugged Lizzie and disappeared, leaving Lizzie surprised but happy.

Lizzie walked to Avon Street and then down to the end tavern where she was to meet Matthew. He was just finishing a pint of ale and a pie and nodded briefly at her when she entered the inn. She sat and waited for him in a quiet corner. A woman pushing her hair up into a mob cap and yawning asked her if she wanted anything but, when Lizzie shook her head, made her way sleepily out to the back again. Characteristically,

164

once Lizzie had decided that she would go to Bradford, she had not allowed any contrary thought into her head. But now, waiting in the gloom for her lift, she wondered if the whole enterprise was not completely foolhardy. It was true that she missed her mother and her sister and even, at times, her father, who shared her tendency towards pig-headedness. But what if she got all the way to Bradford and they did not want to see her? Where would she go? What would she do? Aunt Mary had insisted that all would be well, but really, it might very well not be. Still, she was committed to it now and must take her chance. She shook the memories of shouting and tears, of blood and a tiny body, out of her mind and rose as Matthew indicated that he was ready to leave.

She stood by patiently as he harnessed Betsy, his horse. His loads were already secured and he held out his hand to pull her up onto the front of the wagon. Her nose was red with the cold, but she felt a gladness in her heart as they made their way out of Avon Street and up through the sleepy city of Bath. The moon lay at the edge of the sky and it was still almost dark in the narrow streets. The hard frost encrusting paving stones and roof tiles began to glow as the sun rose in a pink sky and the horse's breath came out as a white plume as it plodded forward. As they turned into the London Road, brown fields and bare trees rose dramatically to the left and right. To their right, the river flowed lazily, glinting occasionally as the sun moved higher in the sky. Lizzie found herself leaning against the waggoner, both for warmth and balance, although the horse kept a steady pace and ignored people and other horses on the road. They stopped at Batheaston to deliver goods and then splashed through the ford at Bathford, where they stopped again. Matthew jumped down to unload and asked Lizzie if she would come in with him for some refreshment. She shook her head.

'Come now Lizzie, come and get warm at least. We've some way to go yet.'

So she nodded her head and jumped down. And she was glad of the warmth of the inn as she ate her bread and cheese.

Then they started the long slow climb up through the woods and by the time they emerged, the sun was as high as it was going to get and everything looked washed clean in the bright but austere winter light. Matthew was not a talker and the steady clop of the horse's hooves combined with the rhythm of her movement caused Lizzie to fall into asleep against his shoulder. When she woke up, she found they were on the outskirts of Bradford and preparing for a descent as precipitous as their upward progress out of Bathford. They dismounted and Matthew led Betsy gently down and round into the town. Now the sun was dying on the other side of the sky and Lizzie felt a chill fear as the evening died. Matthew concentrated on his horse. 'Steady girl, steady.'

The river, wide and slow here, shone eerily as Matthew turned the wagon to stop by the row of weavers' cottages adjacent to it. Lizzie felt her limbs stiff and cold while her heart raced.

'Thank you.'

He nodded.

'Remember me to your father.'

'I will.'

'I'll be back to Bath in four days, if you've a mind to travel with me.'

She smiled and nodded, not at all sure that she would be that long in Bradford.

She watched as he turned Betsy and then jumped back up onto the cart. He waved and she watched him go before sighing and turning to the row of cottages. She stopped in front of one and knocked on the door. There was no sound for a minute or two and she knocked again loudly. Then the door opened and a woman stood there in shadow, peering out. Then someone came behind her with a candle and held it up. The woman gasped.

'Lizzie, my dear Lizzie. God be praised!' and Lizzie stepped into the warmth of the cottage and her mother's embrace.

12

The door opened directly into the main room of the cottage. A weaving loom with two stools took up most of the space. The person holding up the candle put it down and embraced her sister.

'Dear, dear Lizzie — I have missed you so much.'

Lizzie embraced Becky, who did not want to let go of her newly-returned sister. Her mother had slipped out of the room. 'I missed you, too.'

'How goes it in Bath? Do you see fine ladies in the fashions? Oh how I wish I could go.'

Lizzie laughed. 'Yes, I see the ladies in their fine fashions, and a lot of work they make for folk like us. They must have us running after them day and night! And there is filth and sadness too. You are better here with Mother and Father.'

'I still wish I could go. 'Tis so quiet here.'

They sat down on the two stools, Becky still clasping Lizzie's hands as a tear rolled down her cheek. They were quiet for a moment and could both hear the voices in the back room, one sharp, the other persuasive.

'Don't mind him, Lizzie. He'll come round. He misses you, too,' Becky said.

'Hm.'

'No, really. It's his pride. Mother will soothe him.'

The conversation next door ceased and Lizzie looked up to see her father standing in the doorway. She stood up.

'Father.'

'Lizzie.'

Neither moved towards the other. Appearing behind him, Lizzie's mother gently put her hand on her husband's arm and he stepped forward to let her into the room. The candle flickered. Her mother nodded encouragingly to her and Lizzie said, 'I am right glad to see you, Father.'

He nodded. 'How did you get here? Did you walk all that way?'

'No, Matthew the waggoner brought me. I'm to give you his respects.'

Her father nodded again. 'Aye, he's a good sort. Well, wagon or no, ye must have a hunger and thirst on you.'

He looked at his wife and she nodded happily. 'Come into the back, Lizzie. We must find you something to warm you,' she said.

Once they were in the back room, she turned to a pan suspended above the range and spooned out some stew into a dish, which she put on the table in front of Lizzie.

'Eat, child.'

Lizzie obeyed and felt some warmth return to her body. Her father did not speak, but he sat in the corner of the tiny room and listened.

'Mary says you have good employment now,' her mother continued.

'Aye, I deliver water for Mr Leslie, an apothecary.'

'Why do they want water?' asked Becky.

169

'It's from the place where the hot water comes up from the ground. People believe it does heal.'

Her father raised his eyes. 'Some folk will believe anything.'

'The doctors, though, they do recommend it. The sick folk bathe in it too!'

Becky's eyes widened.

'It's a wonder,' said her mother. 'And you live with the apothecary and his wife?'

'I do. They are kindness itself. Mr Leslie . . .' she hesitated and then ploughed on, 'is teaching me my letters.'

'Well, mercy be!' said her mother.

Her father nodded but said nothing. Lizzie felt, though, that there was some pleasure in his silence. It became clear during the conversation that Aunt Mary had kept her mother well informed of her progress, but that all this was news to her father.

'I have things to take to Uncle Silas.'

'But when is Mary coming? Silas is sick to the heart.'

'Within the two weeks, I am certain. She fears to leave Mr Harding without help, but he will not stir himself to find someone till she goes, she thinks.'

Her father snorted but then there was silence.

All four were thinking of the shouting and the tears, the birth and then the death. They were thinking of Lizzie's silence in the face of her father's wrath, stoked ever higher by her refusal to beg forgiveness. At the time all she would say to them was that she was home again from the big house — that she had been got with child and then dismissed. After that, she got up every day and helped with the weaving as she had in the days before her father got her the serving position with the squire. She was largely silent in the face of her father's harshness and her mother's concern.

'Speak to him, Lizzie. Ask for forgiveness and he will relent,' her mother had repeated over and over again. But not a word passed Lizzie's lips. And when the baby started to come, she also remained silent, stuffing the sheet into her mouth to stop her cries until Becky ran to her mother and the midwife was called to deliver the little dead thing. It was only when Aunt Mary came and held Lizzie in her arms, without questioning or berating her, that she cried, tears and milk mingling on the front of her chemise. And then Mary, practical as ever, got her to Bath and presented a wet nurse for poor motherless George to Mr Harding, who was as silent and motionless in his grief as Lizzie had been in hers.

The next day, Lizzie visited Uncle Silas and assured him that Mary would be on her way soon. Walking back to the weaver's cottage, she dawdled by the river and thought about her time with George. There had been times, when it was dark and no-one else was about, that she had slipped into a reverie that the baby suckling at her breast was her own dear son. And then when she had sung songs to soothe George and felt his tiny fist close around her finger, she had allowed a few tears to fall. But as George got bigger and no longer needed her milk, she had hardened herself as she knew she must, in order to survive.

171

She knew that Aunt Mary had suggested she be kept on and she knew Mr Harding had dithered then told her he would no longer need her services. He had been a little shamefaced and she thought perhaps he suspected her of some misdemeanour he was unable or unwilling to discuss. She had been deaf to Aunt Mary's suggestion that all would be forgotten at home. She could quite easily go back to the weaving.

No, she had decided. She would fend for herself, whatever became of her. And then she had met Jack.

Curled up together at night with her sister, Becky gleefully recounted the local news and gossip while Lizzie drifted off into sleep.

'Mr Harding came here, Lizzie, a few days ago.'

Lizzie was suddenly wide awake.

'Why did he come here? What did he want?'

'No, not here. To the George and Dragon. To enquire of Miss Emily of Road.'

'Miss Emily?'

'Squire Pocklington's daughter — her that has run away. We heard all about the squire — how he did shout and bawl when she didn't come home.'

Lizzie propped herself up on her elbow.

'Becky — tell the story properly. Why did Miss Emily not return home? Where was she coming from? What is this?'

'She went to Bath — surely you knew of her?'

Lizzie sighed. However many times she explained that Bath was a big place and that she did not know of everybody's comings and goings, Becky expected her to know of every little trifle that had taken place there.

'No, I told you, I do not mix with the gentry except to deliver water to the sick. Tell me what has happened.'

'Miss Emily had an admirer and the squire got a choler on him and said she must come home. There was talk of a duel — can you imagine?'

Becky was quiet for a few moments, dreaming of duels and admirers. Lizzie shook her. 'Becky — why did Mr Harding come to Bradford?'

'Squire Pocklington came back to Road and then sent the coach for Miss Emily and her aunt Jane.'

'And?'

'The coach stopped in Bradford for the horses and Miss Emily and Miss Jane took some refreshment and they set off on their way.'

'And?'

'When the coach got back to Road, it was empty!'

'How can that be, and why was Mr Harding concerned? Why did he come here?'

Becky was a little confused. 'No-one knows how it came to be — 'tis a mystery! Some think magic!'

'Fie — what nonsense. But why was Mr Harding involved?'

'They say he stopped the duel.'

'Oh.' Lizzie felt something she could not quite put her finger on.

'And, he came with another gentleman . . . '

Lizzie stiffened. 'Mr Castlemaine?'

'I don't know. They're all the same to me.'

173

Becky was beginning to doze off. Lizzie shook her. 'They went to the inn to ask after Miss Emily . . . '

There was a long pause and then a gentle snore. Lizzie shook her sister again. 'But why is Mr Harding concerned with Miss Emily?'

'I don't know, Lizzie. Is it true there was a poor soul found in the river in Bath?'

'How do you know about that?'

There was quiet for a few minutes, then Becky stirred and said sleepily, 'There's another young girl got with child at the hall . . . that young . . . '

She tailed off into sleep but Lizzie lay quiet, thinking for a long time before sleep overtook her.

★ ★ ★

'Enter not into judgement with thy servant, O Lord,' Harding intoned and invited the Abbey congregation to acknowledge and confess their sins and to ask for the mercy of God, which they did. He pronounced their absolution and a psalm was recited. He read the prescribed verses of the Old and New Testaments and led the people in the recitation of the creed and the Lord's Prayer but all the while his mind was elsewhere, turning over the events of the past few days. The sermon was preached by the Rector of Bath and it was not at all unusual for Harding's mind to wander when this happened. But on this particular day it was sadly the case that he would have been hard put to recount, if asked, a single point made by that good gentleman. As the service moved to its conclusion, Harding moved mechanically through the familiar words, praying for peace, for grace, for the King's Majesty, for the Royal Family, for the clergy and people, finally dismissing the faithful with God's grace and processing down the nave, to stand by the great west door and bid good day to them.

His responsibilities for that day discharged, he began a round of visits that he had decided to make. The night before, on their return to the city, he and Castlemaine had discussed the findings of their investigation and the more they did so, the more Harding began to feel sure that the coincidence of the disappearance of Emily and the appearance of the body in the river was something that could not be ignored. That Captain Cosgrove had not been seen since suggested to him a dark and unpleasant explanation. Yet he had no evidence at all to support an accusation and he feared that his suspicions would be dismissed as idle conjecture. When he had spoken to Castlemaine, his friend had thought for a moment or two and then had strongly urged Harding not to abandon his quest. Harding should, he suggested, put it before the authorities. This he had now decided to do.

Mary scrutinized the kitchen. Anyone surveying the scene would have been hard put to detect a speck of dirt or a whisper of disorder, but Mary was very particular about her realm. Even she, though, was satisfied. The pots gleamed; the surfaces were whitened with scrubbing; the pot suspended above the just-made fire was warming nicely, and its contents would begin to cook at just the right moment. She sighed and pulled on her cloak. She had no desire to leave her domain on this dismal day, but she had determined that she would pay a visit to that most unsalubrious place and make a few enquiries. And she wanted to do it whilst Lizzie was away.

On arriving in Avon Street, she headed straight for Mrs Pardoe's tavern. The woman was surprised to see her — indeed no-one would have expected to find Mary Yeo in such a place. Mrs Pardoe waited for her visitor to speak first.

'Good day to you.'

Mrs Pardoe nodded.

'I believe my niece, Lizzie, was a tenant of yours.'

'She 'as gone,' Mrs Pardoe said sharply. 'Up to Cheap Street. You must enquire there for her.' She turned away.

'I know she dwells in Cheap Street,' Mary rejoined just as sharply. 'But before that she dwelt here.'

'Aye.'

'Have you seen her lately?'

'What is this 'have ye seen 'er, have ye seen 'im' business? Don't you people think I have anything to do with my time except answering ye?'

'Who has been asking for her?'

'No-one.' Mrs Pardoe was very clearly exasperated but she had met her match in Mary. 'She, that Lizzie, 'as been here, asking, asking. We mind our business here.'

'Who was she asking for?'

176

'Nancy and Jack. I don't have time for any more enquiries. Ye must ask another!' She stormed off into the back room.

Mary stepped outside the tavern and thought for a moment. She had never asked Lizzie how she kept body and soul together between her employ with Mr Harding and that of Mr Leslie, but she had a pretty good idea. Lizzie had mumbled something about serving in a tavern and getting a bed for her pains but Mary knew that even employment that began like that in Avon Street, didn't remain so for very long — not for a young woman. Someone was following Lizzie, Mary was convinced, and she wanted to find out who it was. It was strange, though, that Lizzie should have come here asking questions. If she was threatened by someone, why would she come halfway to meet him? Lizzie was stubborn, but foolish she was not. Suddenly Mary remembered a woman she had met once when Lizzie lived here — a seemingly respectable woman, even though she dwelt in this squalid place. She opened the tavern door again and called to Mrs Pardoe, who had come back in as soon as she had left.

'Where does Abigail dwell?'

'Three doors down — it's swept outside. Now begone unless you want to drink!'

Mary laughed and closed the door.

Abigail looked at her enquiringly. Her house had been easy to find. The path immediately outside its doorway was, as Mrs Pardoe had indicated, free from detritus, the only house like this that Mary could see.

'Yes?'

'I think you know my niece — Lizzie Yeo.'

'Well, heaven be, what is afoot? One day it's young Lizzie here enquiring of folk she'd left behind her. Next her aunt comes a calling!'

But she was smiling and she opened the door to let Mary in. 'Speak low, my husband is sleeping. Sit down.'

Mary sat.

'Now, what do ye want of me? I told Lizzie all I knew of Jack and Nancy. There will be no more I can tell you. But what do ye want of them anyways? Folk like you don't come asking for Jack or Nancy.'

'Who is Jack?' How does my niece know of him?'

Abigail looked down.

''Tis not for the likes of respectable folk,' she mumbled, 'to be asking about Jack. He is what he is and I would not pass the time of day with him, although my husband will drink with him all hours.'

'Ah. But why was Lizzie asking for him?'

'I know not. He was not pleased when she left. But I think it was Nancy she was concerned with.'

'Nancy?'

'They were friends, shared lodgings — and young Jenny with them. She's gone, too.'

'Gone?' Mary looked up sharply. Abigail laughed.

'No, found better employment like young Lizzie.'

'Difficult to find worse!'

'Aye. Got away the pair of 'em. Good for 'em,

I say! There's not many can pull themselves up once they find themselves here.' She sat quietly for a moment, head down.

'And Nancy?' Mary persisted.

'Well no-one thought of it till Lizzie came asking. But we haven't see much of her for a while — and not of Jack for a few days.'

Mary thanked her and gratefully got back to her kitchen.

★ ★ ★

When Matthew knocked on the door of the cottage two days later, Lizzie was ready. She had a bundle from her mother who hugged first Lizzie and then Becky, who was convulsed by sobs.

'Lizzie, come again. Don't be gone so long.' Becky said through hiccoughs. 'Oh Mother, I shall be so lonely again.'

Lizzie's father shook his head in exasperation and went to speak to Matthew. Lizzie patted her sister and then walked towards the wagon. She stood patiently while the two men discussed the weaving and delivery trades. Presently Matthew said, 'Well, young Lizzie, we must be off now. It will be well dark before we arrive.'

She nodded and stood for a moment by her father. 'Goodbye, fa . . . '

He hugged her brusquely and then went to stand next to his wife and disconsolate younger daughter. They waved her off as she walked alongside Betsy, while she negotiated the hill out of Bradford.

13

David Rees, the blacksmith, who had helped to pull the body from the river and who doubled as the constable of Widcombe, had a smithy which stood at the foot of Widcombe Hill, and it was here that Harding found him. While all around, the day was dull, damp and cheerless, the smithy was warmed with the heat and fierce red glow of the forge. The ring of hammer on iron and the roar of the fire when pumped with bellows provided a powerful contrast to the unmoving air outside. Rees was working in his shirtsleeves, shoeing a complacent shire horse and mopping sweat from his forehead with a rag. Harding waited patiently till he had finished his job, stood back, and nodded to him.

'Good day to you, sir.' He looked questioningly at Harding.

'Good day to you.'

Harding hesitated but, although he was a person who could take an unconscionable amount of time to come to a decision, he was steadfast once it was made. And so he ploughed on. 'About the woman found in the water . . . '

Rees nodded from time to time as Harding explained his doubts, and when the cleric had finished, he nodded and paused before answering, 'Well sir, this is how it stands as I see it.' In his capacity as village constable, he was unable, or disinclined to be of any help to Harding. If a crime were committed and someone accused of it, his duty was to arrest that person and bring them before a magistrate. In this case it was far from clear that there had been any crime, except the one against God, and He must be the judge of that. And even if an accusation were brought, he could hardly arrest a man whose whereabouts were unknown. If he had heard rumours or gossip like that from the baths, he kept that to himself. He was respectful towards the parson whose kindness in the matter of the burial he acknowledged, but he tried to discourage him from pursuing the matter further, noting that the doctor at the inquest had identified the body as being from the lower classes. That the woman who laid out the body thought otherwise was a matter of no interest to him, on the grounds that she was a woman, and not only a woman but an old woman, and a silly, fanciful old woman and indeed not so far from a witch as made much difference.

Despairing of making any progress here, Harding reluctantly tore himself away from the forge's warmth and returned to the city.

His next call was on the coroner, Mr Strang, who was polite and friendly, gave the clergyman a very pleasant glass of Malmsey wine, and calmly advised him to drop the matter. Speculation as to the girl's identity was fruitless. Most corpses dragged from the river were never identified. The woman was probably a stranger to the city. He thought it most unlikely that there was any connection to the Pocklington family matter. Why, anyway, should Cosgrove do away with the girl? If he had not wanted to run off with her, he could simply have left her to her father. What was more, Strang continued, it was not good for Mr Harding's reputation to continue to involve himself in this sordid business. There were already those who thought his behaviour in arranging the funeral inappropriate, even unfitting for a man of the church, he implied. The further pursuit of this matter would undoubtedly add to idle gossip, a commodity in which Bath was already as rich as it was insatiable. These words once again gave Harding some pause for thought. Any gentleman had at all times to consider his good name, and in his profession that was doubly true. Not only his standing but his very livelihood depended upon it and he took his leave of the coroner with a heavy heart.

Still, as he walked through the streets by the hospital and past the Abbey, Harding thought again of the body lying in St Mary's churchyard. If she was Emily Pocklington then surely it were best that her family should know the truth, hard as that would be for them to bear. And if she were not, then he was back at the point where he had resolved she should have a Christian burial, and now thought she deserved the dignity of a name on her tomb. But if she was a common girl, what had the old woman meant? She had spent more time with the body than Dr Gumble, whose examination had been cursory at best. Yet Dr Gumble was a respected professional man, trained at one of the great London hospitals, and surely knew his business. The more he thought about it the more his head swam. Finally, he decided to make one more attempt to interest the authorities and turned into Quiet Street to find the house of Alderman Lewis, one of the three city magistrates.

Quiet Street was quite inappropriately named at this time, for the far end of it was little more than a huge building site. Carpenters, stonemasons, bricklayers, roofers and their attendant mates, apprentices and labourers, were plying their trades noisily and calling to each other over the noise of their own work. The air was thick with yellow stone dust that clung to everything, not least Mr Harding's coat. Reaching the house of Mr Lewis, he knocked at the door, which was opened by a manservant who admitted him to the parlour and went to inform the Alderman of his visitor. Bath had three senior justices of the peace who were also its chief constables, overseeing the beadles, watchmen and, when required, the reserve force of the sedan chair men, all of whom served as special constables in times of emergency or riot. One magistrate was always the city mayor and another normally the previous mayor. The third must also be an alderman of the city. Harding knew the mayor only slightly. He knew his predecessor rather better but had not found him a sympathetic man. Mr Lewis, however, he knew quite well, he having previously been a churchwarden at the Abbey. Harding thought it likely that he would at least be prepared to discuss the matter.

In this he was not disappointed. Alderman Lewis was a large, friendly man who enjoyed company and was pleased to see Harding. He came into the room hastily pushing on his wig and sent his man to the cellar for brandy.

'Why, Harding, delighted to see you! Sit down, sit down my good sir.'

He explained to Harding that he had a particularly fine drop of the French Stuff, having recently been paid a visit by certain gentlemen of his acquaintance. The servant returned carrying a decanter and two glasses on a tray and set them down before retiring discreetly. Lewis settled into an armchair as he examined the amber liquid against the light from a large window and enquired as to the purpose of Harding's visit. The magistrate was of course aware of the recent events in Widcombe, although, being outside the city, it was not within his sphere of jurisdiction, as well as of the strange affair of the disappearance of Emily Pocklington, which had also taken place away from the city. He was also well abreast of the talk in the town about Harding and the funeral, but he himself dismissed any suspicion of impropriety, knowing the parson to be a kind and honourable man. He listened to Harding's thoughts and speculations calmly and with interest, and sympathised with his confusion. Then he gave his opinion.

'The village constable is correct to say that it is not clear that any crime has been committed, except perhaps one against The Lord.' And here he bowed his head and paused for a moment. 'And that if one has, there is no person to hand who may be accused of it. There remain two mysteries which may or may not be linked. It is of course true that victims of drowning are more often than not unidentified, but that is partly because no one attempts to do so. Will you take another glass, sir?'

'Thank you. It is an excellent spirit.'

'The gentlemen see me well provided. Now what is to be done? In London and elsewhere now, I understand, there are magistrates who can actively enquire into criminal matters, but that is not the case or tradition here in Bath. Nor do I or my brother justices have at our disposal any forces to undertake such a matter. I do, however, have the assistance of the chair men and I will enquire among them for any information that may assist you if you intend to continue your search. Would that be of use, do you think?'

Harding was most relieved to be taken seriously by someone in authority and this, coupled with a third glass of brandy, made him feel positively content for the first time in days, as he made his slightly unsteady progress back to Duke Street. Later that evening as he was sitting in his study, feeling quite lethargic, a note arrived from the magistrate. One of the chairmen had been able to tell him that a man fitting Cosgrove's description had taken the post chaise to Bristol on the day that Miss Pocklington departed Bath. He had sent word of this to a colleague in Bristol, who he hoped might make enquiries as to whether Cosgrove could be found there, and had also alerted Squire Pocklington of this news. Harding felt that at last something was being done and that he could finally get back to his sermons and his household concerns. These would have to wait until the next day, however, as he was feeling unaccountably sleepy this evening.

★ ★ ★

Mary, sitting in her kitchen with Lizzie, decided not to tell her that she had been to Avon Street. Lizzie could be quite stubborn and given to quick anger when she felt herself undermined or controlled. And anyway, the good news of the reconciliation with her brother, Lizzie's father, was not to be sullied with talk of prostitutes and bodies. Lizzie was completely unaware of how changed she seemed to Mary — almost carefree and positively chattering about her stay in Bradford.

'Becky said Mr Harding had been to Bradford, asking about Miss Pocklington. Now why would he do that?' Lizzie looked enquiringly at her aunt.

'I don't know, my dear.'

'With that Castlemaine,' she hesitated, 'gentleman.'

'Yes, they do meet together a deal.'

'Becky said Miss Pocklington and her aunt Jane stopped in Bradford while the horses were watered, but when the coach arrived at Road, they were quite gone.'

'It's a mystery my dear, what these gentlefolk get up to. Now, Mr Leslie will be mightily glad to have you back. I fear Dorcas has been found a little wanting in her duties.'

14

Mary served Jonathan Harding his dinner.

'Thank you, Mary. Did Robert bring the coal?'

'Yes, Mr Harding. It's all safely in. He will bring the ale tomorrow.'

Harding had no doubt whatsoever that Robert would deliver and set up whatever was needed — and, under Mary's watchful eye, be quick and clean about it. Perhaps he would be able to manage with him and Eliza? But no — 'under Mary's watchful eye' was the key. He would need another watchful eye. He finished his meal and Mary came in to clear. She hovered.

'What is it, Mary?' He feared he already knew.

'Lizzie went home to Bradford.'

'To stay?' His voice betrayed his surprise.

'No, she is back now. She took some victuals for Silas.'

'Ah.'

'And took a message from me.'

Harding nodded.

'That I will be with him within the two week — which is one week now.'

'Ah. How did she find him?'

'Poorly but much cheered by the news.'

'Good.'

Mary still stood there. Harding looked up at her. 'I will make shift, Mary. I give you my word.'

Mary nodded but she didn't move to leave.

'Lizzie made peace with her father.'

'Praise be!' Harding was genuinely delighted. 'That is good news indeed.'

Still Mary stood. 'Would you like to sit down, Mary?'

'No sir, I must be about my work, but I wished to be clear.'

'Yes Mary, you are clear.'

'Lizzie's sister told her that Miss Pocklington disappeared between Bradford and Road.'

Harding sighed. 'That is true, I am afraid. She is nowhere to be found. 'Tis a sad business.'

'Perhaps . . . ?'

He nodded. 'We have no way of knowing till some investigations are completed. Captain Cosgrove may be in Bristol.'

Harding was conscious of crossing some sort of line in talking to Mary like this. But there were occasions when the requirements of class and etiquette wearied him. And he was tired of the thoughts that circled round in his brain. And, besides, Mary would soon be gone. He knew she had not come yet to what she had to say, so he waited.

'I visited Mr and Mrs Leslie last week.'

'They are goodly folk.'

'They are. They think someone may be following Lizzie.'

Harding's face shot up. 'Following Lizzie? Why?'

'She has not been at ease for some time. She is silent and looks about her much. I heard she had been inquiring about an old friend, a girl she lodged with after she left your employ.'

188

Jonathan Harding did not speak, but nodded, biting his lower lip.

'She is not to be found. The friend, I mean. I believe Lizzie fears . . . '

'I will go to speak to the Leslies. It is the best I can offer.'

'Thank you, Sir.'

★ ★ ★

Now he really did have to address his dilemma. Mary's only advice had been to reiterate her view that Lizzie should replace her. Mary would soon be gone as, he had to admit, she had told him many times she would. Soon there would only be Eliza and Robert, and he had no experience of finding or engaging servants. He did not feel that any of his colleagues at the Abbey or friends around town had anything useful to say on the matter. His new friend Castlemaine, whilst being quite adamantly opposed to the idea of his taking on Lizzie, who he considered a thoroughly disreputable character, was new to Bath and his attitude to servants tended towards the archaic. Harding feared that if he took Castlemaine's advice no-one would be good enough. Finally he decided that he must stop dithering and take action. George would be home from his Latin school in a few days, and would stay in Bath for some months before taking up his scholarship at Rugby. To remain another week without a housekeeper ready to replace Mary was untenable. Although he thought of himself as more of a philosopher than a man of action, even he could see that the time for putting off the decision had run out. He must assess the situation and take the best course of action he could devise. The choices came down, essentially, to two: either he should try to engage Lizzie or he should advertise publicly for a housekeeper. He weighed the matter up.

He knew Lizzie to be honest and hardworking. George loved her dearly and would be delighted to find her back in his father's household. Taking on a stranger would involve considerable time and trouble, and a successful outcome could not be guaranteed. The thought of having his household run by someone he did not know was deeply unpleasant. On the other hand, it could not be denied that Lizzie's reputation was not ideal for a clergyman's housekeeper. She was young and pretty, which would lead to gossip. She had borne a child out of wedlock and had until recently lived in a thoroughly disreputable part of town. How she had lived at that time was not something he cared to consider too closely, but merely to be resident in Avon Street was, for a woman, bound to result in a suggestion of loose living and morals. Then there was the question of whether she would be happy to accept the post. Mary had told him that there was no doubt that she would accept it, but it could not be denied that between himself and Lizzie there was a coolness amounting to discomfort. Why, he reflected, had he been reluctant to keep her on in his service when George left for school? Mary had asked him to retain her, he had procrastinated, eventually

Lizzie had chosen to leave and he had not acted to keep her. Then he had felt guilty and was horrified to discover where she had gone. When the matter of her employment by Mr Leslie had come up, he had been fulsome in his character reference to the apothecary, partly out of a sense that he owed it to her to put something right in her life. It was no doubt to enable him to resolve this aspect of his dilemma that Mary had suggested he go to speak to the apothecary. And so with a heavy heart but also a sense of determination, he found himself on Cheap Street, knocking at the door of Mr Leslie's apothecary shop.

Mr Leslie was pleasantly surprised to see his visitor, since he was not a frequent worshipper at the Abbey and Mr Harding had no occasion to take physic. He showed his guest into the parlour and offered him refreshment, which, since it was early in the morning and he felt more than a little bilious, Jonathan Harding declined, coming straight to the purpose of his visit.

'How is Lizzie coming on in her work?'

'Well, sir, she is a quick and ready girl who shows aptitude. I missed her greatly when she was visiting her family. We had a girl — Dorcas — whilst Lizzie was away, but she is slow to learn and makes many mistakes. Lizzie is a good worker and, I believe, a good woman. She has more than lived up to the character you gave her.'

'I am very pleased to hear that, Mr Leslie. And yet it may be that that makes my next question to you unwelcome.'

Harding outlined the position in which he found himself following Mary Yeo's departure. 'I am nearly persuaded that I should ask Lizzie to replace her, yet if she is happy here and you are content with her . . . '

The two men discussed the matter. Mr Leslie was unhappy to think of losing Lizzie, yet at the same time he knew that the move would be very much to her advantage. After some consideration, he formulated a proposal that might suit everyone.

'I am sure, Mr Harding, that Lizzie would be more than capable of keeping your house, and I would not wish to stand in the way of her advancement. You have said, however that you are uncertain she will take to it and I am loath to lose her help completely. May I suggest this course of action? Lizzie shall come to you and keep house in her aunt's stead, but also continue to take a small number of deliveries for me, at least until she has taught poor Dorcas to do so without mishap. Then if she proves unsatisfactory to you,' here he paused — it would have been quite improper to acknowledge that Lizzie might be the one to cancel the arrangement although both men knew it to be possible — 'then she could return to us with no harm done.'

Harding was astonished that so seemingly intractable a dilemma could have such a straightforward resolution. 'I wonder, though . . . ' He could not quite put into words the possibility that a serving girl might refuse his offer.

'You might propose it to young Lizzie as a

temporary arrangement,' Mr. Leslie said. 'Mary Yeo will advise her to take the opportunity and I will add to that advice. I think all will go as we hope.'

The apothecary's common sense and calm confidence worked a sea of change on the clergyman's state of mind, and he left the shop feeling that at last there was a chance he could settle to his regular life once more. His good spirits were raised even higher on his return to Duke Street. Eliza gave him a letter delivered by hand that afternoon, inviting him to dine a few days hence with the bishop, at the palace in Wells.

15

Lizzie opened her eyes and stared at the ceiling.
She sighed. Another new bed in another new
place. Well, of course, not strictly a new place.
She had lived here before — sleeping in a bed in
Master George's room. How, she wondered, had
she found herself back in Mr Harding's
household after all these years? How was it that
Mr Leslie, one of the few people in life she
trusted, had spoken so quietly and so certainly of
this, as though it were the obvious thing to do?
How was it that Mrs Leslie helped her gather her
few belongings and walk the short distance to
Mr Harding's house in Duke Street? And how
was it that her aunt had so quietly kissed her,
taken the box from them, and walked before
Lizzie up the stairs to the attic room that had so
recently been hers? Why had she, Lizzie of all
people, sat so docilely in the kitchen while Aunt
Mary went through the routines of the house?

Mary had fed Lizzie, settled her in what had
been until that day her own bed, lain on the floor
beside her for a few hours and then disappeared
before Lizzie woke. She had boarded the post
chaise, paid for — he had been most insistent
— by Mr Harding, and was on her way to
Bradford and her ailing brother. So here Lizzie
was, in the attic room of the Reverend Jonathan
Harding's house, his temporary housekeeper as
well as deliverer of water for Mr Leslie,

apothecary of Cheap Street, and unwilling teacher of young Dorcas — the object of this being to make herself redundant to that task. Still, she was here now and had best bestir herself. Hot water and breakfast would be needed soon, and Eliza was probably already on the way to the ferry.

★ ★ ★

In order to deliver his charity sermon on behalf of the foundling hospital, Harding set off early and rode briskly to Wells, with only a short stop for some refreshment for both himself and his mount. He arrived at the Bishop's Palace mid-afternoon, left his horse with the ostler, and was shown by the bishop's chaplain to a room on the second floor where he was to sleep. The chaplain explained that evensong was to be said at five o'clock and that Mr Harding's sermon was due to begin at around half past five. A maid brought him water and towels, a cup of chocolate and a small decanter of Madeira. At a quarter to five, he walked across the green towards the imposing west end of the great medieval cathedral, adorned with statues of the saints. It might have seemed that to do so was to step back into the middle ages, although Harding knew that the magnificent golden stone edifice would, at that time, have been painted in bright colours. What seemed timeless to the modern sensibilities of the mid-eighteenth century was quite different from the riot of colour that would have greeted a visitor four hundred years earlier.

He had composed his sermon by developing the one he had disinterred some days earlier concerning the parable of the Good Samaritan. The crux of his message was that Our Saviour had told the story in response to a question, not concerning the love and charity that should always characterize the behaviour of any Christian, but rather that of the identity of one's neighbour. The point was not so much to praise the actions of the Samaritan, which, noble as they were, were simply what would be expected of any compassionate man, but rather to answer the question — 'who is my neighbour?' — with another one — 'who, in this specific incident, truly behaved as a neighbour?' Our Lord's point, Harding asserted passionately, is that we do not choose the neighbour we are to love; rather that neighbour seeks us out and is identified by his or her need. The fault of those holy men who passed by on the other side was not that of failing to know their duty, rather it was that of failing to see to whom it was due. With the remorseless logic for which his homilies were justly famed, he led his audience along the argument — that it is not for us to choose to whom we should show Christian charity, or at what time, but to recognise that demand when it arises, and our neighbour as he who is in need. In conclusion, he urged his listeners to take heed of Our Lord's ringing instruction to his questioners, 'Go thou and do likewise'. It was not lost on many of his congregation that this was his response to those who had gossiped and questioned his actions in giving Christian burial to a stranger. Nor was it lost on the bishop, who smiled indulgently before bringing the service to an end with a blessing, and taking the speaker back to his palace for dinner.

The Right Reverend Dr Septimus Wellbeloved, sometime Dean of Emmanuel College, Cambridge, and now Bishop of Bath and Wells, presided over a table famed throughout the West Country for its magnificence. He and Harding ate their way through boiled beef, roast duck and a saddle of venison, washed down with a robust claret and quantities of exceptionally fine, old port. Harding had been Wellbeloved's protégé at Cambridge and soon after becoming a bishop the great prelate had summoned his former student to be his agent in a great struggle, as he saw it, for the soul of the Church of England. It was the younger man's already well known talent for a telling combination of logic and rhetoric that had secured him this role, and it was the threatened rise of what was coming to be called Methodism that occasioned it.

The bishop's grave dislike and distrust of a religious movement based on impassioned emotion, led him to undertake a campaign to defend the moderate, rational and conservative religion of England, and to conscript the younger man in this war against a tidal wave of 'enthusiasm'. In pursuit of this crusade, he had procured for Harding the three livings that provided his relatively comfortable income and the canonry of the Abbey that afforded him his principal platform.

'Mr Wesley is nothing short of a hedge priest,' proclaimed Dr Wellbeloved. 'He conducts what he is pleased to call his revivals in fields and on hillsides. He rouses crowds of the lowest orders of society with ranting and blathering. He makes grotesque claims of divine communication — 'inspiration' he calls it, as though the Holy Spirit were talking to him as clearly as I am now to you. Superstition and magic, I say!'

'Mr Wesley is, of course, an Oxford man,' commented Harding.

For these two men that signified an intellectual weakness — a form of reason fatally undermined by the failure to pay sufficient and proper attention to the study and practice of mathematics.

'Worse, sir, worse. A man of Rome, I say. With his howling and shrieking — rousing up common labourers and farm hands to think themselves chosen by the Higher Power without even conceding the proper authority of the church by law established.'

His grace went on at some length to summon up a blood-curdling vision of ravening hordes of Wesleyans overturning all social order and handing over all of protestant England's freedoms, laws and rational religion to the Young Pretender and the Society of Jesus.

After some time in this vein, and another bottle of old port, the storm abated and Dr Wellbeloved turned his attention to the private concerns of his young colleague. Harding had hesitantly expressed some disquiet at the possible misinterpretation of his recent actions,

198

being understandably worried about the possibility of doing anything that might undermine the relationship upon which his livelihood depended. But the bishop was quite untroubled by these events.

'Sir, a clergyman cannot be ruled by the witterings of the mob,' Wellbeloved replied. 'Our place is to lead them, not to follow. Anyway, more will see you in a creditable light than otherwise, I believe.' He paused as he took a large mouthful of port. 'I do think, though, that you should marry again. A respectable clergy wife is a great asset to the public reputation of a man of the church and one who will manage your household will leave you free for the duties of your office.'

'I have engaged a new housekeeper, Your Grace. I am confident she will take over all the daily cares of my modest establishment.'

'I know of her, Harding. Bishops hear immediately of such matters, you may be sure. I am glad to hear of it. I understand her to be young and comely.'

Harding coloured.

'She was my son's nurse, sir. She is a respectable and practical girl.'

'The more reason to have a wife to keep an eye on her. But enough. I see you will manage your own affairs. Did I tell you, by the way, what I heard my brother Salisbury say to one of those damned puritan curates we see so much of now?'

Harding knew the story but was wise enough not to interrupt.

'Seems this fellow was visiting the bishop who

199

asks, 'Will you have a glass of wine, Mr So-and-so?' 'Why, My Lord,' he replies, 'I would as soon commit adultery as take strong drink in the afternoon'. 'A man after my own heart!' says his grace, 'But let's have a drink first, eh what?''

The Bishop laughed generously at his own joke and Harding joined in fulsomely, thinking it ill-advised to tell Dr Wellbeloved that not only had he heard the tale told before, but that on that occasion it had been told not of the bishop of Salisbury, but of the bishop of Bath and Wells.

★ ★ ★

Lizzie had settled into Harding's household quite well. At first she had struggled, realizing very quickly that whilst she had been nursemaid to Master George, she had been almost oblivious to everything that happened around her. She thought often, and ruefully, of Aunt Mary's calm and efficiency and how she had never realized or acknowledged quite how skilled her aunt had been. But Mr Harding was patient and kind, utterly relieved that Mary's departure had not resulted in total chaos in his household. Eliza and Robert's comings and goings helped to remind her of what might be needed next, and she was beginning to get the hang of things. She was lucky, she mused, that Mr Harding was not a great entertainer. He rarely had guests and the few he had, he entertained in a quite subdued way. She shuddered to think how one catered for parties of ten or more, wanting six or seven courses — by bringing in help, she assumed, but it would still require her to oversee things. She was very busy, it was true. Dorcas was slow, but Mr Leslie was sure she would get there in the end, and Lizzie realized with a smile how skilfully she had been managed into this place. Whilst she still did some water delivering, she felt that she had a choice in whether to stay at Mr Harding's, but the longer she was a housekeeper, the better she liked it. And this is no doubt what Mr and Mrs Leslie and her aunt had in mind when they manoeuvred her and Harding into taking what was by far the most sensible decision for them both.

★   ★   ★

Harding, on his return to Bath, was quite tired from the evening's carousing but in good spirits. The weather had improved and although the ground was sodden underfoot, he rode along in pale spring sunshine, reached the stables at Widcombe before dark, and took the ferry back home to find a warm dinner waiting for him. To be sure, boiled mutton washed down with a glass of ale was simple fare after the glories of the bishop's palace, but it was very welcome after two days' riding. Lizzie was proving to have much of her aunt's skill in the kitchen and Harding noted that Eliza seemed to have been inspired by the new regime; her manner was prompter and more attentive and her apron was spotlessly clean and starched. Lizzie had, in fact, both by her own instinct and on the advice of her aunt, taken care to establish her authority

201

quickly in the household and left the girl in no doubt as to the high standards that were now to be expected of her if she was to continue in Mr. Harding's service.

After dinner, Harding was to meet Radleigh and Castlemaine in the Assembly Rooms. He had been almost out of the door in his second best coat, when Lizzie brought him his best, freshly sponged and pressed. She was determined that if her master was to mix with people of quality, they should not find his housekeeper to be negligent in ensuring his proper appearance among those people. When he arrived at the Rooms, his friends remarked upon how well turned out he was.

Castlemaine opened the conversation by asking Radleigh if there was any news of the famous actress, Mrs. Maltravers. 'We had heard she was to accompany you here and to play Lady Macbeth this season. Is she coming or no?'

Radleigh coughed uncomfortably and mumbled that he knew no more than anyone else about the whereabouts of the glamorous artiste. Harding tried to press him further but he insisted on changing the subject. Was there, he wondered, any further news of Miss Emily Pocklington and her aunt? Did they think that either of them might be the woman now lying in Bathwick churchyard? Were they also aware, he asked, that another woman was missing in the town? At this both men looked up sharply.

'What do you mean, Radleigh?' asked Harding.

'I am sure you don't mingle in circles where

there's low gossip,' Radleigh smiled. 'But I fear in my profession it is hard to avoid. By all accounts one of the girls from Avon Street — Nancy, I think she's called — has not been seen for some weeks now and there have been people asking about her whereabouts to no avail. Her pimp's disappeared too, it seems.'

'So the doctor might have been right all along!' Castlemaine cried. 'I saw that fellow, Strang, the coroner, here earlier. I wonder if he knows of this latest news.'

He went off in search of the coroner, returning with him some minutes later. Strang had more news for them.

'Miss Pocklington is found,' he informed them. 'She was living in a poor place near the docks in Bristol with that blackguard Cosgrove. He'd sold some of her jewels already but she still had most of them when the magistrate's men ran them to earth. Seems he'd fed her some story with promises of marriage and starting a new life in America and needing the money for the passage. He ran off when the officers challenged him to produce the papers for the voyage, and hasn't been seen since. Miss Emily is now on the way home to her father, no doubt to be kept under closer watch than before.'

'And is she . . . ?'

'She is a respectable girl, I believe. She has kept herself for marriage. It was her money he wanted, not her.'

'And what of the 'magic' at Bradford? The disappearance?' Radleigh could hardly contain his excitement.

'Oh, 'twas achieved with the aid of Cosgrove's mount and a waiting waggoner.'

'They went in one door of the carriage and out the other?' asked Harding, remembering what the stableman had suggested.

'Yes, and into a serving wench's room until the carriage was gone. Then swiftly to the waggon with Cosgrove riding along, all the way to Bristol.'

'But Cosgrove was known to have taken the post to Bristol,' said Harding.

'Ah, 'twas another of his tricks. He took the post but alighted at Saltford, where he hired a mount and rode to Bradford. 'It was all arranged quite cunningly.'

'And her aunt, the girl's chaperone?' Radleigh asked.

'Oh, that's the cream of the story, sir! It seems she had for some time been buying up ribbons and fancy lace and has now taken this opportunity to leave her brother's house with what jewellery she had of her own, sold it and has set herself up in business in a ribbon shop in Bristol! The squire is outraged, of course, but it is all her own money and there's nothing he can do but rage and swear that when the business fails and she's penniless, he'll have none of her.'

'Then may God be thanked,' said Harding, 'for their safe delivery. So now it seems there is only one missing woman . . . '

'A common prostitute,' interrupted Radleigh.

'Our Lord befriended common prostitutes,' said Harding mildly.

'Anyway, there's another,' Castlemaine laughed. 'Your friend the actress hasn't been seen for days, either!'

Radleigh reddened. 'Why you know not of what you speak! Mrs. Maltravers has not yet arrived in Bath, let alone gone missing here!'

Harding put his hand on Radleigh's arm and the other saw that all had been in jest. He quickly recovered his composure and added with a smile, 'Do you know, Harding? This reminds me of nothing so much as your dashed mathematics problems. Here you have A, B and C. C is missing. Where is X? What is the value of Y? Can you not cast it like a sum in arithmetic to bring out the answer for us? Let us call for more wine whilst you ponder the problem!'

This restored the mood of good humour and the men ordered more wine and toasted the safe return of the squire's daughter and the spirit shown by her aunt. But Harding was struck by his friend's jest. It seemed that indeed there was a problem to be solved and that a man might solve it if he could lay out the facts and apply clear logic to them. As he walked back to Duke Street, his mind turned over this idea.

16

Harding finished his more than adequate supper, put his knife and fork together, and sighed with contentment. It was true that he missed Mary's pastry and that occasionally he called for Lizzie and found her out delivering water, but it could have been so much worse. So many months of anxiety had been resolved, it seemed to him, in the twinkling of an eye. He had been a fool, he realized, to procrastinate so weakly, swaying this way and that. And he had been far too influenced by his new friend who, when all was said and done, knew nothing about Mary, Lizzie or George — or really that much about Harding either. He was a good sort and generous, but on this matter he had been decidedly wrong. There was a knock on the door and Lizzie entered.

'Thank you, Lizzie — an excellent supper.'

She smiled shortly and nodded while she removed the plates and cutlery.

'Would you like some port, sir?' she asked.

'Thank you, I will take a glass in the study.'

As she turned to leave, he spoke again. 'Lizzie?'

He was not really sure what he wanted to say but there was some feeling in the back of his heart that he had used her ill and, although he was always concerned, as a clergyman must be, with his reputation, he had let this concern get in the way not only of good sense, but also of Christian charity.

'Yes sir, is there anything else?'

'No, no . . . Merely that I hope you are settling in well.'

'Yes sir, you are not displeased with anything?'

'Not at all. Not at all. You are managing Dorcas and the water as well as your duties here?'

She sighed. 'Yes sir. Dorcas is slow to learn, but Mr Leslie believes she will get to it in time.'

Harding nodded. He searched for a way to say what he wanted to say in a manner that would be appropriate. 'And . . . other things are well with you?'

She frowned. 'What other things, sir?'

He was getting in too deep and regretting it.

'Nothing, nothing. Your aunt was a little worried about you, that is all. She and Mr and Mrs Leslie,' he floundered, 'thought you anxious about . . . about . . . something — or someone, perhaps?'

She raised her eyebrows. So this is how things had been! She looked at Mr Harding for a moment or two while she decided how to answer. Castlemaine, Harding thought ruefully, would have said it was in an insolent way.

'I have been worried about an old friend, sir. That is all. But I am sure 'twill all be well.'

'Why worried, Lizzie? Is she ill? Can I help in any way?'

'No sir, I do not think she is ill. It is just that I have not seen her for quite some time. May I go now?'

'Yes, of course you may Lizzie. I have no wish to keep you from your duties.' But he could not let it go and, as she turned away again, said, 'A friend from Avon Street?'

Lizzie did not turn back. She did not want him to see her face. If it was impudence let him dismiss her!

'Yes sir, from Avon Street, where many struggle to find a living.'

'I understand, Lizzie. Thank you.'

Oh no you don't, she thought as she closed the door behind her.

But when Harding was settled in his old leather chair in front of a fire laid by Eliza early that morning, and lit by Lizzie in plenty of time for his study to be warm and comfortable after supper, he was thinking something else. He was thinking that the prostitute — Nancy was it? — from Avon Street, who was missing was a friend of Lizzie's. He was thinking that it was said that the girl's pimp could not be found either, and that the Leslies had told him they feared Lizzie was being followed.

'No,' he told himself. 'This is no business of mine. I was quite wrong to question her. I shall proceed with logic and keep the detachment that is right and proper.'

★ ★ ★

Castlemaine and Harding were riding. It was a crisp, dry morning and from the fields on Widcombe Hill, the city looked compact and cheerful with its yellow stone and orderly streets.

The Abbey looked beautiful and peaceful, beneficent in the heart of it all. Both dirt and poverty were invisible from here, and the friends felt free from the anxieties of their everyday lives as they cantered across the fields.

'So, sir, we finally ride unencumbered by thoughts of death!' Castlemaine said cheerfully as he trotted by Harding's side.

Harding smiled. 'That is true, my friend. It is good to be out in the air on such a fine morning and to have crossed the river without incident.'

'And now we know young Emily is safe and back with her father, it will be well with us to forget the whole business.' Castlemaine grinned and then galloped off.

Harding followed at a more sedate pace, but smiling at his friend's exuberance. Castlemaine wheeled round and trotted back to Harding.

'Ah, my dear friend, your city is lovely and I would not speak ill of it. But there are times when I would wish myself back in the country of my birth. A man can ride there all the day long as speedily as ever he may and never see another soul. He can stand alone with the hawks wheeling above him and look down on acres of God's creation and never have to engage in polite conversation!' He sighed. 'But there are no healing waters there for my beloved wife and I must admit that the entertainments are rustic and quite without elegance. And I should never hear the sermons of my good friend Harding again were I to return to my homeland!'

Harding smiled as they both turned their mounts back towards the village. He had not felt so content in some while.

After returning the horses to the stable, their faces flushed with cold and fresh air, both men cheerfully crossed back on the ferry and Harding invited Castlemaine to come in for a warm rum punch before returning to his own house.

They settled down in front of the fire, each cradling a warm glass in his hand. Lizzie had kept her eyes down and her demeanour respectful in front of the jovial Irishman.

'Will there be anything else, sir?' she said to Harding.

'No, thank you Lizzie.'

So she bobbed and left them to their drinks and conversation.

'How goes it with the charity school?' Castlemaine asked.

'Ah, well sir, well. At least it started well and now it slows rather. But that is always the way with these things. We shall, I firmly believe, achieve our aim. If only more men were as generous to the poor as you have been.'

'Oh, it was a trifle. I, a stranger, have been made welcome here. I must contribute what I can.' He leant back in his chair and sighed happily.

'And your wife continues to make progress?' Harding asked.

'She does, she does. I do believe she will be able to come out into society in the near future. She has progressed beyond my most devout hopes. I hope that you and she shall meet soon. I speak often of you to her. She hopes to hear you preach in the Abbey before long!'

Harding bowed his head modestly and there was contented silence for a while. They finished their drinks and Harding looked enquiringly at Castlemaine who nodded slightly. Harding rang the bell and Lizzie re-entered.

'We will have two more of these, Lizzie. They are excellently warming.'

Lizzie nodded and left the room, returning in a few minutes with more of the punch she had kept warming by the range in expectation. The two men sipped their new drinks quietly.

'I have heard from my friend Pocklington.' Castlemaine broke the silence. 'All is rejoicing there, although I fear young Emily will find herself under more watchful eyes in the future. As for Miss Jane Pocklington, I fear she will never grace his doors again, come what may. She will wish she had never played her part in so devious a scheme.'

Harding nodded, but then said quietly, 'She will find the world a hard place to make her way in. 'Tis not easy for a woman on her own and past marriageable age.'

Castlemaine harrumphed. 'Then she should not have abused her brother's kindness in taking her in and then playing the deceiver with his daughter. We must all pay for our wickedness.'

''That is true,' Harding agreed quietly. 'But some, it seems to me, pay more than others.'

'Ah, let us not cast a pall on our day with talk of wickedness. The lady is found and our fears were groundless. Let us be glad!'

'Yes, you are right,' Harding replied. 'We must give thanks that she is safe. There is still, of

211

course, the question of the woman in the water. If she is not Emily, then who is she?'

'Oh, she is some low woman, as we first thought and as Radleigh has reported to us. It is no business of ours now.'

Lizzie knocked on the door at that very moment, removed the glasses and closed the door quietly behind her, having established that the gentlemen required no more of her for the time being. Castlemaine looked towards Harding, but he was looking into the fire.

'Lizzie tells me a friend of hers has not been seen for a while,' Harding said and immediately regretted it.

'We have spoken of this before, Harding. You know how I stand on this business. That girl, I believe, is trouble and brings dishonour to your house. You are a true Christian and an honourable man. But, it is possible that others abuse that honour in you.'

'We must continue to disagree on this matter, my friend,' Harding smiled. 'Do not forget that Lizzie was in my employ before and proved herself a good and honest servant.'

'Aye, you have spoken of it. But I shall continue in my feelings. We shall see. Well, sadly I must be about my business.' He rose. 'Many thanks for your hospitality and companionship.'

'It is my pleasure,' Harding replied as he opened the door of the study for Castlemaine.

'Lizzie, Mr Castlemaine's coat, please.'

Lizzie got the coat and bobbed respectfully as she handed it to Castlemaine. Harding turned back to the study and then turned back towards the door, thinking he heard conversation on the doorstep. But Lizzie closed the door firmly, bobbed and returned to the kitchen. If she looked a little flushed, it was not his business. Perhaps she had been sitting by the range. And if, during the evening, he heard noises — pans banging, he thought — from the kitchen, then that was none of his business either.

★ ★ ★

The overly emphatic moving of cooking pots in Harding's kitchen was a direct result of the conversation he thought he had heard on his doorstep. Castlemaine was not the sort of man who engaged in light banter with servants. Indeed, he did his very best, along with most of his class, to ignore their existence while they went efficiently about their business. It was not his place to consider the labour involved in providing the hot water for washing his face or the food for filling his belly unless it was done tardily or in a sloppy manner. Gentlemen were gentlemen and servants were servants and between them existed the gulf that God had ordained. He liked his new friend and found his company engaging but on this business of his relaxed — one might say lax — attitude to the inferior classes they would never agree. So, in a few words and without giving her chance to reply, he had made it clear to Lizzie that he considered her presence in the Harding household a disgrace that would cause trouble for his friend and that neither he nor Harding could possibly have found anything to interest them in the comings or goings of whores from Avon Street. Turning on his heel, he had left a red-faced Lizzie fuming at both his opinion that her very presence in his house besmirched the reputation of a good man, and the realization that Harding had shared her information about Nancy with this man.

But later, when the pans were back in place and she was sitting by the range, she determined that since there was no way she could defend herself against the Irishman or raise the subject with her employer, she would have to find out for herself what had happened to Nancy.

And so the next day she found herself in Avon Street again, going from tavern to tavern as she had before. The same wearying answers came — surely she knew that Jack's girls wouldn't be out and about at this time of day, nor Jack neither, was she wanting some work to be asking after him, wasn't she getting a bit old — and with the same smirks and attempts to grab her. And then again — come to think of it, Jack hadn't been around lately but a bad penny always comes back and he will when he pleases. She even gritted her teeth and tried the hovel in the alley again — standing well back from the door after she had banged on it. But her thumping and calling was met with silence. There was not even a twitching of the filthy rags at the windows. And then suddenly, at the eighth tavern she entered, and just as she was turning to leave, a man looked up from his ale and called after her.

'Who's asking then? Who's after Jack?'

She turned and approached the man. He was large and had a mop of unruly brown hair. His face was red and fleshy and he had bloodshot eyes peering belligerently at her. He lunged toward her, slopping his ale.

'I said who's after Jack?' before steadying himself on his stool and taking a large draught from his tankard.

'I'm asking for him.' Lizzie stood where she considered she was just out of arm's reach and looked him in the eyes.

'Why?'

Lizzie had planned a little better in advance this time and had decided she needed suitable bait to flush Jack out if he was still in Bath.

'I owe him money.'

'Oh, do ye now? Then give it 'ere and I'll pass it on.'

Lizzie didn't reply to such a facetious remark but continued to regard the drunk steadily. 'I must put it in his hands myself.'

The man closed his eyes and started to fall, very slowly, sideways. But just as she thought he would slump to the floor, he righted himself, opened his eyes and slurred, 'Then come ye 'ere tomorrow eve and he'll be 'ere.'

How on earth was she going to slip out in the evening? And what a foolish thing it would be to do even if she could effect it. Lizzie dismissed the idea and returned to Duke Street, half annoyed and half relieved. She was very busy for the rest of the day.

But the next evening, Harding left the house to discuss with Mr Strang some financial intricacies involving the donations to the Girls' Charity School, and Lizzie realized that if she were going to meet Jack, this was her chance. She secured the bag containing some of the money she owed him inside her petticoat, put on her brown cloak and slipped out of the house. She reassured herself that the whole thing was a wild goose chase. The drunkard probably hoped to cheat her of her money, and anyway, it really did seem as if Jack had not been out and about as usual. She shivered in the cold and also in the realization, the one she had been steadfastly refusing to allow into her head for days and days, that it would be a dire situation that caused Jack to leave town when he was owed money. No, she reassured herself, it could not be. And how much harm could she come to in a tavern, however disreputable? She would not spend the rest of her life being afraid of Jack. And she would find out what had happened to Nancy. She pulled the hood of the cloak around her and walked resolutely along the street.

She stepped into the tavern, which was crowded and extremely noisy. Nobody bothered to look at her at this time of day. She stood and looked carefully around her. The drunkard was on the same stool, just as if he had never left. He was alone. She breathed a small sigh of relief. No Jack then. She scanned all the groups of men in the room, but he was not amongst them. Jack

216

was always in the middle of a group, laughing and brawling. Somehow he seemed to achieve this night after night without ever losing sight of his girls and their clients or the awareness of precisely how long they were gone with them. She was about to leave and was just scanning the room for the last time when she saw him. He was sitting in a dark corner quite alone, staring moodily into a pot of ale. Suddenly Lizzie was overcome with a sense of the utter foolishness of what she was doing. However angry she was with Harding — and whatever was the point of being angry with a gentleman, they came and went as they pleased, her life meant nothing to them — putting herself in the way of her former violent pimp was beyond folly. But just the thought of Harding passing on her concerns about Nancy so casually to Castlemaine fired her up and she made her way through the knots of men over to Jack. She stood in front of him for a moment before he saw her. All the old bluster seemed to have drained out of him. He was oblivious to her presence.

'Jack.'

He slowly raised his head and then his eyebrows when he saw her. 'Lizzie. What are you doing here?'

'I owe you money.'

Suddenly the old fire was back in his face. He grabbed her wrist and forced her down beside him.

'And since when did Lizzie hoity toity seek out old Jack to pay him?' he hissed.

'Let go of me and I'll get out the money.'

'No, you stay 'ere nice and quiet for a minute.' His grip tightened and he tipped up the tankard, finishing the ale in one gulp. 'What d'ye really want? You were always a tricky one, a liar.'

She did not answer for a moment but his grip tightened painfully, so she spat at him, 'Where's Nancy?'

His eyes widened and for a second he loosened his grip. She took her chance and pulling free, pushed through the tavern customers towards the door. But he was close behind her and as she opened the door, he pushed her from behind out into the street and pinned her against the wall.

'Where's the money, then? Let Jack see it if ye've a mind to settle your debts,' he snarled.

'I have it, but I can't reach it like this.'

He pushed her harder against the wall but then released his grip and allowed her to reach into her petticoat and pull out the pocket.

'I can't pay all yet. Here.'

She handed him the money and he looked down at it in his palm. With the other hand, he gripped her round her throat, still pinned to the wall.

'Be off with you then.' His face came close to hers. 'And don't be asking after Jack if you value your life.'

She didn't move. Her limbs felt like lead and her head was spinning.

'Where's Nancy?' she persisted.

He tightened his grip and she began to choke.

'Nancy don't want the likes of you askin' after 'er neither. Be off with you!'

Her throat constricted and the coughing quietened to a wheeze. Jack's face began to swim before her eyes. Then he suddenly released her throat and, grabbing her arm, pulled her roughly behind him still wheezing. He turned suddenly into a narrow alleyway between two houses near to the river and pushed her up against another wall.

'Pay me the rest and don't come 'ere askin' after folks again.' Then he turned abruptly and opened the door of a tiny house. He pulled her inside after him. A tallow candle spluttered in the sudden draught and its flickering light revealed a small room with a fire burning at one end, in front of which was a woman sitting on a stool. She looked up in surprise as a panting Lizzie tried to see who it was.

'Jack?' the woman asked.

Jack nodded.

'Aye, I'm back.'

'Lizzie? Is it you? What are you doing here?' the woman asked in surprise.

'I came to pay Jack the money I owed.'

Lizzie stepped towards the woman across the uneven but well-swept floor and then knelt by her. Her eyes were circled and her face sallow, but there were no bruises, new or old. She wore a red ribbon in her hair. She looked at Lizzie for a moment, nodded slightly and then looked down again with a small smile on her face.

'What's its name, Nancy?'

''E's called Jack,' she said as she continued to nurse the baby at her breast. 'And,' smiling shyly in Jack's direction, 'we're goin' to keep 'im.'

Lizzie was dusting in Harding's study. On the desk lay open a great Bible, surrounded by sheets of notepaper covered in handwriting, which she understood to be the notes he made for his sermons. Harding's scrawl was indecipherable but in the big book she could make out some of the letters that Mr Leslie had begun to teach her, although to put them together to make words was still quite beyond her. With a start she realized someone had come into the room and spun round to see Harding watching her from the doorway. She snatched up the duster and made to leave the room but he stood in her way and smiled.

'Mr. Leslie told me you were starting to learn your letters with him,' he remarked. 'I should be happy to help you continue learning here if you would wish that. Especially if it is the scriptures you wish to read.'

Lizzie was crimson with anger and embarrassment. She looked down and would not meet his eyes.

'I am kept quite busy by my work here, Mr. Harding' she replied. 'And shall be even more when Master George is home. Besides, I shall have them all read to me in the church, shan't I?'

Lizzie knew from her previous time in Harding's service that regular Sunday attendance was a requirement of the position, although she rarely had occasion to set foot inside the Abbey since that time, except as a short cut from Stall Street to the Orange Grove.

She saw that Harding was rather put out by this response and, to cover the embarrassment of both of them, she thought of a way to change the subject quickly.

'You know, sir, how you've been inquiring into the whereabouts of them that's gone missing hereabouts. I thought you'd want to know that the girl Nancy from Avon Street is alive and safe. I know she was one of them you'd asked about.'

Harding was now taken aback in quite another way. He had not realized that Lizzie was aware of his investigatory actions, but he was very interested in her news and pressed her for more information. Lizzie told him the facts but didn't explain how she had come by them. She still smarted with anger at the way Harding had casually shared the information he had wormed out of her with that friend of his.

'May I go now, sir?'

'Of course, Lizzie, of course,' he answered absently and she slipped quickly out of the study.

17

It had been raining hard all night and there was no sign of it easing up in the dismal morning that followed. The wind which had howled through the dawn also continued to blow, spitefully hurling water into the faces of those who ventured out, their cloaks and coats drawn inadequately about them, their hats clutched to their heads. Lizzie had lain for some time listening to the downpour as a grey light inched up the lowering sky. She went through her morning duties like an automaton, distracted and pale.

Harding did not notice, so excited was he at the thought of the imminent arrival of his son. George was to travel home on the mail coach, having been safely deposited on it in Devizes by his Latin master. He thought about the activities he could engage in with his son in the weeks before his admission to Rugby. Lizzie, of course, would see to the lad's physical requirements, as well as overseeing the preparations needed for his entry to the school. But Harding was looking forward to evenings reading with his boy, to riding with him on the hills around the city, and to taking him on a tour of the new buildings in Bath. George's infancy had been lost to him. He remembered little of it, cloaked as he had been in a fog of grief and confusion. Mary and Lizzie had seen to the boy who, for some time, he could barely look at, so closely did he resemble his Jane. Things had improved once George was old enough to engage in activities Harding could relate to, rather than mewling with the women. But still, he had continued to think of the lad as a loaf in the making, mixed, kneaded and proved in the warmth of the kitchen, down with the women. He would not be properly finished for a while, of course. That was for Rugby and Cambridge to effect, but he would be solid enough by now to hold proper conversations with his father. Harding fully intended to get closer to his son.

But while he paced in his study, anxious for the hours to pass, Lizzie sat staring into the fire in the kitchen, preparing her heart for another disappointment. Master George would not, she thought to herself, remember her. He would be a young man now, educated and eager to take his place in society beside his father. She was the housekeeper, a servant, someone on the periphery whose function was to cook and supervise the cleaning and efficient running of the household. The little baby, smothered in white linen, suckling at her breast or rocked by her foot in his wooden cradle, who had taken the place of her poor dead boy was gone. And the infant with his white dress and golden ringlets who had laughed when she spun his top and clutched at her when he had nightmares was now a young man who would not be able, nor want, to remember those days. For the rest of his childhood she had been absent, apart from a few precious minutes here and there when visiting her aunt Mary. She had been deemed to be surplus to requirements.

At four o'clock, as the day, such as it had been, was already dying and, as the rain and wind continued to howl and lash, Harding called down. 'Lizzie, bring my coat and hat, please — not my best, the weather is filthy. I must go to meet the mail.'

'Sir.' She handed him his coat and hat.

'His room is prepared? He will be tired. And we should eat when we return, I think.'

'Sir. Everything is prepared.'

Harding smiled, utterly oblivious to the subdued nature of her responses.

'Then, I shall return with Master George. The mail may be late, of course. There will have been much mud.'

'Sir.' She opened the door.

'Yes, yes, of course. I must be there.' And he stepped out into the rain as she closed the door behind him.

As Harding had expected, the mail was late and a sorry sight when it at last came into view. The horses, when pulled to a halt, were utterly exhausted and covered in mud, standing with their heads down as the rain ran off them. And so were the outside passengers and the coachman, all of whom dispiritedly dismounted and hurried straight into the inn, wet and bedraggled, without a word. Harding stepped forward, but the door of the carriage opened from the inside and a young man jumped down.

'Father!' He stepped towards Harding and then, checking himself, held out his hand.

'Father, I am glad to see you.' He bowed his head a little as he took Harding's hand.

Even with the rain dripping from his hat and his shoes covered in mud, he was, Harding thought, a fine sight with his frock coat and britches, his tricorne and snowy white cuffs. Harding hesitated for a moment and then pulled his son towards him and hugged him. George bore it for a moment and then turned away to receive his trunk, thrown down by the taciturn coachman who had come out of the inn again to discharge his duty.

'Let us get home,' Harding said, picking up the handle on one side of the trunk as his son took the other.

'Lizzie will have a good fire and victuals ready to warm us.'

George looked across the trunk inquiringly. 'Lizzie?'

Harding nodded.

'The very same. Mary had to leave me and Lizzie has come back to us.'

When she opened the door to them, Lizzie tried not to stare. Both Harding and his son had got soaked through in the walk to the house. But she observed enough as they came in and removed their wet hats and outer coats, to see a handsome lad of eight years, with plenty of hair, still curly, but brown now rather than golden, tied back in a ribbon above his black frockcoat and camel waistcoat. The brass buttons on his cuffs were highly polished and he bore very little resemblance to the child she had known. She had done well to prepare herself. To Master

George she was now a maid, not a mother.

'Is there hot water, Lizzie?' Harding asked.

'Yes, sir,' she bobbed. 'In your rooms. And fires lit to warm you and supper ready to be served.'

'Then,' he said to George, 'I shall see you in the half of an hour in the dining room?'

George nodded and Harding went up the stairs.

'Will there be anything else, sir?' Lizzie asked since the boy did not follow his father.

'Oh Lizzie, please don't 'sir' me,' he said and she smiled to hear his voice, a boy's treble, once his father had left them. 'I must be a man for my father, but please let me still be your George.'

Lizzie smiled as she looked at his anxious face. Neither spoke as they hugged and the years fell away.

★ ★ ★

Later that evening, after a hot supper and some appropriate answers to questions concerning his studies, George begged tiredness and retired to his room. And Harding, also tired, but already thankful for some time to himself, went to his study and closed the door behind him. He sat down at his desk, took up a new goose quill and cut it to shape a nib, took a new sheet of vellum, dipped the quill into a pot of ink and began to write. Radleigh's remarks about solving the mystery of the woman in the water like a mathematical equation had been spoken in jest, yet Harding had begun to think that if he was ever to get to the bottom of the matter, something of that kind might be the way forward. He set out the situation:

X = identity of deceased

Possibilities thus far proposed:

A = Miss E Cosgrove
B = Miss J Cosgrove
C = Missing woman from Avon St
D = Someone else, unknown, from Bath
E = Someone else, unknown, from elsewhere

Here Harding paused for a while, frowning, and then added:

F = Mrs Maltravers

It felt disloyal to his friend to include someone who was associated with him, since if it were Mrs Maltravers, Radleigh himself would be under suspicion. The value of setting out the problem mathematically, however, was precisely to assess all possibilities without prejudice. He resumed writing.

A, B & C = already disproven.
F = I cannot believe my friend would be involved in something so terrible. He has sometimes a disreputable manner but he is not capable of great evil. Yet it seems scarcely conceivable that she should have arrived in Bath unnoticed, or that Radleigh could be

unaware of her arrival, since it would have been immediately known to others at the theatre, indeed to all fashionable Bath. If she had indeed gone missing in a way that admitted of no simple explanation, this would have happened somewhere else and there could be no reason to bring her body to Bath for disposal. Not, impossible, but extremely unlikely.

Thus either X = D or X = E

D = if from Bath why has no one missed her? She would have to have been known by someone who then decided to keep their knowledge of her secret after her death. Yet it is hard to see how such a thing could be achieved. If she were an idiot, perhaps, she might have been locked up, but even so it would be hard to conceal someone so absolutely.

E = if from outside the city, why come here alone and then die immediately, with no identifying possessions? She must have, at least, spoken to somebody or bodies, and she must have had some possessions to dispose of.

The unknown woman, then, cannot be completely unknown. Somebody must be concealing information. From this premise come three more possibilities:

a = somebody in the city knows of the woman and is keeping quiet in order not to compromise the woman's reputation;

b = somebody in the city knows of the woman and is keeping quiet in order not to compromise their own reputation;

c = somebody in the city decided to dispose of the woman in order to save themself from disgrace — or for some other nefarious reason.

Harding spent the next hour reading and rereading what he had written. As he did so, the mystery seemed to him to deepen at the same time as some more sinister possibilities opened up. Most people had by now dismissed the matter as simply a case of common tragedy such as occurs from time to time among the lower orders, but, set out like this, it seemed plain to him that something was unresolved and that only more information could change that. But how was that information to be found? Reasoning alone could only go so far. At length, still troubled, but clearer in his mind as to the nature of the problem, Harding folded the paper carefully and placed it in the drawer of his writing desk. Then he went to bed and a troubled sleep.

★   ★   ★

Despite an extremely busy morning — after overseeing breakfast, fires and deliveries, setting Eliza to work on the silver, enduring another attempt to impress upon Dorcas the importance of collecting the used bottle at the same time as delivering the new, and paying a quick visit to

Nancy, big Jack and little Jack with a pie she had made to help Nancy keep up her strength — Lizzie was smiling as she served Harding and his son their lunch. Since his return, George had been on a number of improving outings with his father, attended divine service on several occasions, and had been tested nightly on his Latin verbs or had read aloud passages to his father, which they then discussed. In between, and whenever his father was out, he had spent as much time as possible in the kitchen with Lizzie, making her laugh with his irreverent tales of his fellow pupils and the tricks they played on their masters, and making her gasp at his descriptions, embroidered for her benefit and to make himself the hero, of the level of roughness in both horseplay and discipline he endured. Lizzie, for her part, filled in the boy with an edited version of her own history in the years they had been apart, making much play of the eccentricities of the gentry to whom she delivered water and giving an elaborate description of Beau Nash's funeral, which George was very sorry to have missed. They both kept an ear open for Harding's return during these times — not because they wanted to deceive him or to be disobedient to his wishes, but because they knew that Harding's peace of mind was easily disrupted by suggestions of irregularities in the organisation of his household.

On this particular afternoon, however, they were to visit a seamstress in the centre of town to begin the process of getting George a suit made for his entry to Rugby School. Lizzie had found a good woman, on the recommendation of Jenny, who was well acquainted with the many workers who were employed in clothing the fashionable in this city of fashion. Her mistress was as inconsistent in her choice of person to execute her whims as she was in her ideas of how to embody the latest styles. Her state of constant dissatisfaction and indecision left Jenny with a working knowledge of practically every seamstress in the city. So now, Lizzie and George found themselves walking together to Mrs Green's shop for the first of his fittings. The day was grey but dry and the subdued weather matched George's mood.

''Twill be fine, Master George,' Lizzie said as they walked along. 'A young lad needs the company of other boys.'

'Aye, Lizzie,' he replied. 'I must do as my father wishes — how could I do otherwise? But I would like it better if we could go on as we are.'

'We will go on as we are in the holidays, George. You cannot stay a child,' said Lizzie, realizing ruefully that she had just committed herself to remaining Jonathan Harding's housekeeper for the foreseeable future. She also reflected that George would not continue to feel like this for long and that she should make the most of it.

'Here we are,' she said as she stopped outside a sparklingly clean bay window. A woman sat in this window — making the most of the light — as she picked out very fine embroidery on the edge of a bodice. She looked up as Lizzie and George stepped down into the shop and turned her head to call out.

'Mrs Green. Young George Harding is arrived.'

She nodded at Lizzie and George, smiled and then returned to her painstaking work. A middle-aged woman came into the front of the shop and bobbed to George. She wore a plain, dark blue dress with white lace at her cuffs. Her modesty piece and her cap were also white. She took a pair of spectacles from her nose and rubbed her eyes, before wiping the eyepieces with a linen handkerchief then letting them dangle on the blue ribbon attached to her waist. She looked tired but cheerful.

'A good day to you, young sir.' She smiled and nodded at Lizzie. 'So, the young man is off to school then?'

'Aye. He's away to Rugby in a month.'

'Then we must make sure that he is a credit to his good father. Come along.' She turned, indicating that Lizzie and George should follow her. George, fiddling with his hat, stood in indecision but Lizzie lightly touched him on the arm and followed Mrs Green into the back room, with George behind.

In the back room, a large trestle table dominated the space. On this, a number of pieces of material were carefully arranged. Behind the table, two large windows were set into the wall. A woman, measuring and arranging the pieces, looked up for a moment, bobbed, smiled and then got back to the task in hand. Along the side wall were two more tables and on all of the walls were hung dresses, jackets, petticoats and waistcoats in various stages of manufacture. On two chairs by the windows, two young girls sat sewing. They had been quietly talking, but at the arrival of customers they fell into silence. Mrs Green indicated a chair for George to sit on and retrieved from a small cupboard some drawings which she showed to Lizzie.

'Aye,' Lizzie nodded, as the woman showed her the drawings. ''Twill do nicely. It must last, mind. Boys will be rough.'

'Come.' Mrs Green led Lizzie into a storeroom where bales of cloth were stored on shelves. She took down a roll of black.

'Feel,' she said.

Lizzie felt and nodded.

'And these?' Mrs Green handed Lizzie a box of brass buttons.

'Aye, 'twill all do well. The linen?'

Mrs Green took a roll of coarse white linen from another shelf and Lizzie wrinkled her nose.

'It will soften,' Mrs Green said. 'Or there's this — but 'tis more costly.'

'How much more costly?'

By the time they emerged from the storeroom, all was settled to Lizzie's satisfaction and within Mr Harding's budget. One black suit. Four white shirts and a nightshirt — none of which would itch.

'Now, young sir, I require a few measurements and then we shall set to. Follow me, if you please.'

George looked up at Lizzie, who nodded slightly, and the boy stood up. Just then, they heard the sound of the outer door being opened and of a conversation held between the woman sewing in the window and another woman who had entered the shop. Mrs Green held up her hand.

'Pardon me for a moment, I will not delay you for long,' she said and went out to the front of the shop.

'Ah, Mrs Dudgeon, a very good day to you. I will need another day and then all will be finished. Will it be possible for the lady in question to come for a fitting?'

Lizzie could not hear the reply.

'Well then, we must do our best. If all is not to Mrs Castlemaine's liking, then you must return the items and we will try again.'

Again the other woman said something that Lizzie could not quite catch and then the outer door opened and closed. Mrs Green came back into the workshop sighing. Lizzie looked at her questioningly and Mrs Green shook her head and grimaced.

'Was that Mrs Castlemaine?' Lizzie asked. 'I heard she was too ill to be out and about.'

'And that she is,' Mrs Green replied. 'That was her housekeeper. She brought me dresses last week to be let out. But it is difficult when I am not to see the lady herself. I was hoping that the improvement in her health that has occasioned the need for dresses, might have allowed her to visit for a proper fitting, but apparently this is not yet the case. Now Master George, if you would like to come into this little room, I shall set about the measurements.'

George's palpable relief that this indignity was not to take place under the watchful eyes of the two young girls caused Lizzie to smile. 'Go George, and then we will be on our way.'

When George and Mrs Green emerged from the little side room five minutes later, Lizzie nodded to the seamstress.

'In a week?'

'Aye, that will do nicely. Bring Master George.'

'Of course.'

And with that, George and Lizzie left the shop.

★ ★ ★

When Nancy opened the door, Lizzie thought she saw someone move hastily at the end of the room. Little Jack's cradle, caught in a ray of sunshine, seemed suddenly to be rocking gently.

'Come in, Lizzie.' Nancy smiled.

Lizzie looked behind her as she entered, from habit she supposed, since she no longer had anything to fear from her old enemy. Jack had clearly decided that, since there was no way she was to be put off, the best way to deal with Lizzie was to allow her to visit her old friend. The two women could dandle the baby, Lizzie often brought food and, anyway, she still owed him money. Nancy's face had filled out and she had done her very best to clean herself and her clothing with the poor facilities available. There were still no bruises — new or fading — on her face. The purple rings under her eyes lessened every time Lizzie saw her. Lizzie was not a woman who held much truck with stories of sudden conversion, or even much change in

235

character at all. People were what they were, she thought, and very unlikely to change. Still, it could not be argued. Here was Jack at home and not in the tavern and, unless she was very much deceived, had until her arrival, been rocking the baby's cradle.

'Jack.' She nodded.

'Aye,' he replied. 'I'll be off then.'

'You won't be late?' Nancy asked.

'No,' he replied quietly, with the merest hint of bristle. And the door closed behind him.

Lizzie tried to suppress a smile but suddenly both women were clutching each other, laughing raucously just as the baby set up a wail.

When Lizzie left an hour later, having played with the baby and drunk a pint of ale which Nancy had fetched from the nearest alehouse, she turned to kiss her friend at the door.

'Nancy . . . You won't have to . . . ?'

Nancy shook her head. 'Not for now.'

'But later?'

'I know not, Lizzie. It has all been a great surprise. You are a housekeeper for a reverend, I have given birth to Jack's child and he hasn't pushed me out of an evening since. Who can tell where next year will take us?'

'Nancy — you mustn't. You mustn't go back.'

'I will not choose it, Lizzie. I have a boy now, and I want to be a good mother to him. But . . . we must eat and if Jack fails me, then I cannot promise. But I hope not. I hope not,' she said as she closed the door.

It was dark and the alley was unlit. Lizzie hurried back into Avon Street and homewards.

There were always shadows, she thought once or twice — especially in this part of town. They could not be anything to worry about now. They were shadows, she supposed, from the past.

18

It was half past four in the afternoon and already dark. Lizzie, like most other people, was beginning to long for spring. Just to see that glint in the sky as evening came on and to know that soon it would not be night almost as soon as it was day, would be a fine thing. She was hurrying, as she so often was. Really, it was too much, trying to manage the Harding household, as well as rushing out twice a day to attempt what she now thought of as the impossible — to teach Dorcas how to deliver the water. But needs must. It was her own fault to some extent. They had offered her choice, knowing how she hated to be caged, and to keep the choice she had to persevere with Dorcas.

She had moved on to an attempt to shadow the girl rather than standing over her as she delivered the bottles, and this is what she was doing when it happened. Dorcas had finished the last delivery. Lizzie had sent her back, again, for the empty bottle and now Dorcas was returning to the apothecary's with Lizzie following several yards behind. She was concentrating on the girl and the light was bad, but even so, she castigated herself later, she should have had some awareness of another presence before it was too late. This is what came of soft living, she thought. She was losing her edge. But who on earth could now wish her harm? It had been a sharp blow to the head and she had crumpled beneath it. Dorcas, as she would have expected, was completely unaware that her guardian was no longer present as she went into Mr Leslie's shop. Lizzie was not sure how long she was on the ground, but when she came to, she was dizzy, disorientated and felt a deep, dragging cold in her bones. She felt immediately for the pocket concealed beneath her skirt, but it was still there. She touched her head gingerly and drew away fingers wet with a sticky substance she assumed to be her blood. A couple of passers-by looked at her with curiosity, but none offered to help. They supposed her drunk, she thought in an unfocussed way and closed her eyes again. Just as she thought she might lie there for a while until she felt better, she heard a welcome voice.

'Lizzie, my dear, whatever has happened?'

Mr Leslie went back for his wife and between them, they helped Lizzie into the apothecary's shop. Mrs Leslie bathed her head and Mr Leslie gave her brandy. Dorcas hovered anxiously.

'Go home, Dorcas, my dear,' Mrs Leslie said. 'Lizzie will be soon mended. Go now. We will see you in the morning.'

So the girl left.

'You should lie down, my dear,' Mrs Leslie said to Lizzie as the younger woman struggled to get up.

'No, I must return to Mr Harding's. There is supper . . . '

'Mr Harding will not worry about supper when he knows what has happened,' Mr Leslie reassured her.

239

'No.' Lizzie immediately regretted the attempt to speak loudly and screwed up her eyes in pain. 'Please sir, I beg of you, do not bother Mr Harding with this.'

Mr Leslie looked at his wife.

'It will worry him and it need not.'

'But who do you think it was, Lizzie? Who wants to harm you?' Mr Leslie asked.

'No-one, sir. I give you my word. 'Twas a mistake, I am sure of this.'

'But . . .'

Lizzie's head swam and she wished they would be quiet. But this was important. They must not make him doubt her. Through the fog in her brain, she realised she had to tell these good people a little about what had been going on.

'What you saw before . . .'

She was quiet for so long that Mr and Mrs Leslie began gesturing to each other that they should move her to a bed. But then she resumed.

'What you saw . . . I had some trouble, some money was owed. But 'tis over. I have paid. I do not want Mr Harding to know. Please.'

Neither of the Leslies had ever seen Lizzie in a weak or unguarded state, and they felt their hearts go out to her.

'Do not tell him,' she pleaded.

'If you will agree to rest quietly here with us for a while, then we will send to Mr Harding that you are delayed with the water.'

'You will not . . . ?'

'No, we will keep our counsel for the time being. I will not promise more than that.'

'Thank you, sir,' she said and allowed herself to be led into the back of the shop.

For the next two days, Lizzie felt as if a great iron anvil was clanging in her head. And so she was extremely pleased that Mr Harding was very busy and that he dined out on both evenings. George chattered away without apparently noticing anything and she managed to conceal what had happened. Despite what she had said to the Leslies, she did not think this was a case of mistaken identity. But she was at a complete loss to understand what exactly it was. Her life in Avon Street, her way of earning her living, the necessity of ducking and diving — these could all easily be contributory factors in making enemies and in exciting grievances in others. She couldn't, though, for the life of her, imagine what this one might be about. On the third day — a bright and sunny morning — she felt a little better, but was still very glad when Mr Harding announced that he planned to take George on a visit to one of the places that had been a regular attraction for the young man in earlier days. Lizzie had neglected a few chores in her hazy state and would have a chance to catch up while the Hardings, father and son, set off for Combe Down to watch the quarry railway at work.

George was dressed in his frock coat, from which Lizzie had removed the mud of the post chaise journey, and was under strict instructions from her to take great care to keep it clean and smart. As they walked along, Harding felt quite moved to see how much his son resembled his late wife. There was no picture of the adult Jane

Harding, no painting nor even a pencil sketch, and it was a shock to the clergyman to realise that he had forgotten some of her features that he now saw again in those of his son. The lift of the cheekbones and the curve of the eyebrows seemed to him to hold a bittersweet reminiscence of lost joy. George, meanwhile, was very pleased by the respect with which his father was treated by the ferryman, who addressed them as 'Your Reverence' and 'Young Master Reverence'. In truth, though George did not know it, all Bath was divided between those who judged his father's recent actions as exemplary of Christian virtue, and those who thought him a fool to waste his money or, worse, suspected him of some hidden scandal. Lizzie, of course, was well aware of the state of town gossip but would not for a second have dreamed of speaking to her master or his son about it.

Harding and George climbed up the hill and along the path beside the railway, stopping once or twice to take in the view over Prior Park, Ralph Allen's country house. The magnificent house and its two impressive wings rested at the top of the hill, and before it a great landscaped garden sloped down towards where they stood. They had frequently walked here during George's childhood, when Harding would stand by the wall that ran all the way down the hill with Prior Park on one side and the railway on the other, and lift the boy onto his shoulders to view the house and its grounds. They both said, 'Good day' and tipped their hats to a number of men and women out on such a fine day — for this was a popular walk for locals and visitors alike, combining as it did the opportunity to enjoy magnificent views across Bath and to experience an example of a famous engineering achievement. To the people of Bath, it was Ralph Allen's railway. To the men who built it and worked on it, it was John Padmore's railway. For, while it belonged to Squire Allen and was employed by his workers to transport blocks of his stone from the quarry to the river, it was the creation of the great civil and mechanical engineer of Bristol. The notion of wheeled carts travelling within grooved tracks or along wooden rails was not new; such devices had been employed for many years at the tin mines of Cornwall. But as the mechanics who maintained and operated it would point out with unconcealed pride, such constructions were crude and primitive by comparison.

'Mr Padmore's notion was a great one, George,' Harding said.

'Yes, sir, I remember,' his son replied. 'The wheels of the trucks are not made of wood are they?'

'They are not.' Harding smiled.

'They are made of iron and they have a . . . a . . . '

'A flange, George.'

'Yes, a flange which keeps them on the rails properly.'

'It makes the running smooth,' his father replied. 'And reduces the wear on the rails. There is much less danger of the carts derailing and spilling the stone blocks.'

At the top of the hill, quarrymen used large levers to load the stone blocks onto the trucks, two or three blocks to each. At the bottom, a slewing train, also constructed by Padmore, lifted the stone into barges to float downriver to the port of Bristol. So, Ralph Allen could sell his stone not only to the developers of Bath itself (who collected their blocks more prosaically by horse drawn drays directly from the quarry) but to many destinations in the country and beyond. At the rear of each railway truck was a platform on which the brakeman rode. His task was to regulate the speed of the truck's descent, and to prevent it from accelerating out of control and crashing into the crane at the bottom, by operating a lever that lowered a wooden shoe onto each of the rear wheels to slow them down. In this way the stone was delivered to the barges by the force of gravity, moderated by the ingenuity of the engineer. The empty trucks could then be drawn back up the hill by horses to collect another load.

The railway had held an undying fascination for the young George who had begged regularly as an infant to be taken to see it and Harding wanted to find out if this interest still exerted its power. When they reached the top of the path, George stood with his father watching the quarrymen levering huge blocks of yellow stone onto the trucks and the brakemen riding them downhill to the crane at the riverside. Mr White, the overseer of the works was a man known to Harding as an honest fellow and a hard worker. He was not a worshipper at the Abbey. Like most of the workforce, he attended services at one of the dissenting chapels, but his wife was sometimes to be seen attending one of Harding's sermons. He turned away from his work for a moment in response to Harding's 'good day.'

'Why, good day to you, sir. What a pleasure to see you here.' He tipped his hat, which was covered in stone dust, as was his coat and shoes. 'And this must be Master George, quite grown! How goes it with you?'

'Well, thank you sir,' George replied.

'D'ye remember your visits when you were an infant? You were mightily impressed!'

'Yes I do, sir.'

'Perhaps Master George, now he is grown, would understand a little more, were you to show him again?' Harding added.

'Be most glad to, sir, most glad,' Mr White replied.

And so, after a word with his under manager, he led them to the top of the railway and began to explain the braking mechanism to a newly fascinated George. There were, in fact, two sets of brakes — the wooden brake shoes used to control the speed of the vehicle and a pair of iron spikes which, controlled by a lever, could be passed through the rungs of the cast iron wheels to immobilise them completely. He encouraged George to pull the levers used by the brakemen but the boy, strong as he was growing, found them all but impossible to move. A brakeman, he concluded, must be one of prodigious strength in the arm. After the overseer had finished his explanation, George and his father admired the view across the city to the north and the horizon beyond which the River Avon flowed down from Wiltshire below the ancient, proud crest of Solsbury Hill. Then they walked down to the inn and took a small glass of ale before returning across the river for dinner.

★ ★ ★

On their return, Lizzie served them a meal of cold pork accompanied by something of a luxury for a weekday, potatoes. Harding drank a glass or two of claret and his son some small beer. Soon after the plates were cleared away and Harding and George had retired to the study, Lizzie knocked on the door and entered.

'Mr Castlemaine is here, sir. He says he knows 'tis an unexpected visit, but 'twere you to be at leisure to receive him, he'd be most glad to meet young Master George.'

'Oh, show him up, Lizzie, and bring up the good port.'

Harding was delighted to be able to introduce his son to his new friend and Castlemaine asked George how he had taken to school and how he was looking forward to attending Rugby. Lizzie knocked and entered with a tray on which was a decanter and two glasses, which she put down on a side table.

'That will be all, thank you, Lizzie,' said Harding as Castlemaine looked away.

'Yes sir,' she replied and bobbed. But just as she reached the door, she turned and addressed Castlemaine, 'Meaning no disrespect, sir, it is very good news to hear that your good wife is soon to be well enough to partake in society.'

Harding looked up at Lizzie in puzzlement.

'When Master George and I were at the seamstresses,' she replied in answer to his questioning look, 'Mr Castlemaine's house-keeper came in for news of Mrs Castlemaine's new gowns.'

Harding turned to his friend. 'Why, sir, this is excellent news. We must drink a toast!'

In response, Castlemaine made no clear answer but growled in an angry way. As soon as Lizzie left the room he exclaimed, 'That wench is too forward! She will bring disrepute on your house, I say again. A servant should speak when she's spoken to, by G . . . ' He swallowed the blasphemy, conscious of his host's profession and the presence of his son.

Harding was both puzzled by Lizzie's behaviour and more than a little shocked by the vehemence of Castlemaine's outburst, feeling that there was something he did not understand about the exchange. But his immediate attention was taken by the rush of anger he saw in the face of his son. Before George could speak, his father told him firmly to take his Latin exercises up to his room to finish them, while he and Castlemaine discussed matters of business in the study. George stood but did not speak until he saw the raised eyebrows of his father.

'I bid you good night, sir,' the boy said to Castlemaine, bowing as he closed the door behind him.

It had been Harding's intention to show

Castlemaine his mathematical description of the puzzle of the dead woman's identity, but now he felt reluctant to do so. For a second, after the Irishman's outburst, he had wondered if Lizzie was, in fact, acting improperly, but that feeling passed quickly and was replaced by some annoyance that this man should presume yet again to tell him how to run his household. Their conversation was restricted to matters of the charity school and Castlemaine, clearly discomfited, left after a short time.

19

The next day Castlemaine made his way along the Parade towards the Assembly Rooms. He was admiring the views of the city and the surrounding hills, when he saw Richard Radleigh walking towards him. Since Radleigh was not required for that day's rehearsal, they both found time to continue to the Rooms, to take some wine and to hazard a little money at the card tables. When both men had lost enough to retire from the tables respectably, they took a seat near the windows and settled down to conversation.

'I see,' Castlemaine began, 'that the famous Mrs Maltravers has still not arrived in Bath, nor is to be seen anywhere else to public knowledge.'

'Emma Maltravers will make her appearance soon enough I am sure,' opined the actor. 'She is to play the lady to my lord in the Scottish play here this month, and I do not doubt she will arrive just late enough to worry the theatre management considerably, but not quite so late as to induce them to replace her. These grand actresses are of a cut, sir, believe you me. I know 'em.'

'Well,' Castlemaine replied with a twinkle in his eye, 'I am beginning to wonder if you have not done away with her! Perhaps she is the unfortunate woman in our friend Harding's unnamed grave?'

Castlemaine laughed loudly but Radleigh was unamused and changed the subject abruptly.

'Mr Harding needs a wife, do you not think?' he asked.

'All Bath thinks so,' Castlemaine replied, 'Especially the mothers of a number of young women now approaching the age of thirty and as yet unwed.'

'I have a proposition, Castlemaine. There's a new young widow in town, a Mrs Woodforde, chaperoned by some old maiden aunt. She's to take the waters and look for a new husband, I think. I met her at dinner last night. She has an income, I believe — not a great one, but it would not go amiss for our friend.'

'More to the point, with an income, he'd not think her a prospector.'

'Why my friend Harding is too kind and innocent a man to think that of anyone. No matter, I propose we effect an introduction. You must invite Harding to accompany you to see me give my Scottish lord next week,' he continued, warming to his scheme, 'and we'll see to it she's there as well. Does the idea appeal to you?'

'It does so very much, Mr Radleigh. Only today I had cause to be concerned for Mr Harding on account of the conduct of his maidservant.'

Radleigh was surprised. On the only occasion he had called on Harding since Lizzie's appointment, he had considered her polite and — more importantly — rather pretty — a distinct improvement, he thought, on Mary Yeo.

'She is a pert baggage, Radleigh. She speaks to her betters without respect to their rank. She's of bad reputation, consorts with all sorts of low life. She is a friend of prostitutes and like as not one herself. She's been searching after one of her acquaintances who's gone missing — probably that woman in the river.'

Radleigh's eyes widened and he was about to express some interest in this new aspect of Lizzie's character (having found himself more than once in Avon Street in the course of a night's revels), but he broke off to draw Castlemaine's attention to a new arrival. 'Why, here is the Mrs Woodforde, of whom I spoke.'

The woman in question cut an imposing figure: tall, tending just a little towards plumpness and dressed in the height of fashion. She sported a wig that was eighteen inches high, beribboned and powdered in the French style, and she looked out at the world through the very latest style in spectacles.

'The glass of fashion,' murmured Radleigh and led his friend across the room to meet her. 'Mrs Woodforde, it is a great pleasure to meet you once again.' He bowed like an Italian and lifted her gloved fingertip extravagantly to his lips. 'Allow me to present my friend Mr Castlemaine. Mr Castlemaine is a great gentleman in Ireland, Madam.'

'I had not been aware of many great gentlemen in that country,' she replied. 'Be that as it may, we are all of a level here in Bath.' She nodded formally to Castlemaine and continued, 'I was saying so only this afternoon to my good friend Lady Caroline Bough. She is a fine lady, you know.'

For once, Castlemaine was amused rather than offended. 'Well, as we are all of a level, madam, you will, I hope, permit me to offer you some refreshment?'

'Oh, but I cannot drink wine, sir. I am on a strict regime here of Bath water day and night, and no strong liquor at all of any kind. My health, you see, is most delicate.'

Both men reflected that they had seen few people who looked in ruder health, but they adopted expressions of concern and hastened to find the delicate lady a seat and a small bowl of fruit, before engaging her in close conversation about fashionable matters.

★ ★ ★

And so it was by a great and benevolent providence that on the following day, Castlemaine should chance to meet Mrs Woodforde at divine service. Jonathan Harding had preached a fine sermon and Castlemaine was waiting by the great west door of the Abbey to compliment him on his preaching.

'Madam, I am delighted,' he said as she stopped on her way out of the church. 'The sermon of my good friend Mr Jonathan Harding was a delight to the ears and to the heart, was it not?'

'Indeed, sir, a most uplifting homily.'

'Would you wait for a moment or two that I may introduce you to him?'

'I will.'

'He is a man of great talents,' the Irishman

252

told her, 'But his life holds a great sorrow. He is a widower of ten years and has a small son but no companion in his life, and no one to care for him but a slut of a maid who I consider to be a great disgrace to him. The fact is, he should marry again, but he will hear nothing of it — I feel sure the girl's poisoned his mind to the idea, for what reason I cannot think.'

'It is a great shame for him to be alone so long, and at the prompting of a servant too! But perhaps his circumstances are such that he cannot afford to remarry?'

'Oh, no, Mrs Woodforde,' he assured her. 'His circumstances are most comfortable, I believe. He has the living of three parishes and is held in much esteem by the Bishop of Bath and Wells himself. Why, I suspect he may be a bishop himself one day.'

Mrs Woodforde permitted herself a moment's reflection on the comforts of life in a bishop's palace. Before she could reply, the object of their interest appeared in the doorway.

'Harding — a fine sermon once again.'

'Thank you Castlemaine, you are too kind.'

'Allow me to introduce Mrs Woodforde. She has recently come to Bath for her health.'

'You are most welcome to our city, Mrs Woodforde. Do you intend to stay here long?'

'I am of comfortable means, sir, and my time is my own. I mean to stay as long as suits me and as my health benefits. I anticipate that I shall make the acquaintance of many of the people of quality hereabouts. This lady — ', here she indicated the small woman who stood behind her and had until this moment been unnoticed by either of the gentlemen, 'is my aunt, Miss Anne Downing, my companion.'

Harding and Castlemaine politely acknowledged Miss Downing's presence, though it was clear that Mrs Woodforde did not expect her to make any contribution to the conversation.

'Mrs Woodforde and I were discussing your sermon, Harding. I believe she would like very much to have the opportunity to discuss the ideas in it with you.'

Harding was aware that a trap was being set but he could see no way of avoiding it without causing offence.

'Mrs Woodforde, I would be delighted if you and your aunt could take tea with me one day soon,' he said, somewhat reluctantly.

'Why Mr Harding, that is too kind of you. We would be delighted to do so. Would tomorrow afternoon be too soon?'

So the trap was sprung and a somewhat irritated clergyman made his way home to tell Lizzie to expect two guests for tea the following day.

★ ★ ★

The event itself was tedious but not worse than that. Tea was served by Eliza, Lizzie being out on an errand accompanied by George, who was spending as much time in her company as he could when not with his father or working on his books. Mrs Woodforde's conversation was largely confined to accounts of her acquaintances in the better classes of society. Indeed her supposed theological interests were quite absent from their talk. Miss Downing said nothing except in answer to direct questions. Mrs Woodforde's conversation particularly concentrated on the number of her friends who had influence within the church. She knew, it appeared, a number of people who were on good terms with bishops, as well as with parliamentarians and members of the royal household, all of whom might be able to mention a person's name at the right time when vacancies occurred in the establishment.

To Harding, who aspired to a bishop's mitre about as much as he did to a general's helmet, this was a dull subject, but he remained polite. After about an hour and a half, the tedium was relieved when Lizzie and George returned home and she brought the lad in to be introduced. Mrs Woodforde's demeanour towards Lizzie was frosty, but this didn't surprise her, accustomed as she was to the behaviour of many of the great and good of Bath. Harding, too, considered it of a piece with the lady's general conduct, although he did not think it was a sign of good breeding to be rude to social inferiors, and certainly not to one's host's household. George patiently underwent a catechism from the grand lady about his schooling and his future plans before escaping as quickly as he decently could to spend some time with his Greek primer. At length, the ordeal came to an end and Harding summoned Lizzie to show the ladies out. As Lizzie opened the door, Mrs Woodforde, to Lizzie's astonishment, turned and spoke in a low and angry voice to her.

'I can see your game clearly enough, Miss Lizzie. You will bring disgrace to a fine man and his son here. The sooner you are sent packing the better, and when I am mistress of this house, I shall make it my business to see that you are!'

Lizzie stood in silent amazement, her cheeks burning. Castlemaine was one thing, she had never understood Mr Harding's friendship with him, but his attitude to her was of a piece with his general pomposity. But now this woman as well? Was this how she was talked of in the city? As someone who brought disgrace upon Harding and George? And was Mr Harding thinking of making a proposal of marriage to this woman? Surely not! Was she to be cast again from the Harding household? Tears of injured pride appeared at the corners of her eyes and she hurried to her room before anyone could see them.

★ ★ ★

Lizzie was on her way back to Harding's house from another frustrating expedition with Dorcas. She had not slept well for days, the words of Mrs Woodforde turning over and over in her mind and infecting her dreams. She glanced over her shoulder for the tenth time and sighed. There was no-one there, so why did she need to look so often? She entered the house by the back entrance and had only just removed her cloak when George clattered down the stairs and into the kitchen. She smiled wanly at him.

'Lizzie, I shall die of boredom! Latin, Greek, Greek, Latin and the scriptures. Now my father speaks of mathematics. Tell me what is there in the town? Is there anything to be seen?'

'The same, Master George,' Lizzie sighed. 'Nothing of interest.' She scrutinised him for a moment. 'You need the company of other boys, not that of a servant.'

'Oh, for a ball to kick,' he agreed.

'There'll be balls aplenty at Rugby,' she replied.

'Aye.' Suddenly he was lost in his thoughts. Lizzie sat and looked into the fire. 'I must away, Lizzie. Back to the books before Father comes home.' And he left her, clattering up the stairs, making as much noise as a whole yard of footballers.

Lizzie sat for a few more minutes and knew she must pull herself together. She had not survived thus far to be cast down by a snobbish woman and a spiteful man. Besides, they would surely soon be gone. Mr Harding had indicated no displeasure in her own work or presence. On the contrary, he seemed to go to some trouble to make her feel that all was well. The ill humour she was experiencing must, she thought, be the effect of the blow on her head. And this, surely, had been a case of mistaken identity. And, what's more, she told herself severely, there was no-one following her.

20

Lizzie was running as fast as she could. She was terribly afraid. Someone was close behind her and gaining ground. In her arms she held a bundle and it was the terrible fear of dropping it that was slowing her down. It was foggy and hard to see where she was going. It was also hard to breathe. She turned a corner and leant against a wall, panting, catching her breath. Looking down at her bundle, she saw a mass of blood and screamed. Then, whoever was following her turned the corner and caught her. She clutched the bundle to her breast as a sheet was wound round her, tighter and tighter from her feet, up her legs and then round her stomach. Not a word was spoken. When she could no longer move her arms or legs, the winding moved up to her face and she started to cough. She couldn't breathe and she knew for certain the end was near. Soon she would be in the river and it would all be over.

The cough that woke her felt as if it would rip her chest in two and she tore the sheet back from her face. The room was full of smoke, she was covered in sweat and the rest of her sheet had become entangled round her body like a shroud. She realised with horror that while she had been running from her pursuer in her dreams, in the real world the house had caught fire. The sparsely furnished attic room had only a bed, a chest and a stool in it, but on the stool was a bowl and in the bowl was some water. At least, she thought there still was. She had washed her face in it this morning and thought, 'I must bring up some more tomorrow.' What there was would have to do. She crawled towards it, feeling her way, hacking, desperately struggling for breath, found the bowl and the cloth beside it, soaked the cloth in the remaining inch or two of water and put it over her head, covering her face. She wanted to lie down, to lie down and rest from the fight to get air, but she forced herself to crawl towards the door, to open it and to descend the stairs. Smoke swirled around. She could not see anything but she felt her way down the stairs one at a time, determined to reach George's room.

Inching her way along the wall, she found his door and pushed it open, racked as she did by another bout of intense coughing. George was fast asleep in his bed and did not want to be roused. Dimly, through the haze of smoke and panic, she heard noises. But she could not think. She could not think about anything but drawing her next breath and the overwhelming need to wake George. She could not speak and only the cloth, drier now but still slightly damp, enabled her to keep going. She was running in sweat. Through the dim fog in her brain, she thought again of water, reached round the room till she found George's bowl, lifted it, made her way to where she thought the bed was and threw the water at it. There was a groan. Then Lizzie felt her way to the window and struggled to open it.

A blast of cold air revived her a little and she was aware of people below shouting. She gripped the window sill and looked out. Her eyes stung and a film seemed to have formed over them. She thought she saw Mr Harding in his night shirt and a coat that was far too big for him amongst the crowd, but she could not be sure. Then she felt a drop of water on her face and realised that a man with a bright red neckerchief was holding a hose from which water shot up and onto the house. Behind him other men with the same red scarves, pumped furiously by a large tank on a cart.

'Lizzie, Lizzie!' someone shouted but she closed the window, turned away from it and back to the bed.

The smoke still swirled around her but the breath of air had revived her. Some dim memories of Mr Harding's talk when she had entered his service made her close the window. It hadn't made sense to her but he was quite adamant. In the case of a fire, close the windows and get out. He had shown her the red plaque on the outside wall, as well. This was the company to send for, he had stressed, not that it would probably ever come to that if they were careful. There was another groan from the bed and Lizzie addressed herself to the task in hand.

George still did not want to wake, but Lizzie slapped him hard, over and over, till she got a response. Then she pulled and pulled at him till he had no option but to come with her. She ripped a piece from his sheet and tied it loosely round his face. Then she dug her nails hard into his arm and pushed him towards where she thought the door might be. She opened it and pushed him out. In the stairwell the smoke was even worse and she was conscious of heat and some alarming cracking sounds. But there was no other way out, so they must take their chance. She moved in front of him and stepped gingerly down one step at a time, pulling her charge behind her. When they came to the final step, they heard a terrifying bang and stood still in the swirling smoke and crackling heat. The fire, Lizzie realised, was in the kitchen below them and they did actually stand a chance of getting out if they were quick. But George was sitting on the stairs with his eyes closed and she had hardly any strength left. She pulled the lad forward and pushed him onto his knees, crawling behind him, pushing and poking till he was forced to move. They moved, inch after laborious inch, towards where Lizzie thought the door was, seeming to get nowhere. Then suddenly there was another loud bang, the front door flew open and flames became visible, licking up the stairs from the kitchen. Harding and a crowd of men were suddenly there and Lizzie felt herself lifted just as she fainted away.

★　★　★

Two days later Eliza and Lizzie were both on their hands and knees on the kitchen floor, scrubbing at the blackened stone. The younger woman looked up and wiped her forehead with a sooty hand. She hesitated for a moment and

Lizzie looked up as well. Surveying the room might well have induced despair in anyone else tasked with cleaning it, but the two women knew that it had already improved beyond all recognition.

''Tis hard work, Eliza, but we must keep at it.'

'Aye, Miss Lizzie, I know.' She hesitated again, still looking troubled.

'What's the matter, Eliza?'

'I didn't leave no candle burnin', Miss.'

'No,' Lizzie replied grimly, 'and no more did I.'

'Maybe 'twas a spark?' The girl turned her eyes to the range but Lizzie shook her head.

'No, it was all shut down. I'm quite sure.'

'Then 'tis a mystery,' Eliza said as she returned to her task, clearly relieved that although strange spirits might be involved, she was not to get the blame.

In fact, the damage was largely cosmetic. Two beams were badly blackened and had obviously become very hot during the fire. This accounted for the two loud cracking sounds. But Robert inspected them and pronounced them safe, while Harding stood at the foot of the ladder in his old coat nodding sagely. On the first morning after the fire, he had appeared in shirtsleeves, to the astonishment of the servants, and stood around making a nuisance of himself till Lizzie was able to find an excuse to get rid of him. Instead, and much more usefully, Robert's wife and Eliza's father had come in to help get the bedrooms aired and clean enough to sleep in and enough of the kitchen usable to make cooking a possibility.

Mr and Mrs Leslie had walked round twice with a pot of stew. George coughed for days, but was thoroughly enjoying the excitement and the necessary break from his studies. Sadly, his books, though grubby, were intact.

He was sitting at the dining table with his father when Lizzie brought in the Leslie's latest offering.

'I shall be able to cook tomorrow, sir,' Lizzie said.

'That will be wonderful, Lizzie,' Harding said, and then added hurriedly, 'Not that the offerings of our friends have not been very welcome.'

'No, sir, they are kindness itself, but back to normal will be good.'

'To think, Father,' George said, 'I might have been burned to a cinder if it were not for Lizzie!'

Both Harding and Lizzie paled.

'Yes George, Lizzie was your saviour and has our heartfelt thanks for her bravery. Now, though, we must get back to study and an even life.'

George's face fell.

'Sir.'

'Yes, Lizzie.'

'I have questioned Robert and Eliza and we are sure no-one left a candle.'

'The range, then? A spark could so easily have jumped.'

'I do not think so, sir. I checked it before going to bed.'

'My dear Lizzie, I am not looking for to blame here. Accidents happen in the best run households and we must thank the Good Lord

263

that we are all safe and not much harm done. You know, the fire men were called for even before I knew what was happening? It is a wonderful thing. And there were beer men a plenty to pump. We were most fortunate.'

'Yes, sir, that is true.'

But Lizzie was troubled as she descended the stairs, and she continued to be troubled as she coughed her way through the next few days.

She was still troubled and deep in thought when Mrs Leslie visited a few days later.

'Come in, Mrs Leslie. How kind you have been! We are almost straight again.'

'And young Master George?'

'Oh, well as ever and still talking of his adventure!'

'Ah, the young. 'Tis a bright lad.'

'Aye. He has stopped coughing. Mr Leslie's tincture was a blessing for us all.'

'And you, my dear? Are you quite recovered?'

Lizzie nodded. 'Aye, but I cannot fathom this fire. I can find no reason.'

'We cannot always find reasons,' Mrs Leslie said quietly. 'Accidents come upon us and we must be thankful to our Lord when we are well.'

'Aye. So says Mr Harding. Still, I cannot but think . . . '

Mrs Leslie didn't answer and they both sat quiet for a while. Lizzie looked up as if she were going to speak and then seemed to think better of it.

'What is it that troubles you, my dear?' Despite her words, Mrs Leslie also had the shadow outside the apothecary shop on her mind.

264

'Well, 'twill sound foolish to you, but I wonder if there was malice in it.'

'Have you been threatened?'

'No. I thought my trouble was settled.'

'Then?'

'Only Mrs Woodforde,' and Lizzie laughed when she looked up to see Mrs Leslie's astonished face.

'Mrs Woodforde? In town for the waters with her aunt?'

'Aye, the same,' Lizzie replied. 'She told me I was a disgrace to the household and that she would be rid of me when she was mistress!'

'Well! And a lady! Is she to be mistress?'

'Mr Harding did not seem to think so — although who can tell?'

'Lizzie, you must stop this. Mrs Woodforde is looking for a husband and may well find one. But gentlefolk do not start fires and certainly not to spite a servant.'

'No, 'tis foolish.' As soon as Lizzie had articulated the thought, she had realised it made no sense.

'But . . . '

'But what, my dear?'

'What if there is someone? What if my presence is a danger or a disgrace to Mr Harding and George? Should I not look for another place?'

Mrs Leslie pished in exasperation. Lizzie was normally so level headed. The fire must have affected her more than they had allowed for. She sighed.

'Lizzie,' she said patiently, 'listen to me. You

are a fine housekeeper to Mr Harding and perhaps we would all be grateful if he were not again so soon to be placed in the position of looking for a new one!'

Lizzie smiled. 'Aye.'

Mrs Leslie laid her hand on Lizzie's.

'My dear, you saved George's life. Mr Harding will always be in your debt. Get about your work and forget this. Tomorrow I will come to help with the last matters. Then 'twill all be as if nothing happened.

Lizzie smiled and nodded. 'I will do as you advise, Mrs Leslie. And I will always be in your debt.'

'Tsk. Till tomorrow, then.'

And Lizzie did her best to do as she had been advised. Except, she still felt quite sure that there had been no spark except one created through malice. She kept this thought, however, to herself.

★ ★ ★

For Jonathan Harding, the days following the fire were a strange mixture of upheaval and contemplation. His study had not been greatly affected by the fire, save that everything in it, like the rest of the house, smelt strongly of smoke. So his schedule of preaching at the Abbey continued uninterrupted. Beyond that, he felt a great restlessness. That his own life had been endangered was not a great concern. That he had nearly lost George was an almost over-whelming thought. That the cause of the fire was unknown gave him some concern but he was reconciled to accepting that he would never know the answer.

On the very day after the fire, his friend Castlemaine had begun to suggest that it must be carelessness on the part of a servant, and that this would be a good time to review his circumstances, discharge his domestic staff and take on new ones, while at the same time seeking to remarry, a wife being sure to manage servants more closely and effectively than any widower could. He had not got far in expressing this opinion when Harding, uncharacteristically angry, held up his hand and cried, 'If it were not for Lizzie, my son might now be dead!'

The Irishman withdrew his remarks immediately, astonished to see such passion in the normally placid clergyman. And after that, he kept his opinions on the matter to himself.

★ ★ ★

The next time they met, Castlemaine brought news and an invitation. Mr Radleigh's leading lady, Mrs Maltravers had at last arrived in Bath and was to open the following Tuesday as Lady Macbeth at the Theatre Royal in Orchard Street. Castlemaine had secured a box for the first night and expressed the desire that his friend would accompany him. Harding was still cautious about the suitability of a clergyman spending an evening at the theatre. He had enjoyed plays when a student, having attended more than one in which Radleigh had performed. But now he had to consider that he was a figure of some moral standing in the city and that he had already to some extent risked endangering his reputation in the matter of burying the mysterious woman from the river. Eventually he was persuaded that, whilst he would hardly consider it proper to attend some vulgar pantomime like Mr Gay's Beggar's Opera, which had recently played this very venue to packed and appreciative houses, attending the performance of a play by England's great national poet was quite different. The story of Macbeth, in which immorality leads to destruction and punishment, seemed quite in keeping with Christian teaching, and he decided to accept his friend's kind offer. His thoughts then turned to the other import of the news of Mrs Maltravers' arrival. He went to his study and took out the paper on which he had set out his calculation concerning the deceased woman's identity. It was with great relief that he scored out Possibility F. Although he had never thought it possible that his old friend could be involved in so horrible an affair, he was glad, none the less, to establish this as a fact. Once again he was left only with D and E — someone unknown from Bath or elsewhere. Someone with something to hide.

★ ★ ★

The following week, Mr Harding arrived at the Orchard Street theatre. He was wearing his best coat because, although he had intended not to dress in any way suggestive of a vanity unbecoming in a man of the cloth, when he went to get his second best coat, he found that Lizzie was in the process of mending a tear in it. Unaccountably, it seemed that the buttons on his best coat, like the buckles on his shoes, had been recently and highly polished although he had given no instructions for this. Despite himself, he could not help feeling some pleasure in catching his reflection and seeing himself as a well-appointed gentleman. Anticipation was high in the theatre when he entered. It was full to capacity and in the pit in front of the stage, people stood, closely packed together in a dense crowd. The three tiers of wooden boxes lining both side of the auditorium were similarly crowded. Luxurious dark red curtains hung across the front of the stage. Harding, feeling cheerful and quite excited, looked around for his friend. Seeing Castlemaine wave from a first floor box just up to his right, he exited the stalls and went up by the stairs to find him. Having exchanged pleasantries with their companions, a squire and his wife up from Devon to take the waters who Castlemaine had met in the lower Assembly Rooms and already made welcome with his ready smile and convivial chatter, Harding settled down to enjoy the evening.

The tapers in the auditorium were extinguished and the curtains parted to reveal a dark and brooding landscape. Candlelight flickered against the dark foliage of the backdrop and the pillars that ran along each side of the stage. As Harding's eyes became used to the dim lighting he saw what had looked like three boulders suddenly come to life, revealing themselves as three hideous hags who declaimed in a sonorous united voice, 'When shall we three meet again, In thunder, lightning or in rain?' followed by cackles that sent shivers down his spine. A hush fell over the previously raucous audience.

'The witches, sir,' whispered Castlemaine and Harding nodded, completely absorbed in the drama before him. When Radleigh entered in full military dress and an impressive frockcoat, his wig curled and high, Harding almost gasped. What a fine figure he cut on this blasted heath! How clearly and dramatically he gave his lines! It was years since he had seen his friend in his true metier and he felt suddenly ashamed of the way he had questioned himself as to whether it would be to his detriment to be seen consorting with him at all. All Radleigh's shabbiness was gone here, all his fly-by-night humour and manner of living; all his love of gossip and fine wines similarly absent. Here he was magnificent. At 'Is this a dagger I see before me?' Harding had a tear in his eye, as much for shame at his own pride at the way he had thought of his old friend, as for the tragedy of unchecked ambition unfolding before his eyes. Why, he asked himself, was he so consumed with worry about his reputation? He had looked down on this actor and he had looked down on a young woman who had gone on to save his own son's life, putting her own in danger in the process. As the evening progressed, Harding felt, in equal measure, both pleasure in the evening's entertainment and penitence and sorrow for his own arrogance and thoughtlessness.

Mrs Maltravers was equal in every way to Radleigh and gave a stirring performance as Lady Macbeth. But although Harding felt gripped with terror as she begged to be filled from the crown to the toe full of direst cruelty, he also became suddenly and unpleasantly aware that the next box was occupied by Mrs Woodforde, her companion and an elderly lady and gentleman he later found out were her parents, paying her a brief visit en route for London. Throughout the last scenes of the first half of the play, his attention was divided between Radleigh's and Mrs Maltravers' bravura performances and the unmistakable feeling that he was the subject of a whispered conversation between Mrs Woodforde and her father. His apprehension became intense when, at the interval, Castlemaine invited the Woodforde party into his box to drink a toast to Harding's safe delivery from the fire. For a while, they made polite conversation about the play and the city, but just before the recommencement of the drama, Mr Woodforde took Harding aside and spoke quietly.

'I understand quite,' he murmured, 'that a man in your position has to be very circumspect and I shall say naught to any until you and Maria make your plans known publicly. I wish you to know, though, sir, that her mother and I are wholly pleased with the notion of our families being joined.'

Harding was speechless and profoundly

relieved that the end of the interval came at that precise time. As the Woodforde party hurried back to their own box, he returned his attention to the play, but his enjoyment of the second half was marred both by the constant glances of Maria Woodforde towards him, and by the ghastly sight of Banquo's ghost, which turned his stomach with nausea and memory of another dead soul, rather than thrilling him with its effect. At the end of the performance, he rose and made for the door, apologising and saying that for him this was a late hour and that he had urgent appointments early the next day. Before he could escape completely, however, Castlemaine gripped his arm and said, 'I am delighted to tell you my friend, that my wife and her doctors are at last determined that her health is now so recovered that she may slowly return to society. With that object, I would be delighted were you to join us for a soiree on Tuesday next at our house in the High Street.' He smiled in a conspiratorial way. 'Mrs Woodforde has already kindly agreed to join us.'

Harding was not at all happy at the thought of any more contact with Mrs Woodforde, yet at the same time could think of no way to decline the invitation without giving offence. He was also delighted by his friend's news and wanted very much to meet the lady of whom he had heard so much.

'My dear friend, this is good news indeed,' he said.

Accordingly, he accepted the invitation with enthusiasm and made his escape as swiftly as he could. On the way home, he was struck by the thought that he had hardly noticed the bloody end of the Scottish usurper.

21

On Tuesday, following the three o'clock evening prayer, at which he led the prayers and endured the rector's sermon, Harding left the Abbey by the south door and passed between the market stalls that clung to the walls of the church like beggar children at their mother's skirts, on to the Orange Grove and from there to the High Street. He passed the Guildhall, where the council chamber perched, in a style of architecture old fashioned when it was built over a hundred years before, above the arches and columns that housed the noisy market investigated by Molly a couple of weeks earlier. He glanced up at the statues of the old kings, Cole and Edgar, then hurried across to the house that Castlemaine had taken for himself and his wife during her treatment.

The door was opened by a maid who took his hat and showed him in to the dining room, where the rest of the company were all assembled. Besides Mr Harding, Castlemaine had invited Mr Arbuthnot, the Girls' school Beadle, who was dressed in a splendid coat of blue and gold brocade, Dr Sloane from the hospital with his wife, a small, quiet lady with an impressive wig that towered above her like the mast of a ship in full sail, Mrs Woodforde and Miss Downing. Harding was very relieved to discover that Mrs Woodforde's parents had continued their journey to London, but he was nonetheless discomfited to find himself seated next to the widow for dinner. He was, however, delighted to meet at last Castlemaine's wife, now much recovered from her illness. He knew how hard it was to fret over a sick wife. His own experience had not ended so happily and he felt pure delight that his friend had had better luck. Invited to say Grace, he gave thanks to God for the healing properties of the spa water that had effected this cure, as well as for the dinner they were about to eat.

There was boiled beef, a leg of mutton, a goose, a great tureen of broth, plenty of Burgundy wine, port and old French brandy. As the dishes kept arriving, Harding began to wonder if he should not have been more fulsome in thanking the Lord for what was put before them. He was, however, considerably less delighted by Mrs Woodforde's conversation — a long and detailed account of the influential friends her father was visiting in London, and particularly of their ability to secure advancement within the church. Her father, she explained, had informed her that the present administration of Lord Devonshire could not last long under the new King George. Harding nodded politely for a while but his attention began to wander as she explained in great detail what this might mean for an ambitious churchman. Indeed, he became quite mesmerised as she droned on. Her face was large and angular, her forehead high and shiny. She had a loud voice and big teeth.

'He tells me that Bute is the coming man, and Bute, sir, has the favour of the king. What think ye of that?'

Harding started as he realised he was expected to reply.

'I'm sure it is true, madam,' he mumbled.

'Oh, my father was quite sure of it,' she answered triumphantly and rattled on. The low church party would find itself out of the sun and the high churchmen would be in the ascendant. There was a vacancy in the see of Salisbury. The Archbishop of York was very ill. There were appointments to be made and the new king would look to the Tories, not the Whigs, for advice in their appointments. Mr Woodforde had the ear of a number of men close to Bute and other senior Tories. This was a good time for a clergyman to seek preferment.

Harding watched her teeth and nodded from time to time, fearing that the evening would be a long one. For not only did Harding's complete lack of interest in the politics of both church and state render her conversation of no interest to him, but he had also heard recently from his patron, the Bishop of Bath and Wells, the true inside story on these matters. Bute was unable to secure the majority needed to form a government, the new king secretly favoured the continuation of the present government, and Salisbury was promised to Hay Drummond, the present bishop of St Asaph, an announcement being imminent. It had seemed tedious to Harding when his bishop told him about it. Mrs Woodforde's version, less well-informed and considerably more long-winded, made him long for the end of the meal.

Across the table from Mrs Woodforde sat Mrs Castlemaine. She was a tall, good-looking woman with a rosy complexion and a winning smile. Harding could quite understand how anxious Castlemaine had been for her return to good health. She was pale and there was just the trace of a little darkness under the eyes, but apart from that she appeared quite recovered. As the widow pressed on with her outline of the ways an ambitious cleric should be courting the favour of the powerful, Harding observed his host's wife chatting merrily to the beadle and the doctor's wife about the miraculous effect of the spa waters and the various entertainments of Bath which she now hoped to be able to enjoy. In particular, she was very fond of music and hoped soon to be well enough to attend concerts in the Assembly Rooms and to hear the choir at the Abbey (here she smiled winningly at Mr Harding).

Mrs Sloane chose this moment to interject. 'Why, Mrs Castlemaine, I believe you have musical talents yourself, do you not? I saw as we arrived that you have a spinet in the adjoining room. Do you play it?'

'Only a little, in a very amateur way,' Mrs Castlemaine demurred, looking towards her husband.

'Perhaps you are not quite strong enough for that, my dear?' Castlemaine asked as he covered her hand with his. 'We must not tire you.'

But Mrs Sloane and Mr Arbuthnot now

assured the couple that even the shortest recital would be quite delightful to the company and it was decided that as soon as the brandy were despatched, the hostess should play for them. As even Mrs Woodforde would find it impossible to talk during the performance, Harding was in full support of this plan. As the party moved into the music room, Mr Castlemaine, brandy glass in one hand and decanter in the other, spoke to Harding in an embarrassingly loud whisper.

'Why, sir, the widow is much taken with you, I am sure. You should think what prospects there are for a well-connected churchman in these days.'

Harding stepped sideways to allow Mrs Woodforde to precede him into the room and then carefully placed himself firmly at the other end on a chair between the beadle and the doctor's wife.

Mrs Castlemaine began by playing, hesitantly at first and then with growing confidence, a selection of short pieces by Mr Handel, mixed in with two tunes that were new to Harding. She explained to her audience that these were composed by the Coventry organist Mr Capel Bond. She followed these with a version of one of Mr John Hebdon's concertos. As more brandy was taken by the guests, however, she was persuaded to play more lively pieces and gave a more than passable rendition of some songs from the popular theatre of the time, notably two numbers from *The Beggar's Opera*: 'Can Love be Controlled by Advice?' and the rather risqué 'How Happy I Could be with Either?' Finally, as the evening was drawing in, at the request of Doctor Sloane, she led them all in singing the satirical ballad 'Lillibulero'. And so the party passed enjoyably with, to the pleasant surprise of the guests and the wholehearted relief of Harding, a whole forty minutes of music. They then all departed for their various homes with the sound of Mrs Castlemaine's playing ringing in their ears and the profound disappointment of Maria Woodforde that somehow Mr Harding had left before she could suggest a further meeting.

On returning to Duke Street, Harding was greeted by Lizzie who had laid a fire in the study where Harding sat to talk to her. He gave an animated account of the evening, passing lightly over Mrs Woodforde's presence, and expressing his delight at meeting Mrs Castlemaine and at her wonderful return to health.

'She played the spinet, Lizzie. We had both sacred and popular music. She is quite the accomplished lady.'

'Really, sir? 'Tis a blessing she is so revived to health,' Lizzie replied, but she seemed a little preoccupied.

'Are you well, Lizzie?'

'Oh yes, sir.'

'Cough abated?'

'Yes sir, I am quite well.'

'Then I shall not need anything else tonight.'

'Goodnight then, sir.'

And he settled down in his study with his books.

★ ★ ★

The next day Lizzie went to the seamstress' to collect George's suit. Just as before, she was greeted cordially by the woman sitting sewing in the window and just as before, Mrs Green answered the woman's call and came out to meet her.

'Come into the back, my dear,' she said smiling. 'The items are quite ready. I think you will be well pleased.'

The two girls stitching in the back room nodded at Lizzie as she approached the table where the suits were laid out. She found the room, and indeed the whole shop, very pleasing. The light, the quiet, the air of peaceful industry, the crisp linens hanging around the walls, all created a calming ambience that almost silenced the nagging worries that had afflicted her for much of the night. She had told herself each time she woke that it was none of her business. But still — it was all very puzzling. She felt the fabric of the jacket and the shirts and she was indeed pleased. George would look quite the young gentleman in them — and he would be comfortable as well. She nodded happily at Mrs Green who motioned to one of the girls to wrap the clothing, and then to Lizzie to sit for a moment.

'You will miss Master George, I think?'

'Aye, but we have another week or two. He is a fine young man.'

'And a credit to his father.'

Lizzie nodded.

'It was a sad business when Mrs Harding died.' Mrs Green was cut off by the sound of the bell at the door.

'Excuse me, my dear. I am expecting Mrs Castlemaine at last.' But she returned a moment later. 'It was not she.'

'I heard that lady was out in society,' Lizzie said. 'And a fine player of the spinet too.'

'Yes, she is quite recovered, it would seem, a great blessing. But 'twas a most trying moment for me! The measurements I had been given were quite awry. I have had much lengthening of sleeves and hems to attend to.'

'Mrs Castlemaine favours the new high heel perhaps?'

'She does, she does. Still, 'tis all work and I should not complain of it. Ah, here are the goods.'

Lizzie took out the leather purse secreted in her skirts, paid the seamstress with the money Harding had given her, and said her goodbyes. As she stepped into the front room, the outer door opened and a fashionable lady entered the shop. Her fair hair was piled high on her head in great curls and with a red velvet hat trimmed with black lace perched at a jaunty angle on top. Her coat was of a similar material, pinched in tight at the waist with a voluminous skirt which impeded her entrance into the shop. Her heels were vertiginously high. Ignoring Lizzie, she spoke imperiously to the woman sewing. 'Fetch Mrs Green, if you please.'

But there was no need for the order. Just as Lizzie put her hand on the outer door, Mrs Green came into the antechamber and greeted the lady. 'Mrs Castlemaine, do please come through, madam. We are quite ready for you.'

'I do hope so, Mrs Green,' the lady in red replied as Lizzie turned her head to watch. 'I do hope that all is well this time.'

Mrs Green bowed her head politely and led the woman through to the back as Lizzie stepped into the street and almost into Mr Castlemaine, who turned his back pointedly on her and stared into the distance.

By the time Lizzie was back in the house in Duke Street, she had made up her mind. It was a rash decision — not the first she had made, but she was quite determined in her resolve. Individually, each incident did not amount to much, she knew. And it was hard to articulate quite what was wrong, as she had found when talking to Mrs Leslie. But put them altogether and, she was quite sure, they added up to something deeply awry. There was no point in speaking to Mr Harding. He could be as stubborn as she was and when he didn't want to see something, he simply ignored it. Apart from which, she preferred not to throw herself on the mercy of others and she did not trust her so-called superiors. They could be kind, she owned, but when it came to the crunch, you were nobody and nothing. They were all of a piece, she thought bitterly, these ladies and gentlemen. She would pursue this mystery alone.

Dorcas looked surprised to see her waiting outside Mr Leslie's shop.

'Oh miss, I thought I was to take the water myself today,' she said uncertainly.

Lizzie pulled her away from the door. 'No, not today, Dorcas,' she said. 'I will take Mrs

Castlemaine's water.'

'Oh, but Mr Leslie said . . . ' She trailed off.

'Said what?'

'That I must take it by myself.' The girl was red-faced and deeply unhappy.

Lizzie frowned. 'Why?'

'Well, that Mr Castlemaine did take on so . . . '

'What about?'

Dorcas' voice quavered. She was quite clearly about to cry. 'Well, I don't rightly know, miss. Maybe you should ask Mr Leslie? I shall only get it muddled.'

'There now, Dorcas, don't cry,' Lizzie said but her face was set. So, Castlemaine had spoken about her to Mr Leslie had he? Not content with badmouthing her to Harding and setting the widow against her, he was now telling the apothecary she was not fit to deliver his precious water!

'Dorcas, I must just take the water one more time and then you will do it on your own. You've come on well,' she took the girl's arm and received a smile in return. 'I am right pleased with you — and so is Mr Leslie.' The smile widened. 'But just this once, I must deliver a message.'

Dorcas looked terrified. It was bad enough knocking on the doors of those great houses and handing the bottles to the housekeepers. But speaking to them — she shuddered and, speechless with awe, handed Lizzie the bottle.

'Now,' Lizzie said as the girl turned back to the door of the shop. 'Go home. Mr Leslie will not need you anymore today.'

Dorcas hesitated for a moment and then turned tail. She didn't think she would ever get the hang of this water delivering.

Lizzie didn't allow herself to hesitate on Castlemaine's doorstep. As soon as the housekeeper opened the door, she stepped over the threshold. The woman started to protest, but Lizzie cut her short. 'I have an urgent message for Mrs Castlemaine,' she said.

'What possible business could you,' the housekeeper's eyes passed dismissively over Lizzie, 'have with Mrs Castlemaine?'

'It is a message from the apothecary,' Lizzie replied, her voice bold, her heart full of fear. ''Tis important. I must speak with her.'

The housekeeper hesitated for a moment — it was easy to get things wrong in the Castlemaine household — but she was persuaded by the certainty in Lizzie's voice and turned into the parlour, shutting the door behind her. In a flash, Lizzie was up the stairs and into the first room she came to. It was a woman's dressing room, neat and peaceful. Paper, ink and pen lay on a small table in front of the window. Lizzie closed the door and tried the next room. She thought for a moment it was locked, but the door gave when she put her weight against it and she entered. This room was not clean or tidy. The curtains were closed and the air was full of dust. She almost tripped on a large trunk as she moved to the window and pulled back the curtains. Quickly she knelt and opened the trunk, finding it full of women's clothes. Lizzie pulled out a dress, stood and held it up against her as dust motes swirled around. It barely came to her shins — the woman who had worn this was very short — but the sleeves were very long. Long enough, Lizzie thought, to cover a deformity. She knelt again, hearing sounds and knowing she had but a moment. The door flew open just as she pulled out a pair of satin shoes. They were extremely small with low heels.

'What the . . . ' Castlemaine stepped threateningly towards her. 'What are you doing in my house? In my wife's rooms?'

The housekeeper appeared behind him. 'Sir, I did not know. She said she had come with a message from the apothecary. She came up here when I went to get the mistress. I had no idea, truly sir.'

'Get out of my house and never come back,' Castlemaine roared at the terrified woman. 'And as for you . . . ' He grabbed Lizzie by the hair and propelled her out of the room and down the stairs, not loosening his grip as he grabbed his frock coat and opened the door. 'We will go to see the apothecary and then I will go to see Mr Harding. And by the end of the day you will be whoring in Avon Street again, where you belong.'

It was a painful walk to Mr Leslie's shop. Castlemaine dragged her behind him and roared for the apothecary. Even more painful to Lizzie were the expressions on the faces of both the Leslies as they emerged from the back of the shop.

'How dare you send this strumpet to my house!'

'Sir I . . . ' Mr Leslie began. But his words were drowned out by Castlemaine's bellowing. The man's face was quite crimson and Lizzie looked down mortified to see the alarm on Mrs Leslie's face as she put her arm on her husband's.

'I made my wishes quite clear to you. I shall make complaints, I tell you, sir. I shall shut you down. I am away to my good friend now to apprise him of this deception. You are a disgrace to your profession, sir,' and he slammed out of the shop.

A shocked silence fell for a few seconds. Mr Leslie sat down and put his head in his hands.

'Lizzie,' Mrs Leslie began. 'How? Why? After all we have done . . . ' She looked worriedly at her husband.

'Mr Leslie,' Lizzie said.

He did not answer.

'Mr Leslie, it is very important.'

He raised a dazed face to hers, shaking his head.

'Please sir.' Lizzie bent her hands round on themselves, knuckles touching, before the amazed faces of the couple. 'Please sir, can the waters cure this?'

'Lizzie are you quite out of your senses?'

Lizzie had never seen Mrs Leslie angry, but she persisted. 'Please, sir, it is very important. You shall see. It is not as you think, I give my word.'

She thrust her hands in front of him. 'Can the waters cure this?'

'Well . . . '

Lizzie forced herself to stay calm while she imagined the tirade that Harding would be listening to at this very moment. 'Well?' she said quietly.

'We can never say what miracle the Lord might work . . . '

'But have you ever seen it?' Lizzie persisted. 'Have you ever seen this cured?'

He bowed his head. 'I have not.'

Lizzie turned on her heel and ran out of the shop, leaving both the Leslies thoroughly shaken and completely astonished in her wake.

22

Lizzie's conversation with Jonathan Harding was short and to the point, although she had to explain twice.

'Lizzie, this is quite beyond the grounds of credibility. You have let yourself run away with these notions,' he began.

'No sir, I believe I speak the truth,' she answered quietly, and in his heart he knew she was right. The clergyman stood silently for a moment and then made a decision.

'You must come with me, Lizzie,' he said as he put on his hat and coat. 'You are the only one who has had sight of her. 'Twill not be pretty.'

'No,' she answered as she closed the door behind them. She was quite certain that none of it would be pretty.

George, on hearing the commotion downstairs which had preceded Lizzie's arrival, had without regret or hesitation, left his books and started down the stairs. He did not, however, go into the room from which Mr Castlemaine's furious shouts came, having realised some time ago that if he wanted to know what grown-ups were saying, it was better if they did not realise he was listening. So he paused at the foot of the stairs and what he heard made him feel angry. He had known for some time that Castlemaine was no friend of Lizzie and he disliked him for that, but this loud condemnation of her was something new. He was interested to hear how his father responded.

'Mr Castlemaine,' Harding said, 'I understand you are aggrieved that your instructions to the apothecary were not followed, but I cannot see what harm has been done. As to your suggestion that she is not a fit person to serve in my household, I must inform you that I have quite the opposite opinion of her. She saved my George's life, sir, and I bless her for that.'

Castlemaine began to utter a strangulated cry of anger but managed to swallow it. 'Then, sir, I bid you good day!' he cried and stormed to the door, slamming it behind him.

In the silence that followed, George peered cautiously into the room to see his father sunk in his chair with his head in his hands. He was not, George knew, a man to seek out or enjoy conflict. Not wanting to acknowledge he had been eavesdropping, the boy was uncertain whether to go in, and when, a moment later, Lizzie arrived, flushed and out of breath, having run all the way from the apothecary's shop, he decided to stay concealed.

As soon as Harding and Lizzie left the house, George threw on his coat and slipped out after them. His mind was racing in an attempt to understand these extraordinary events. He knew much more about the story of his father's burying the mystery woman in Bathwick Churchyard than either Harding or Lizzie gave him credit for. He was well aware that opinion was fairly evenly divided between those who thought it a kind and Christian act, and those who thought it evidence of folly at best, shame at worst. And although no one had ever voiced the latter opinion to him, he would have been ready to defend his father's honour had they done so. What he now suspected was that Mr Castlemaine, who he already disliked heartily, was in some way connected to the mystery and that this was the matter which his father was now intent on resolving. Certain that, as in any matter of significance, if he showed his interest, he would be told to keep out of it, he followed his father and Lizzie at a discreet distance.

They went first to Mr Leslie's shop in Cheap Street, where they stayed only a few minutes. When they emerged, his father's face was set firm and Lizzie walked with a renewed confidence by his side. From here, they walked briskly into Orchard Street, past the Theatre Royal, and entered a doorway on which, as George read once they had gone in, was a brass plaque inscribed Josiah Strang, Attorney at Law and H M Coroner. Here, George had a longer wait. After ten minutes, the door opened and out came a lawyer's clerk who hurried away and returned some time later, accompanied by two men. They looked like sedan chairmen but instead of a chair, they carried digging tools, two spades, a shovel and a pick. It was very soon after this that Harding and Lizzie, accompanied by the chair men and an imposing figure that George took to be the coroner Strang himself, left the building and hurried away in the direction of the Abbey. As they passed the theatre, the actor Richard Radleigh was arriving and, expecting to pass the time of day with them, greeted them with a smile and a flourish of his hat. But they had no time to stay and exchange conversation and with a cursory word hurried off. They skirted the Abbey, crossed the Orange Grove and made their way purposefully along the riverside to a jetty where a small rowing boat was moored. One of the chair men disappeared into a nearby house and emerged accompanied by another man, carrying oars. George took care to keep out of sight as the group climbed into the boat and were rowed across the Avon and upriver to a makeshift landing stage by the churchyard of St Mary.

For some time, George stood beside the river, looking across, but whatever was going on, was on the other side of the church and he could hear or see nothing. After a while, he decided there was no more to be discovered in this way and walked back into the city. He loitered for a while around the market stalls under the Guildhall and bought himself an orange from a street seller. Soon after he had eaten it he saw Henry Castlemaine in the crowd and decided, on a whim, to follow him. It was quickly apparent to George that Castlemaine was a harder man to follow than his father. He looked about him constantly as if he feared someone might be watching him and George had to make use of doorways, market stalls and the crowd to keep his surveillance secret. The big Irishman walked down through the Orange Grove and onto the North Parade, towards the Assembly Rooms. But before he reached them, he chanced to meet Richard Radleigh and the two men fell into conversation. A line of sedan chair men, waiting for custom, stood outside the assembly rooms and George was able to stand behind one of the chairs, near enough to hear Castlemaine and Radleigh's conversation.

'Good day to you, Mr Castlemaine. I hope you enjoyed our performance.'

'Very much, my dear Radleigh. Mrs Maltravers in particular made a great impression on our party. As, of course, did you yourself, sir.'

'And my friend, Harding, who was with you — was he also entertained? I only ask because I passed him in the street a short while ago and he seemed too busy to exchange more than the briefest of greetings. In strange company too, by my honour!'

Castlemaine's interest was aroused. 'Strange company, how sir?'

'Why, his housekeeper, a lawyer and a band of navvies, I believe, carrying shovels. Some odd sort of gardening party, I thought.' Radleigh broke off. 'Sir, are you well?'

The Irishman's normally florid face had turned pale and he held for a moment onto a doorpost for balance. 'I — I must go!' he cried and turned back, almost at a running pace toward the High Street.

'By God!' mused Radleigh aloud but to no one in particular. 'Everyone is quite mad today!'

★ ★ ★

On arriving in the churchyard, Harding had sought out the sexton, as Mr Snape was not at home that day. The man protested vehemently at what Harding told him, but on reaching the graveside, he was constrained by the authority of the coroner and the intimidating size of the two men with spades, and raised no further complaint. The ground was damp and heavy and the digging was hard work. The men had to dig wide as the sides of the hole were prone to slip back into the grave, and the wet earth slipped from their shovels as they lifted it.

Mr Strang repeated the questions he had already put to Lizzie in his office.

'You say you are familiar with this medical condition?'

'Yes, sir,' she replied, patiently. 'My grandmother Alice White and my uncle Robert both had it bad; well he still does, she's dead ten years.'

'And you really think each case so particular, you can recognise a person by their hands?'

'I am sure of it, sir.' Lizzie was well aware that she must be very clear and calm in her replies. 'They each twist up in their own particular way.'

The lawyer turned to Harding. 'You spoke, you say, to the apothecary?'

'I did,' said Harding. 'He confirmed what Lizzie says and that he was sure that, short of a true miracle, the condition is incurable, by the spa waters or any other medicine.'

'Then if the woman now calling herself Mrs Castlemaine has it not — such that she can perform on the spinet — then she cannot be the same who Lizzie Yeo saw when first she delivered water to that house?'

'It grieves me much, Mr Strang, to think that a man I believed my good friend has misled me, but I am much afraid that is the case.'

'We shall soon see.' The coroner's face was grim as the sound of shovels striking the coffin lid interrupted their discussion.

In the midst of this grisly scene, Lizzie thought about recent events. Her sense of being followed, the attack on her, the fire with no cause all fell into place. The man who had caused the horror now at their feet had also made her his target because she might possibly have seen his real wife on her first visit to the Castlemaine house — the small woman with crippled hands, who now lay in this grave. The men worked with renewed vigour to clear enough earth to allow them to raise the lid, and then used the sharpest spade to lever it off the cheaply constructed box. A horrible smell rose from the coffin, making the gentlemen fear they would retch. Lizzie and the chair men were made of sterner stuff. Holding a handkerchief over her mouth and nose, she peered down into the grave, at the hands crossed over the bosom of the corpse. Decay had set in fast in the dampness of the riverside graveyard, but there was no hesitation in her judgement.

'Those are the hands I saw that day, sir,' she said to Harding. 'I am quite sure this is the lady I saw that time.'

'And you are sure of this even though you did not see her face?'

'As sure as if I had done so, sir.'

294

Harding and Strang exchanged looks.

'This is a terrible thing, sir,' said the coroner.

'What shall we do now?' asked the clergyman

'This good verger must guard this grave. You and I must go immediately to a magistrate. You two,' he spoke to the chair men, 'go to the house in the High Street where Mr Castlemaine lives and do not suffer him to leave there until we arrive.'

Both Harding and Lizzie were feeling quite amazed by the events of the day, but they were yet more astonished to hear the sound of George's voice calling to them and to see him a moment later, running around the corner of the church, followed by the boatman who had ferried them across an hour before.

★　★　★

Following Castlemaine back to his home had been a much easier task for George than shadowing him from it. The big man had looked neither to right nor left but hurried single-mindedly to the High Street and flung himself through his door. Less than ten minutes later, the door flew open again and he emerged, along with his wife, each of them carrying a travelling bag with all the appearance of hasty packing and dressing. As they skirted the Abbey and made their way along the Parade, George's first thought was that they must be making for Duke Street to visit his father, but he quickly realised that they were, instead, intent on taking the ferry to Widcombe. George knew that nothing he said or did would arrest their flight, so he turned about and ran along the river to where his father had crossed. The boatman was sitting on the opposite shore, smoking a clay pipe and, bad temperedly, came back across and brought George over the river. Immediately the boy ran around the church calling out as he ran.

'Father! Lizzie! He is escaping! He is running away. Be quick Father, he is even now at the ferry!'

'Who is at the ferry, George?' demanded Harding, but as the words passed his lips, he knew what was afoot. The Castlemaines were at the ferry on their way to the stables to hire horses and escape. The whole digging party, save for the bewildered sexton, began to run along the riverside down towards the landing stage for the Widcombe ferry.

★ ★ ★

The ferryman had been settling down on a bench outside the inn with a glass of ale when the big man in the red and gold coat ran up, followed by a lady, out of breath and very distressed. His normal practice, when gentlemen demanded he leave his beer to carry them, was to affect disdain, but the guinea that Castlemaine held up to him made him swallow his pride, along with his drink, in an instant and he helped the couple and their bags aboard his vessel.

'Row it faster, man!' demanded the Irishman, but the ferryman kept his customary pace. When they reached the other bank, man and wife leapt ashore, without waiting for him to tie up, and began to hurry toward the village.

Before they had gone far, he saw a group of figures running along the riverside towards the Irishman and his wife. George was out in front, ignoring his father's orders to come back. Behind him ran Lizzie and then came the clergyman and the burly sedan chair men. Some way to the rear, Mr Strang the coroner puffed and gasped as he ran as quickly as his age and dignity would permit.

Castlemaine and his companion turned tail and began to run back downstream, but the ferryman, seeing that something was up, stepped into the path, holding his boat hook. He had realised almost instantly that there were no more guineas to be had from his passenger but that there might well be some sort of reward for a man who apprehended a fugitive. There was only one other path that Castlemaine could take — the road beside the railway up to the quarry. He and his companion flung aside their bags and started to run uphill, but their pursuers were gaining on them as they ran.

At the top of the hill, the quarry workers had manhandled another two great blocks of yellow stone onto a wagon and the brakeman set off on the journey down to the loading crane by the water's edge. He held a firm grip on the handbrake that controlled the rate of descent and then, with a practiced motion of his feet, operated the levers releasing the metal rods that protruded into the spokes of the rear wheels, allowing them to turn. He gently eased the pressure on the handbrake and, as the waggon began its stately motion along the track, he allowed it to pick up a little speed, well within his control, and looked ahead, down the hill. The sight that confronted him was something he had never seen before. A large man in a bright red coat was turning to look behind him down the hill at a crowd of people pursuing him. Beside him a woman had fallen to the ground and was clinging to his coat tails. Running towards them were a boy, a serving wench, a clergyman, two rough-looking workmen and an older gentleman in fashionable city clothes.

They were all safely to the side of the tracks, but the brakeman was about to slow the waggon's progress, when he saw the big man draw from his belt a pair of pistols and take aim at the boy.

'Beware!' cried the brakeman. 'Beware! A gun!'

The man in the red coat turned around at the sound of his voice and the pistol in his left hand discharged. The shot went wildly into the air but the terrified brakeman released his grip and leapt for safety from the waggon which, unimpeded by the hand brake, shot forwards. As he fell, the brakeman's foot caught the control for the right hand wheel brake and the metal rod jerked into the spokes. There was a scream of metal. Running up behind George and Lizzie, Harding was horrified to see Castlemaine, his face contorted with frustration and rage, aim his second pistol directly at Lizzie's heart in a final act of vengeance. But before he could fire, the stone waggon had leapt from the rails and the two great blocks it carried tipped like a giant gambler's dice onto the figures of the man and woman beside the tracks, crushing both of them instantly.

Harding ran forwards and gathered his son and Lizzie into his arms. All three were weeping with fear, horror and relief as the chairmen, the brakeman — holding an oddly protruding right arm against his chest — and, finally, the panting coroner looked down in horror at the crushed dead bodies of Castlemaine and his mistress.

Epilogue

A week later, Jonathan Harding, George and Lizzie again crossed the river by the ferry and walked up the path beside Ralph Allen's railway. The track had been restored where it had buckled as the stone waggon pitched from it. The great blocks had been manhandled back onto a new waggon and taken down to the river to be shipped off downstream to Bristol. Although the path had been raked smooth and the hole caused by the accident filled in, they could see clearly where it had happened, but did not linger to examine it, somewhat to George's disappointment.

Towards the top of the hill, they turned into a lane of cottages and knocked at the third one along. The brakeman's wife opened the door. Behind her they could see three children in clean but patched and threadbare clothes, and behind them the brakeman himself, seated in a chair by the fireside, nursing his broken arm which was splinted and held in a sling.

'We came to see how you are, Tom,' said Harding.

'Thank you, your reverence. It hurts but they say it will mend. I shall be glad when it does. There's no work for a one-armed man and we have still to eat. My Judy has some work at the big house but it's small money compared to the railway.'

'I have brought you this, Tom,' said Harding, handing him a purse. 'I hope it will help.'

'Oh thank you, sir!' cried the woman.

'Had you not called out when you did, I know not whether I should now be mourning the loss of my son, my housekeeper or both. I would not have you starve as a result.'

Lizzie handed the brakeman's wife the basket, containing a veal pie wrapped in a cloth. 'I hope this will help, Judy,' she said.

The cottage was small and cramped and so Tom rose and came to the door. 'Who was they, sir? And why was they running away?'

'He was a murderer, Tom, and she was the woman for whom he killed. Who she was we may never know — the magistrate has made enquiries but so far nothing is found. All I know is that he married for money but tired of his invalid wife. He brought her from Ireland to Bath, where no-one knew her, and kept her hidden from view with the excuse of her illness. When his mistress arrived to take her place, he sent his servants away — for he thought only they had seen the real Mrs Castlemaine. He paid, them, I suspect, to leave Bath. He did away with his wife and threw her in the Avon, bringing out the mistress as his recovered wife. He thought the body would float far away but it pleased the Lord to keep it at the river bank to accuse him. Even so, he hid his sin and it would have stayed hidden but for certain mistakes he made.'

'They say as you found him out by numbers.' The brakeman looked frankly sceptical as to the gossip he had heard.

'No, Tom, Lizzie found him out by her sharp eyes and her quick wits. She caught a glimpse of the real Mrs Castlemaine when she delivered water to her. And for fear that Lizzie would reveal his secret, Castlemaine attacked her and set fire to my house. But for Lizzie's bravery, there would have been more deaths,' and he looked across to George, who was playing peep-boo with Tom's youngest child. 'We could all have died on account of this man's wrongdoing.'

Lizzie in turn looked at George, who might, indeed, have died at Castlemaine's hands, and smiled to see him play so gently with the baby. He thought of the whole episode as an adventure but she still had nightmares about the fire and how she might have lost this boy who was so precious to her. She regarded the city, spread out below them. Stone waggons descended the railway to the boats while across the Avon, the bells of the Abbey began to ring. Fashionably dressed ladies and gentlemen walked along the North Parade and in and out of the Assembly Rooms, seeking pleasure, company, good fortune at the gaming tables or future matrimony on the dancefloor. In Orchard Street the audience were entering the theatre to see the celebrated performance of *Macbeth*.

She thought again of Castlemaine and his mistress enjoying themselves amongst them, while all the while they were wicked murderers, who had, under the cover of darkness, ended the life of a poor invalid and dumped her body in the river. The prostitutes and scavengers of Avon

302

Street were also invisible from here, as were the noisome alleyways behind the golden houses. Nancy, Jenny and folk like the good-hearted Leslies worked quietly in the background to ensure that this parade of finery and sophistication continued on its way. Lizzie, though, knew they were there She knew that for every fine sermon in the Abbey and every ball that took place under the glittering chandeliers, a pimp was beating his girls and someone was cheating at cards.

For the time being though, she was to live on the right side of the coin as housekeeper to the Reverend Mr Harding and his son Master George, and she counted her good fortune as she looked across at the new Palladian buildings spreading towards Lansdown and shining golden in the evening light.

We do hope that you have enjoyed reading this large print book.

Did you know that all of our titles are available for purchase?

We publish a wide range of high quality large print books including:
Romances, Mysteries, Classics
General Fiction
Non Fiction and Westerns

Special interest titles available in large print are:
The Little Oxford Dictionary
Music Book
Song Book
Hymn Book
Service Book

Also available from us courtesy of Oxford University Press:
Young Readers' Dictionary
(large print edition)
Young Readers' Thesaurus
(large print edition)

For further information or a free brochure, please contact us at:
Ulverscroft Large Print Books Ltd.,
The Green, Bradgate Road, Anstey,
Leicester, LE7 7FU, England.
Tel: (00 44) 0116 236 4325
Fax: (00 44) 0116 234 0205